Out of Darkness

By M. A. Richards

ISBN: 9780692162682

Library of Congress Control Number: 2015912077

Independent Publishing Platform North Charleston, South Carolina

Dedicated to my daughters Charity, Zoie,
Violet, and to my son Declan.

Table of Contents

Chapter One

All Brian Porter ever wanted was a normal life, one with friends, girlfriends, and parents who weren't ashamed of him. Instead what he got was a life filled with ridicule and bullying. He watched other kids at lunch as he sat alone, always alone. Brian envied the way they interacted with their friends and laughed. The joy they had in their lives was the joy Brian craved. Often he would sit imagining friends sitting with him, joking with him, friends that would fill the empty loneliness he felt every minute of every day. He would give anything to trade places with any one of them.

The bell rang signaling the end of lunch and broke Brian out of his imaginary world. He knew what was coming. It was the same thing every day: one of the kids would spill their soda "accidentally" on his head. As everyone started to get up to leave, Brian felt the cold, wet stickiness of soda run down his head like a waterfall. *Right on time*, Brian thought to himself.

"Whales can't be out of water too long, or they'll die," the boy said as he poured the soda over Brian. All the kids in the lunchroom laughed as Brian got up and ran to the bathroom. Brian wondered why no one ever got tired of that stupid joke.

It wasn't always this way. Brian used to be a skinny little blond-haired, blue-eyed boy who liked to spend his time playing football, baseball, and any other sport with his friends. Everything changed on his ninth birthday. It started when he was bitten by his family's pet black wolf. It was the weirdest thing, and Brian replayed it many times in his head. The wolf jumped up, bit his arm, and fell dead to the earth. Why? He always wondered what made her bite him. Was she sick? Is that why she died? Not even the vet understood what she died from. It took over forty stitches to seal up the bite in his arm. The next morning Brian woke to find that he had put on a hundred pounds. The doctor said it was just an allergic reaction to the bite, or in other words, he didn't know. The weight never went away, and Brian became the laughing stock of his school. His friends wouldn't talk to him anymore, and they joined in with the bullies making fun of him. Even his best friend had turned on him.

Brian rubbed water through his hair and on his face. *Must be diet soda*, Brian thought. *It doesn't feel as sticky*. When he was finished, Brian stared at his fat face in the mirror. His blue eyes stared back at him. He remembered how his mother used to brag about how he got his blue eyes from her. "You have your mother's eyes," she would say. Now she wouldn't even bring it up. Brian stared at himself and felt nothing but hate and loathing for the kid who stared back at him in the mirror. The mirror showed the six-foot, three-hundred-pound blob that Brian had become. "I hate you," he said to his reflection.

Slowly Brian walked out of the bathroom to his English class. He wasn't in a hurry to get to Mr. Perkins's classroom. The short, balding teacher was always the meanest to Brian. He would make Brian do a book report on *Moby Dick* every year. Every time Brian would get in front of the class and announce the title of his book, Mr. Perkins would laugh so hard that it would bring tears to his eyes. Once Mr. Perkins started laughing, the class usually started laughing too. This was the last day of class, and Brian was looking forward to having an entire summer away from both the teachers and the students. Next year would be his senior year, and that meant one more year of hell before saying good-bye to everyone forever. That was the only thought getting Brian through the day. He didn't know what he would do after next year, and it didn't matter. He was leaving; it didn't matter where to. Brian didn't think his parents would let him stay after he graduated anyway.

Brian hurried through the door of the classroom straight to his seat. He waited for Mr. Perkins to say something in that nasally voice of his. "Just because it's the last day of school doesn't mean you can come in late." That voice didn't belong to Mr. Perkins. It was a deep voice with an accent Brian didn't recognize from any movie he had ever seen. Movies were his only reference to the rest of the world and how people spoke. Brian looked to the back of the class to see who the voice did belonged to.

Sitting on the edge of Mr. Perkins's desk was a tall man with long gray hair. He had a large nose and dark brown eyes. His polo shirt did a horrible job of hiding the muscular physique underneath. He grabbed the clipboard and began to take roll, looking at each of the students as he called out their names. Afterward he announced to the class, "Mr. Perkins will no longer be teaching. Starting next year I will be your new teacher."

Could it really be true? Brian thought. *Could Mr. Perkins really be gone?* Brian could not hide his smile. By the looks of the other students, he wasn't the only one who was happy with the news.

"My name is Mr. Samuel," the new teacher continued. "Before I get the usual questions, no, I don't have a first name for you, and yes, this is my last name."

"I have a question for you, Mr. Samuel. Can Porker still do his normal *Moby Dick* book report?" asked Chris Miller. Chris was the most popular guy in school. He was captain of the football and basketball teams. He stood around six feet and was very lean and muscular. He had brown hair and brown eyes, which Brian believed was because he was full of crap. Chris came up with the name "Porker" instead of calling Brian by his last name, Porter. It stuck immediately, and the whole school now called him "Porker," even the teachers. Brian hated Chris more than anything he could describe. It wasn't because he picked on Brian. It was because Brian believed Chris was living Brian's life. Chris was Brian's best friend before Brian got fat. They played together all the time. Brian was the better athlete and was always in the starting position. When Brian put on all that weight, everything changed. Chris went on to become the star athlete and made fun of Brian with the other kids. He traded his friendship with Brian for popularity.

"We don't make fun of peoples' names or the way they look in my class," Mr. Samuel said. "I would be more worried about your name, Mr. Miller. Don't you know that the name *Miller* is synonymous with mental instability, alcoholism, and the inability to control one's own bladder? I expect to see you pumping gas soon after graduation."

Chris turned red, and the whole class started laughing at him. Brian couldn't believe it. This was the first time anyone had ever defended him, even a teacher. Mr. Samuel winked at Brian and then turned back to the class. He continued talking for another half hour about what the students could expect next year and what he expected from them.

"Now I have nothing more for any of you, so I will dismiss you early. I expect to see you all next year ready and eager to graduate," Mr. Samuel concluded.

The students all cheered at the mention of graduation. The students cleared the classroom quickly, trying to leave before Mr. Samuel could change his mind. Brian grabbed his things and started moving toward the door when he heard Mr. Samuel. "Brian, come here a moment."

Brian turned away from the door and waddled over to Mr. Samuel's desk. "Yes, sir?" Brian asked with his head down. He was expecting to hear some kind of insult or cruel joke to come his way.

Instead what he heard Mr. Samuel say was, "This is your life. Only you can decide if others will ruin it. Keep your mind strong."

A tear almost fell down Brian's cheek. No one had ever spoken nicely to Brian before, let alone words of encouragement. He didn't know how to respond, so he turned, saying nothing instead, and walked to his last class of the day—his most dreaded class, gym.

The gym teacher wasn't nice to Brian, but he didn't go out of his way to be mean either. The short gym teacher would always play dodgeball on the last day of class. He would always make Brian play at least one round, and then Brian could sit it out for the rest of class.

As Brian turned to enter the gym, Chris came by and knocked his books out of his hands. The guy wasn't the most original when it came to bullying. Chris laughed as he ran into the gym. A beautiful blond girl with bright blue eyes saw what happened and ran over to help Brian. She must've been new, because Brian had never seen her before. He would have remembered seeing a girl that beautiful. Brian's eyes elevated from her feet all the way to her head and didn't see one flaw in the girl. She stood around five and a half feet tall and had a round, beautiful face. Brian noticed that her lips were red and full. She smiled at Brian, and her smile made her even more beautiful. Brian got weak in the knees and almost fell over.

"Are you all right?" she asked. Even her voice was beautiful. "My name is Sarah, Sarah Evans. It's nice to meet you."

"You too," was all Brian could think to say. His brain felt like it was tied in a knot.

"What's your name?" Sarah asked.

"Um…My name is Brian," he said. "You probably shouldn't talk to me. They usually give a hard time to anyone who is seen being nice to me."

"Let me worry about that," she replied. "I'm not going to be bullied into who I talk to. I've been here for less than a month, and I have seen the way everyone treats you. I don't like it. I think it's about time you had a friend. Here's my phone number, Brian. I want you to call me this summer, and we'll hang out." She wrote her number on a corner of her notebook paper before tearing off the corner and handing it to him. Brian took the paper as if it was the most priceless object in the world.

Sarah turned and walked away to her next class. Brian watched her walk away and couldn't help but wonder if this was an elaborate prank the girls were playing on him. He really hoped it wasn't.

Brian walked through the gym door, set his stuff on the bleachers, and then joined the other students sitting on the floor. While the students waited for class to begin, they talked about what they were going to do over the summer. Brian already knew what he was going to do. He was going to sit in his room alone watching television or playing video games. His parents would take his brother and sister to Disneyland or other fun places. It bothered Brian at first that he didn't get to go to these places with them, but now he enjoyed his solitude. Being alone meant that no one was picking on him.

The bell rang, and a few minutes later, a tall man walked out of the coach's office. The man wasn't as big as a weight lifter, but he was still the most muscular man Brian had ever seen. He had really short brown hair and dark eyes. His large nose made him look more angry as he glared at the students. The man wore blue shorts and a white tank top, as if he wanted to show off his muscles. He looked like a professional trainer at a gym. One look at this guy, and Brian immediately missed his old gym teacher.

"My name is Mr. Aurelius," he said in a deep, accented voice. His voice sounded European. "I am your substitute teacher for your last day. My only rules are no whining, no complaining, and especially no crying."

The students looked at each other uncomfortably as Mr. Aurelius flipped papers on a clipboard.

"It looks like your teacher had a game of dodgeball planned, so break into teams. I don't care how you do it."

The students divided into the popular kids and the unpopular kids, as if that was a surprise to anyone. Neither team wanted Brian, but the unpopular kids got stuck with him. Mr. Aurelius grabbed the rubber balls and tossed four to each team. He then went and sat down on a bench and blew his whistle for the students to begin.

The first thing everyone did was aim at Brian. Even his own team hit him. They would always say things like, "Porker, you're too fat for us to throw around." The ever-popular one was, "You're so fat that your gravitational field is pulling the balls toward you."

Brian went to sit on the bench, but Mr. Aurelius stopped him. "You can't let those brats push you around like that. Go back out there and hit one of them," Mr. Aurelius ordered.

Brian turned and went back onto the court, only to be hit half a second later. He tried to go out again, but Mr. Aurelius pointed for him to stay on the court. Whenever a ball was thrown at him, he tried to catch it but was just too slow. Finally he got a chance to pick up a ball and throw it. The ball fell straight to the floor. The students all started laughing when they saw that. Even while they were laughing, they didn't stop blasting Brian a few more times.

During the last ten minutes of class, Mr. Aurelius came onto the court and stood by Brian. "Now it's my turn to pick on you kids the way you did this fat one," Mr. Aurelius threatened, sticking a thumb in Brian's direction.

The fear on the students' faces was evident. Mr. Aurelius looked like he could throw a ball through a brick wall. A few of the jocks in class with type A personalities wanted to knock Mr. Aurelius down a few pegs, and that included Chris. They threw the balls as hard as they could, only to have Mr. Aurelius catch them and throw them back at them. Mr. Aurelius was deadly accurate, and it was the first time Brian had ever seen anyone get knocked off their feet by a dodgeball. One boy tried to catch the ball only to have the wind knocked out of him. Mr. Aurelius was showing no mercy. Kid after kid was knocked to the floor. He caught every ball that was thrown at him and returned it to the sender. Brian had never seen anyone move so fast. When one side was down, he switched to the other side, knocking all the other kids down. Brian was the only student left standing.

When the bell rang signaling the end of class, the view looked like the end of a war movie. Students were lying on the floor moaning with pain, and some were hunched over holding their sides. A couple of students were sitting on the bench holding tissue to their noses to stop the bleeding. It didn't seem like anyone was leaving class. "Well, if no one is leaving class, we might as well start another round," Mr. Aurelius threatened. The students seemed to gain new life after that. Everyone rushed to the door, trying to all get out of the gym at once. Mr. Aurelius laughed as he watched them run. "I haven't had fun like that for a long time," he said to Brian. He then turned and walked back to the coach's office, laughing as he walked. Brian watched after him for a moment. Two teachers defending him in one day, and a girl talking to him: it seemed like his luck was changing, and he didn't know if he should trust it. All this good luck could only mean something worse was around the corner.

With gym over Brian was done for the day. He signed up for early release from school so he could miss the last two periods of the day. This made it easier for him to make it home before the other kids got a chance to pick on him.

Walking took over an hour for Brian to make it home, but it was worth it. He was home safe. He lived in a two-story house at the end of the street that backed into a forest. Brian loved it there. His room overlooked the forest, and often he would sit staring out into it. It was beautiful and made him feel like the world wasn't such a bad place. Then the next morning he would wake up for school and be reminded how wrong he was. But now that it was summer vacation, he didn't have to worry about the other kids for a few months.

When Brian got home, he yelled to see if anyone was home but got no reply. He figured his family must have already left on their trip. He walked up stairs to his room and stopped by the staircase to look at the pictures on the wall. He did this occasionally as he went to his room. He didn't know why, maybe he just liked to torture himself. He looked at the picture of his brother and sister. His sister, Janet, had blond hair and blue eyes like he did, and his brother, Craig, had light brown hair and blue eyes. They were born a year apart and were the children his parents always wanted. His brother was a freshman in high school this year, and he was great at sports. His sister was a cheerleader like his mother, and she finished middle school this year. Brian hardly knew them both. They shared the same house, but they never talked except for what they said in passing. His parents and siblings would have dinner together, and he would eat in his room. His siblings never offered him any ill will, and he knew that his parents were the reason that they didn't know each other.

Brian's eyes fell upon the family portrait that didn't have him in it, and he felt angry. The family looked so happy together. His mother with her long, blond hair and blue eyes as tall as the shoulder of his father, with his brown hair and blue eyes, smiling as if everything was perfect. No one would have guessed that they had a third child who was at home when this picture was taken. He wondered if his parents would still be smiling if he were in the picture. The thought made him more angry, and Brian stormed upstairs to his room and slammed the door.

For a while Brian sat on the edge of his bed, looking out the window into the forest. He tried to think about something other than his family to repress the anger he felt. He found his thoughts turning to Sarah. Instantly the anger was gone. Brian went to his dresser that sat in the corner of the room and put the piece of paper Sarah had given him on top. He still didn't know if he was going to be the butt of an elaborate joke, but he was willing to call her and find out. He just needed to wait until he knew she was home to call.

With his family gone, Brian had the run of the house. He went downstairs and raided the fridge and watched television on his parents' gigantic flat-screen. He sat on the couch and looked around, half expecting his father to come into the room and tell him to get upstairs before he's seen by one of his clients. When his family went on vacation Brian felt like this was his home. Other times he felt like a foreign exchange student visiting a family. Yeah, they'll put up with you and be cordial, but it will never be your home.

Around seven o'clock Brian decided to call Sarah. Around eight o'clock he actually called. For an hour he kept turning on the phone and then turned back off again. He had never been so nervous in his life. It wasn't for fear of it being a prank. It was for fear of it not being a prank. Finally, he just went for it and hoped he didn't sound like a dork.

"Hello," a female voice answered.

"I...i-is...Sar-ah...h-home," Brian said, realizing how bad he sounded with his voice shaking.

"This is her. Is this Paul?" she asked.

Great she has a boyfriend, Brian thought. "N-n-no. This is Brian."

"I knew who it was; I was just teasing you," Sarah responded, giggling.

Great joke. Next time you can tell me how fat I am, Brian thought. "You said you wanted to hang out sometime."

"Yeah, that totally sounds like fun. What did you have in mind?" she asked.

Brian froze. He never really thought past this point in the conversation. "I...I...I'm not sure. I'm not used to just hanging out."

"How about if I come over to your place around lunchtime tomorrow, and I'll bring a movie that we can watch?" Sarah asked.

"That sounds great," Brian accidentally shouted in excitement.

Sarah giggled. "I'm glad to hear you're excited. What's your address?"

"Twenty-three, forty-nine Palisade Lane," Brian responded.

"Great. I will see you tomorrow," Sarah replied and then hung up the phone.

Brian hung up the phone and then banged his head against the wall a few times. "Stupid, stupid, stupid," he said repeatedly.

Brian was too excited to sleep that night. He kept thinking about Sarah and couldn't believe she was coming over. He ended up staying awake until early in the morning. He fell asleep on the couch with the television on. He dreamt for the first time of his old pet wolf. She sat staring at him with her golden-yellow eyes.

"Almira," Brian called out in excitement. The wolf sat still, staring at him. "Almira, come here, girl."

"You have proven yourself worthy, little one," Almira said. "Tomorrow your old life will end and your new life will begin."

Brian heard a doorbell ring in the distance, and Almira began to fade. "Wait," he called. "What are you talking about?"

"Tomorrow," Almira repeated.

Chapter Two

A doorbell followed by knocking echoed through the house waking Brian out of a deep sleep. It took a few minutes for him to register where he was and that someone was knocking on the front door. "Root beer and Cheetos, you have done it again. That was the weirdest dream yet," Brian joked sarcastically as he got to his feet and wiped the chips from his shirt. The clock on the wall read noon, and he realized he had slept through the morning. Quickly he ran to the front door and opened it. Sarah stood on the front step with a few movies under her arm. She looked beautiful even in an old, gray shirt and a pair of shorts. She smelled terrific, Brian just stood there staring until Sarah broke the silence.

"Did I wake you up?" she asked.

Brian rubbed the sleep from his eyes. "No…yes," he responded. "I'm sorry. It was a long night. I fell asleep on the couch."

"Too excited to see me, huh?" Sarah teased.

Brian didn't say anything, but he could feel his face turning red. He stepped back from the door and motioned for Sarah to enter. They walked to the living room, where Brian noticed his fallen bag of chips and empty soda cans. Embarrassed, Brian quickly picked up his mess from the floor and moved it to the kitchen.

"You have a nice house," Sarah said, making small talk.

"This is my parents' house," Brian said, making a point that this was not his home. "Make yourself at home; I am going to take a shower real quick, if you don't mind?"

Sarah looked him up and down. "Yeah, you probably should. It's good to look your best to impress the ladies."

Brian's face turned red again, and Sarah giggled at the sight, which made Brian's face redden even more. "I will see you in ten minutes," Brian said.

Brian ran up the stairs to his bathroom and quickly showered. It was the fastest shower he had ever taken. He got out of the shower and looked in the mirror, seeing the large body in front of him. For a few minutes, he had forgotten he was fat. Sarah had made him forget who he was for a moment and believe that he was just like everyone else… normal.

As fast as he could, Brian dried himself and put on deodorant and some of his brother's cologne. He didn't have any—before now, he never needed it. Brian threw on some blue jeans and a shirt and ran back downstairs. At the foot of the stairs stood Sarah, looking at all the pictures on the wall. She studied each one carefully before moving on to the next.

"I see your parents, and I assume this is your brother and sister, but where are you?" Sarah asked, turning to look at Brian.

Brian didn't say anything. He didn't know what to say. All he could do was stare at her for a moment, searching for an explanation. He couldn't hold the stare anymore, and his eyes fell to the floor with embarrassment.

"I'm sorry," Sarah said. She must've seen the hurt in his eyes. "When was the last time you were allowed in the family photos?"

"They're buried in my dad's office. Right this way," Brian said.

Brian led Sarah through a pair of doors off to the side of the main hallway. Inside was immaculate. There was nothing out of place. His father knew where everything was. A solid oak desk sat in the center of the room with oak bookcases lining the walls. His father's computer sat on top of the desk, resting from an extensive year of work.

"Try not to touch anything on the desk. My father has a sixth sense for knowing when someone has touched his things."

Brian went to the bookcase in the corner and pulled out an old, dusty family album from the bottom shelf.

Sarah immediately got excited. "Is that a family album?" she asked.

"Yes, it is," he responded. Brian led Sarah over to the pair of chairs that sat in front of his father's desk—Sarah in one chair, Brian in the other. Sarah scooted her chair as close as she could to Brian.

Brian opened the album of his life before the accident. Sarah looked intently at each picture of Brian. She looked through his soccer and football pictures. She saw him in his baseball uniform and football uniform posing with a younger, nicer Chris. She thought he was so cute being that tiny boy in such a big uniform. Sarah looked through the pictures laughing and pointing at each one. When she came to the last picture, she didn't giggle. It was a picture of nine-year-old fat Brian sitting on the couch with bandages on his arm from the wolf bite.

Sarah looked back at Brian. "What happened to you in this picture?" It looked like she was trying to find a nice way to say, "How did you get so fat?"

Brian quickly jumped in to save her from asking. "You see, I used to have a pet wolf. On the morning of my ninth birthday, I went to feed her, and she jumped up and bit the underside of my upper arm. That picture was taken right after I got forty stitches."

Sarah didn't say anything, but Brian could tell from the expression on her face that she didn't understand why he was fat. She couldn't grasp why he went from a skinny, athletic kid to a fat one.

"The doctor didn't know why I ballooned up; he thought it was an allergic reaction to the bite," Brian explained.

"Are there any more pictures of you?" Sarah asked, changing the subject.

"Not after I got fat," Brian replied. "My father thought it would be bad for business if he was seen with me. I didn't fit into his idea of a picture-perfect family."

"I'm sorry," Sarah said with a tear coming down her cheek.

Brian didn't know what to do. He didn't know how to respond to her crying. It wasn't her fault his father was such a prick. "Let's go watch a movie and leave all this depressing stuff in here," Brian said, trying to put a smile back on Sarah's face.

It almost worked. Sarah wiped the tear from her cheek and put on a weak smile. She followed Brian from the office into the living room, where he put in one of the movies she had brought.

He popped some popcorn and brought out some soda. Chris used to come over every weekend when they were little to watch movies and drink soda. It was the only memory he kept of Chris that made him smile. Some days he would fantasize that the old Chris had come back and he had a best friend again.

Sarah and Brian sat and watched the movie together as they ate popcorn. Halfway through the movie, Sarah put her head on Brian's shoulder. This was new to Brian. Feelings rushed through him that he had never experienced before. He didn't know what to do next, but he did know he did not want this moment to end. He was afraid to even move for fear that she would move away.

After the movie had ended, Sarah got up off the couch and stretched. Brian tried not to make it obvious that he was staring at her. He failed. Sarah looked Brian in the eyes, and Brian turned bright red. "You know it's not polite to stare," she said, giggling. "But I hope you don't stop. What do you say we stretch our legs for a while and go for a walk?"

Let me think, Brian thought. *Stay here by myself, or go for a walk with a beautiful woman? That's a hard decision.* "Sure," Brian replied a little too eager, which made Sarah giggle again. Brian was really beginning to like the sound of her giggling. He took it as a sign that he was doing something right.

The two of them walked down the street toward town. They talked about school and what they wanted to do after college. Sarah wanted to be a doctor. Brian wasn't sure what he wanted to do; he just knew he wanted to get away from here. They talked about anything and everything. Brian never knew that it could be this easy to talk to a beautiful girl.

"Look at that house," Sarah said, interrupting the conversation. "It looks so eerie."

Brian looked at the house Sarah was referring to. It was an old, abandoned house. The grass looked like it hadn't been mowed years. The old blue paint was sun-bleached gray and was chipping away. The roof of the house looked like it was about to collapse. The house hadn't changed since Brian was little. Anytime anyone looked at the house, it just gave them a slimy, evil feeling. It was a few blocks away from Brian's house. Brian was so distracted by Sarah that he didn't realize he was walking down this street.

"You know how some neighborhoods have that one house that's creepy and no one wants to go by?" Brian asked rhetorically. "This one is ours."

"It just gives me such an evil feeling. Let's get back to your house," Sarah said.

Brian wasn't going to argue with her. They turned to go but they saw Chris Miller walking straight for them. That was the other reason Brian avoided this street. Chris lived next door to this spooky house.

"Hey, Porker," Chris yelled to him. "Who is that pretty girl you have with you? Is that your lunch, or is she stuck in your gravitational pull and can't get away?"

"Shut up, you jerk," Sarah yelled back.

"Let's just walk and ignore him," Brian said.

Sarah and Brian starting walking to avoid Chris, but he ran in front of them, pushing Brian to a stop. "Why is she with you, Porker? She should be with a real man, one who won't eat his young."

"Brian is a real man," Sarah yelled. "He is twice the man you'll ever be."

"Actually, he is five times the man I'll ever be." Chris laughed at his own joke.

Brian always thought he looked like a hyena when he laughed at his own jokes. "Chris, just leave us alone. We were having a good time until you showed up," Brian said.

"OK, Porker, I'll leave you alone…on one condition. You walk home alone and leave me with your girl here. She's too pretty to be with a lard like you," Chris said.

"There is no way I'm staying with you," Sarah said, disgusted. "Brian knows how to treat a woman. You probably only know how to rape one."

"Ooh, good one. I hate to inform you, princess. You're not a woman," Chris retorted.

Brian had never really been angry enough to hit someone before, but he could not stand to hear the way Chris was talking to Sarah. "Chris, leave right now!" Brian yelled.

"Make me!" Chris yelled back.

This was the first time in his life Brian had ever tried to hit anyone. He wasn't surprised that when he threw a punch, Chris just stepped out of the way and laughed.

Chris loved seeing Brian angry. He loved knowing that he could get to Brian. "I tell you what, Porker. You prove to me that you are a *real* man, and I'll go. Since you obviously can't fight, why don't you go and touch that house you have always been afraid of…better yet, go walk inside of it. You do that, and I will leave you alone the rest of the summer."

It was tempting to Brian. Chris would leave him alone for the whole summer. That was a whole summer he could spend getting to know Sarah without interruption from the bully patrol. He could walk with her anywhere they wanted and not have to worry who was behind him. It was too tempting not to entertain the idea.

"You don't have to do it, Brian," Sarah said softly into Brian's ear. "You don't have to prove anything."

"Yeah, but, Sarah…a whole summer Chris-free would definitely be worth it. I wouldn't have to hide in my house like all the other summers."

"All right," Sarah told Brian reluctantly. "But you're not doing it alone." She then turned to Chris. "Brian will do it. But if you don't want me to spread rumors around school next year about how the great Chris Miller was too scared to go into that house and Brian wasn't, you will go with him."

Brian looked at Sarah approvingly. She was very mischievous. At that moment Brian felt like he could fall in love with her.

Chris looked at Sarah flabbergasted. He looked like he was about to find some excuse why he couldn't do it until he saw Brian smiling. "Fine, I'll do it," he said defiantly.

Chris led Brian through the tall grass to the front door of the house. As Chris was turning the doorknob, Brian could hear his whispering to himself, "Please be locked. Please be locked." Chris turned the doorknob, and the door opened right up. "Damn," Chris said aloud.

"After you," Brian said, putting on his best and bravest smile. Chris went in first, followed closely by Brian.

A putrid smell raced out through the door and into their nostrils. It smelled like a combination of mildew and cat urine mixed with something they never smelled before. Both of them clapped their hand to their nose and mouth to keep from throwing up. They breathed trying to use their fingers as a filter. It didn't work. The only light coming in the house was from the open door and a few open holes in the ceiling. The light showed mildew stains all over the red walls. They stepped inside before Brian noticed that the walls weren't painted red.

"That's blood on the walls, Chris," Brian pointed out. "We need to get out of here,"

"I'm not going to argue with you," Chris responded.

As they turned to go, the door slammed shut. "You two aren't going anywhere," a raspy voice said. The voice sounded like it came from someone having a hard time breathing. "It's been so long since anyone has strayed into my home."

It took a few seconds for their eyes to adjust to what little light there was in the home. Once their eyes were adjusted, they saw by the front door a skinny old man. He looked like a skeleton that had skin wrapped around him. His eyes were sunken into his head. His hair was long and looked like it had never been washed.

"You better let us out, old man, or you'll regret it," Chris threatened.

The old man let out an evil laugh and pushed Chris with his hand. With little effort from the old man, Chris was sent flying into the wall and then fell to the ground. He slowly got off the floor with astonishment written all over his face.

"Who do you have there, Curtis?" a female voice asked, coming from deeper in the house. It was sweet sounding, almost hypnotic.

Brian turned to see a woman in a black, form-fitting dress walk around the corner. Her hair was long and black like a raven. The dress left little to the imagination, and Brian could see that she had a great body. It was too dark to see her eyes, but Brian would bet that they were beautiful, too.

"Were you going to have a bite to eat, Curtis?" the woman asked.

"No, Delilah. They just wandered in," Curtis said defensively.

"Well, then, I guess it was a good thing I came to check up on you," Delilah said. "I'll tell you what, Curtis. Since you have been so good on your sentence, I'll let you have the fat one. The fat always go straight to my hips. I'll take the handsome one."

She was so fast that Brian didn't know she had moved until she had lifted Chris into the air by this throat. Without thinking, Brian charged forward, hitting his shoulder into Delilah's back and knocking her to the ground. Chris landed on his feet.

"Thanks, buddy," Chris coughed out.

It had been a long time since Brian had heard Chris refer to him as "buddy." He smiled despite the circumstances.

It was a short-lived moment. Curtis pushed Chris down, coming after Brian. Chris fell so hard he hit his head on the floor and was knocked unconscious. Curtis was slower than the woman, but he was still fast. Curtis backhanded Brian with such great force he flew into the air. Brian hit the ground hard forcing the wind from his lungs. Curtis climbed on top of Brian and opened his mouth. Long fangs grew from the corner of his upper teeth. If Brian was afraid before, he was terrified now. Brian grabbed Curtis by the neck with both hands, trying his best to keep Curtis from driving his head down to bite him. The man wasn't giving up, and he was unbelievably strong. Brian was losing the fight.

Just when Brian thought all was lost, a loud noise came from the back of the house, causing the building to shake violently. A massive, furry beast moved from the back of the house into the light. It's eyes were golden-yellow and reflected light in such a way that they looked like they glowed. The beast was at least eight feet tall with gray fur covering its entire body. Even with the fur, Brian could see very large, defined muscles. It had long ears, a massive snout, and long teeth. The beast had long fingers with long, sharp black claws. As it stepped into the room, Brian could see that the beast had a tail that hung down until it was a foot off the floor. Brian realized right away that he was looking at a werewolf. Then he saw that there was another one following behind the first, identical in every way. *This is not my day,* Brian thought.

Curtis forgot about Brian and went to attack the werewolf that entered the room. Curtis was fast, but the werewolf was faster. He backhanded Curtis, sending him flying across the room. Delilah moved to Brian and lifted him into the air like he was nothing. She pulled a knife from the back of her dress. It was anyone's guess where she hid it.

"What should I do, warriors? Should I bite him and give you another enemy?" she taunted.

The werewolves stood looking at Delilah and growled.

"Then you have him," she yelled as she plunged a knife into Brian's chest as easy as if she was slicing butter. She threw Brian at the werewolves, and then she grabbed Chris and ran, dragging him behind her like a rag doll. She ran deeper into the house, disappearing into the shadows. Brian fell to the ground feeling warm, sticky liquid starting to pool under him.

With every breath the world felt like it was slipping further away. With every heartbeat the room grew dimmer. He watched helplessly as Delilah ran off with Chris. Even though they had fought for so long, Brian wanted to reach out and pull Chris back to him. The werewolves stepped closer to Brian, looking down at his body.

Curtis yelled and then charged the werewolves. The werewolf behind the one looking at Brian plunged his claws into Curtis's chest and stopped his charge. The werewolf then leaned forward, snapping his jaws around Curtis's neck and pulling Curtis's head from his body.

Brian watched as the headless body of Curtis was tossed aside like a piece of garbage. The werewolf then joined the first by Brian's side.

"What should we do?" the first werewolf asked. His voice was very deep and sounded to Brian like a bear growl.

"We can't leave him to die," the second werewolf said. "He is the reason that we came here. We have no choice but to change him."

"You can't without the elders' permission," the first werewolf argued.

"We must do this, or else we risk losing him forever. We can deal with the elders later."

"Then at least let me do it."

"No, I must be the one to do it."

"You can't. You are the eldest of us. If you change him, he will have almost all your strength. He would be stronger than every warrior but you. The elders would be furious, and their judgment will be upon us," the first werewolf argued.

"You let me worry about the elders when the time comes. If we do not act now, we risk losing him forever."

The first werewolf backed away, and the second approached. The beast looked into Brian's eyes. "It is all right, little one. Everything will be all right."

When the second werewolf was finished speaking, he leaned forward and opened his massive jaws. Drool dripped from the large white teeth. Brian heard him say, "little one," just like his pet wolf did in his dream. The fear inside him began to melt away. The werewolf then sank his large teeth into his shoulder and then again on his chest. Brian wanted to scream with pain but couldn't find the breath. He could feel his blood pouring onto the floor.

"I bit you twice so that the healing will work twice as fast, little one," the second werewolf said.

"Brian," Sarah called from outside, "are you OK?"

"We cannot be discovered," the first werewolf said.

The second werewolf released Brian. "We must go, little one, but know that we will be close," the giant beast said. The two werewolves ran with lightning speed to the back of the house, and just as quickly as they came, they left.

"Brian?" Sarah called again. Hearing her voice brought a determination to see her. If he was going to die, he wanted to see her one last time.

Pain shot through Brian's body as he lifted himself to his knees. It was too much for him. He was able to pull himself through the doorway before he collapsed. Darkness now blinded his eyes from the world. The last thing Brian heard before losing consciousness was Sarah screaming.

Sarah ran to Brian and tried to shake him for a response. When he didn't, move she tipped her purse upside down, dumping its contents onto the cement walkway. She sifted through the receipts, papers, and junk she collected throughout the week until she found her cell phone. She dialed for an ambulance. She was so frantic that she had to repeat herself a few times for the operator to understand her.

Chapter Three

Brian walked through the long grass with the warm sun on his face. It was a beautiful day. He walked to the edge of the lake and sat down to look over the mirrored surface of the water. Nothing plagued his mind or troubled him in any way. He was at peace.

"Hello, little one," a soft female voice said to him. Her accent was very strange.

Brian turned to see Almira looking at him with her piercing golden-yellow eyes. "How is it you can talk?" Brian asked.

"I could always talk. This place just makes it easier for you to listen."

"This place?" Brian asked.

"Where do you think you are right now, little one?" Almira asked.

Brian looked at the lake and felt the grass with his fingers. How did he get here? He didn't remember. He remembered waking on the couch this morning, walking with Sarah, and Chris bullying him, again. He went into the old, creepy house with Chris and…and he was stabbed. He remembered the werewolf biting him and crawling out of the house to find Sarah. That was the last thing he remembered. If that was the last thing he remembered, then that meant…

"Am I dead?" Brian asked.

"Yes," Almira said.

"So this is heaven?"

"No," Almira answered. "This is the place you go before heaven. This is where your family and friends come to meet you and take you with them to heaven."

"This place is so beautiful and peaceful. I can't imagine a place more peaceful than this. Is…is heaven better than this?"

Almira looked like she smiled, if a wolf could smile. "Oh yes. Heaven is more beautiful than you can even imagine. The peace you feel there cannot be duplicated. It is truly a paradise."

"Let's go," Brian said enthusiastically.

"Not yet, little one. If all the dead went straight to heaven, then no one would ever return to their body."

"So, I must go back?"

"That is up to you, little one," Almira said. "You have a choice. You could leave with me right now and live for eternity in paradise."

"Um…yes, please," Brian said, half joking.

"It is a tempting choice, but I think you should go back," Almira said.

Brian was shocked that she would tell him to go back. "Why would I want to go back?"

"Believe it or not, there really is a battle between good and evil, and right now evil is winning. Holy warriors fight every day, unbeknownst to the humans, to keep them safe. Our enemy has many soldiers and many means by which to fight. The order of holy warriors is crumbling, and not just from our enemies, but from the inside. They are killing themselves, and they are too blind to see it."

"What does this all have to do with me?" Brian asked.

"I never much liked humans. I fought our enemy like I was born to do, but I fought for me and not for them. To me humans were selfish, conceited individuals who cared for nothing but power, riches, and pleasure. They would turn on each other in an instant over trivial matters. I hated all humans. When our enemy changed and our ranks grew thin, we had to recruit from the humans. We were also granted the ability to change our form to hide among the humans. We could change from our warrior form into a human. That was too much for me. I would not change to look like a human. Like you, we were given a choice. We could change form and hide among the humans and continue to fight as warriors, or we could give up immortality and become the wolves you know today. It was a smaller form than I was used to, but I found it was better than being a human. I, along with a handful of others, decided to live a mortal life as a wolf rather than degrading ourselves and taking human form. Unlike the others I was not granted a mortal life. More than likely it was because of my contempt for humans, God's so-called greatest creation. I was to live until I found a human worthy of not only becoming a warrior, but also having the ability to turn the tide in the world's darkest hour. I never thought I would find a human worthy. I lost track of time after a few thousand years. I watched as the warriors' numbers dwindled and bureaucracy took over. It seemed that warriors were not immune to what plagued the humans. Never in the history of time has the warriors' future, the world's future, been darker, and then I found a light. I found you, a human with a heart so noble and pure. I watched as you grew, and your heart never changed. Even after I marked you and others berated you for looking the way you do, your heart stayed true. The time finally came when you were to finish your transformation. A month ago I was able to speak to my twin brother as he slept. I told him of you, and he promised to finish the transformation."

Brian stared over the lake. "One of those big werewolves was…"

"My brother," Almira finished. "Call us warriors. Though werewolf is what we are, it has become a term to denote a monster, something out of control."

"Warrior? If I go back, I will be a were—I mean a warrior?"

"Yes," Almira said. "But a new breed of warrior. I don't know how. All I know is that you will not be like the others. The order of Holy Warriors has to change, and it *is* going to change with you."

"When you marked me—whatever that means—it caused me to gain weight?"

"What it means to be marked is that you were singled out to become a warrior. The moment I bit you was the moment you ceased being human. You were mostly wolf from that moment. To any wolf or warrior you would have smelled like us. Secondly, yes the mark did cause you to gain weight. It was a side effect that I did not foresee. As I said before, you will be a new breed. Your body needed to store enough energy to finish the transformation."

"What happens if I don't go back?"

"Eventually the warriors will be eradicated, whether from their own doing or our enemy, I do not know. With them gone there would be nothing to stop the evil that lies in wait. The world will be destroyed, and there will become a literal hell on earth."

"And I can stop that?"

"Yes," Almira said.

The figurative weight of his responsibility rested on his shoulders. It was too much to bear. He didn't want to go back, but if he didn't, it would be an eternity of guilt knowing what he could have stopped. "I don't know if I can do this," Brian stated honestly.

"You're the only one who can," Almira said sincerely. "I wouldn't have marked you if I didn't know you could."

"Then, I guess, I better go back," Brian said, trying to muster all of his courage.

"I knew you would," Almira said. She nuzzled against his cheek very lovingly. "You will not be alone; I will be watching you. Find my brother; he will teach you what you need to know."

The world around him began to fade away, along with Almira, until only darkness surrounded him.

***

Brian awoke to rhythmic beeping. He opened his eyes to look around and immediately shut them again. The light was too bright; it burned his eyes. Through narrowed eyes Brian made his way to the window, dragging his heart machine and IV with him, but the blinds were already closed. *What's going on?* Brian thought to himself. He felt different. With his eyes tearing up from the sun, he made his way to the mirror with his machines in tow. It took a minute for Brian to realize the image in the mirror was himself. What he saw in the mirror looked nothing like the person he was used to seeing. His hair was no longer blond; it was black as night. His chubby face was replaced with a chiseled muscular jaw. His chest and shoulders filled out his hospital gown. Lifting his gown up, he found his fat was replaced with a muscular physique that was well defined. *I have a six-pack,* he thought, smiling. It was a drastic change from the huge belly that he normally carried. He felt lighter, more agile. Looking down, Brian saw his feet and let out a giggle. It might have sounded girly, but he didn't care. It had been too long since he last saw his feet. He wiggled his toes for good measure. His body might have changed immensely, but the most drastic change was his eyes. Instead of the blue eyes that were just like his mother's, they were replaced with golden-yellow eyes like those of a wolf. They reflected light in such a way that they seemed to glow. Brian smiled. *There is no way anyone will recognize me.* He loved that he no longer resembled anyone in his family.

Voices started to float to Brian's ears, hundreds of them. He heard doctors talking to nurses and nurses talking to patients. He heard families talking and rejoicing over a lifesaving operation. He heard the crying of families that had just lost their loved one. They all came at once, and they were all loud, too loud. Covering his ears didn't help, and it was starting to hurt. Brian lay on his bed, covering his ears with a pillow. That didn't work either, and if this kept up, he was going to go crazy. His ears throbbed with pain as he held his pillow in place over his ears. The heart machine started to beep faster and faster. What was he going to do? How was he going to make this stop?

As he lay on the bed in pain, odors started to become stronger. A scent of rubbing alcohol stung his nose, followed by the smell of blood. The smell of someone reheating their spaghetti for lunch mixed with someone's aftershave. Then the smell of perfume came to him, and it was the same perfume that Sarah wore when she came over to watch movies.

The thought of Sarah came to the forefront of his mind. The way she smiled at him and made him feel like he wasn't just put on this earth to be miserable. As he thought about Sarah, the beeping on the heart monitor began to slow. The loud noises began to fade and all the other scents went away except for the smell of perfume. As Brian focused on the scent of the perfume, he began hearing footsteps and somehow knew that those footsteps belonged to whomever wore that perfume.

The other sounds were still in the background like a fly hovering next to his ear, but Brian found that they didn't bother him. He dismissed the smell of perfume and listened for another set of footsteps. He focused on those footsteps and nothing else. Again the other sounds faded away, and he could hear those footsteps as well as if he was in the same room. He followed the sound of those footsteps and soon heard the voice they belonged to. It was a woman who was on a break and talking on her cell phone. Brian could hear every word like she was talking to him. If he concentrated hard enough, he could almost make out the conversation coming from the other side of the phone.

Brian laid on the hospital bed listening and focusing on different sounds and smells. As he expected the farther away the sounds, the harder they were to hear. Walls got in the way of some conversations.

When someone got onto an elevator, they sounded like they were talking into a soup can. He was having fun with his new abilities until he heard a familiar voice.

Focusing on the voice, he singled it out from the rest in the hospital. "We have nonrefundable tickets," the man said. The voice belonged to his father. Brian could smell the cologne that he always put on.

"Our son is in the hospital! I cannot go on a vacation and pretend to be your good, little wife and suck up to your clients knowing that I left our boy to stay in the hospital by *himself.*" That voice belonged to his mother.

He never heard his mother fight for him before. He always thought it was both of his parents that were embarrassed by him. Now he began to wonder if it was just his father. *Even if it was just Dad,* he thought, *she went along with it. If she loved me, then where was she all these years when I needed her?*

He listened to his father complain to his mother about their vacation and how his clients needed to see him so they would trust him more. It was evident that his mother was not listening. That put a smile on Brian's face. His dad stopped talking when a woman introduced herself to his parents. It was the same woman he heard on the cell phone earlier.

"Hello," the woman said. "I am Doctor Swanson. I was the attending physician when your son was brought in."

"What happened, Doctor? Is he all right?" Brian's mother asked.

"He came in with large animal bites on his upper body. The size of the bites leads me to believe that a bear bit him. I'm not an expert in animal attacks, so I wouldn't be able to tell you for sure."

Close, my dear doctor, but not a bear—a werewolf, Brian thought with a Sherlock impression. The image of that massive beast came back to him. The thought of those golden eyes were terrifying. He looked in the mirror and saw the same golden eyes looking back at him. A shiver ran through his body. He didn't know if he would ever get used to seeing his own reflection.

"We also found a puncture to his heart that looks like he had been stabbed before he was bitten."

"Who would want to stab my son?" Brian's mother asked while she broke down and began to cry.

"I bet it was some kid from his school. I am going to sue that school and every kid in it until I get compensation for what we are going through," Brian's father said boldly.

You mean compensation for losing your vacation, Brian thought, blowing out air in frustration. Brian's father always threatened to sue someone if he was starting to look bad or was inconvenienced in anyway. This time it was both. His father always found out where his biggest clients were going on vacation and would book a vacation to the same place. The family was supposed to pretend it was a coincidence they just happened to end up at the same place. His father would try to do the same activities and suck up to them the whole trip. He loved to march out his perfect family in front of his clients to impress them, hence the reason Brian was never let out of his room. The fat son was too much of an embarrassment to his father. His father once wanted to legally change Brian's last name but decided against it since the people at the court would have to approve the paperwork. That meant they had to see Brian first. His father couldn't risk having them linked together in any way. Sentenced to his room was the best thing for his father.

"Can we see him?" his mother asked, sniffling with tears.

"I will take you to him, but first I need to warn you about something," the doctor replied. "Your son has gone through some changes. We can't really explain it, and his blood work has come back with no answers."

"What kind of changes?" his mother asked.

"Hopefully not like the changes that happened last time," his father said with an irritated concern.

The doctor ignored Brian's father. "His physical appearance has completely changed. Your son will not look the same as you remember."

That's an understatement, Doc, Brian thought, looking at himself in the mirror again.

The doctor continued, "If you would allow us, we would like to keep your son here to run some tests and find out how and why this drastic change has occurred."

"I don't see that being a problem," Brian's father said.

"Absolutely not," Brian's mother said with evident anger in her voice. "Our son will not be used as a lab rat. Show me to my son, Doctor. If he is well enough to leave, then we are taking him home."

The three of them started walking toward Brian's room. He could hear their footsteps getting closer. He could hear their rhythmic heartbeats as they walked. One of them smelled like a gallon of coffee. Brian assumed it was the doctor from working a long shift. Their footsteps stopped right outside his door.

Brian didn't know what to do. Should he stay in bed? Should he stand up and greet them? What was the appropriate way to say, "Hi, Mom and Dad. I know I don't look like me, but it is me. I only got bit by a werewolf, but it's OK because they are the good guys..."?

The door opened, and Brian stood on his feet. His parents and the doctor froze, staring at him. To Brian the room was well lit, but to everyone else the room was completely dark. All Brian's parents could see were his golden-yellow eyes staring at them in the darkness.

Brian thought they were shocked by how he looked and wanted to ease the tension. "Hey," Brian said. He didn't recognize his own voice. It was so deep now. It almost sounded like a beastly growl.

Brian's parents let out a scream and slammed the door. Brian could hear them breathing hard on the other side.

"What was that?" Brian's father asked excitedly.

"I believe that was your son," the doctor answered.

"That can't be my son," his father responded. He controlled his breathing before following up with, "Are you telling me that my son has gone from a tub of lard to some sort of freak?"

"Charles!" Brian's mother yelled. "If that is our son, then we need to help him."

"Oh no, April. If that is our son, then he is never leaving this hospital. Doctor, I will sign off on whatever test you want. I don't care if you have to strap him to a table and cut him open. I don't want him ever leaving this place."

"Charles!"

"No, April. I have made up my mind. That thing in there is not your son anymore. Can you imagine what my clients would think if they saw that freak? No, no, even having him locked in his room will not be enough now."

It looks like my father is in the running again for father of the year, Brian thought. *There is no way I am going to let them lock me up in here and do God-knows-what to me.*

Brian ripped his IV out of his arm and unclipped his heart monitor. He went to the window and pulled open the blinds. The sunlight caused intense pain. Through watery eyes he looked out to find that he was on the second floor.

That's quite a drop. He looked back at the door. *A broken leg at this point will be better than what they plan to do with me.*

He unlatched the window and slid it open. Just as he was about to jump, his mother opened the door and yelled out his name. He looked back at her to see her sad and shocked face. Her cheeks were stained with the tears that she had shed on his behalf. He felt moved to go toward her, but he knew that she always gave in to his father's wishes. There was no way he would be the winner today.

Brian held his breath and dove out the window. He heard his mother scream for the second time.

Chapter Four

Brian fell to the hard pavement but amazingly didn't feel any pain. He got to his feet and looked up to the window. It was higher than he realized.

Score one for werewolf genes, he thought before seeing his mother stick her head out the window. Brian turned and ran down the sidewalk. It didn't matter which direction he went since he had nowhere to go. With the sun burning his eyes, it made it difficult for Brian to run too fast. He kept bumping into buildings and poles as he ran. He could hear people snicker about him as he bumped into them and ran past. No doubt they were getting a nice view of his backside in his hospital gown, but he didn't care at the moment. He just ran until he tripped over something and fell to the ground.

"Hey," a voice yelled.

Or someone.

"I'm sorry. I am having trouble seeing at the moment," Brian said. He couldn't see who he was talking to. The pain was so bad he just shut his eyes as he lay on the sidewalk.

"It's OK, kid. Most people pretend not to see me, but you actually couldn't. Hey, I found these the other day. I think you need them more than I do."

The man put a pair of glasses on Brian's face. Brian opened his eyes and found that he could see a lot better. The pain from the sun was still there, but it was lessened considerably. Instead of burning it felt like his eyes had been scratched.

"Thank you," Brian said, sitting up.

He looked at his benefactor to find a man sitting on the sidewalk with his back against a building. He wore an old army coat that was torn and dirty. He had an old military blanket covering him to keep warm. He smelled like he hadn't bathed in years. He had a gray, scraggly beard and long gray hair. An old green stocking cap covered his head. His face was stained with dirt, and when the man smiled at Brian, he had only a few teeth left. His skin was leathery and stretched thin.

"You shouldn't be walking around in hardly nothing," the man said, reaching into an old, torn rucksack. He pulled out some pants and a sweatshirt. They looked almost new. "They gave me these at the shelter. I was saving them, but you look like you could use them more."

Brian didn't know what to say. This man, who had next to nothing, was giving him everything that he had. Brian took the clothes, humbled by this man's generosity.

"What is your name?" Brian asked as he slid on the pants and took off his hospital gown. He slipped the sweatshirt over his head. The clothes even smelled clean.

"No one has asked me my name in a very long time." The man looked confused, like he was trying to remember what his name was. "It's Jack. Jack Duncan."

"Thank you for the clothes, Mr. Duncan."

"Just call me Jack. I lost the right to be called 'mister' a long time ago."

"I don't think you have. Mr. Duncan, I promise that I will find a way to repay you for all of this."

"You don't have to. I am just glad I could help someone again."

"Again?"

"I used to be a medic in the army. I was pretty good at it, too. I loved helping people. Army downsized, and they didn't need me anymore. So thank you for allowing me to help one more time."

This was the best man Brian had ever met. If anyone would take the time to look at him, they would see it too. Instead they didn't want to look at the dirty, homeless man, and they just walked right by. He knew what it felt like when no one wanted to look at you because of how you looked.

"Mr. Duncan, I promise that I will find a way to repay your generosity. I will be back when I can. If someone comes by looking for me, anyone, even if it's a cop, can you not say you saw me?"

"Kid, I can't condone running away from home. You don't want to end up like me, do you?"

"Would you condone it if the kid's father wanted to lock him up because he was embarrassed by him? Run medical tests on the kid because he looks different? I can't go back."

"Go on, kid, your secret is safe with me."

Before Brian turned to go, he looked at the man and asked, "Will you be here when I come back to find you?"

"Where else do I have to go?" The man laughed, which made Brian laugh with him.

Brian turned and started to run barefoot as fast as his legs could take him. With the sunglasses it made it much easier to see his way. He couldn't believe how fast he could run. The wind blew against his face as he ran down city blocks. As he ran he passed a car that was driving next to him. Fat Brian got winded walking to his classroom. The new, improved Brian was fast and agile. He wasn't feeling winded at all; he felt like he could run forever.

He ran out of the city and into the suburbs. He continued to run through neighborhoods, jumping over fences and running through backyards. He still was not thinking about where he was going. He just wanted to be somewhere his parents would never find him. He saw a forest and ran straight for it. He entered the woods and stopped running. He was amazed that he still didn't feel tired from the long run. Brian loved his new body. If he had this body in school, he wouldn't have been made fun of. He probably would have had some friends, too.

The shade from the forest, plus his sunglass, gave Brian's eyes some relief from the bright sun. He walked around exploring his surroundings. The moist earth felt good against Brian's bare feet after running on the hard cement. He passed over fallen trees and broken branches walking deeper and deeper. It was strange he never liked walking into the forest before. It always creeped him out. But now he felt strangely at home. The moist air smelled of trees and moss, which he found pleasant. The shade felt cool and damp against his skin, which he wouldn't have liked before, but now he enjoyed. He found it a little disturbing that he could smell and hear all the animals around him. That was going to take some getting used to. Brian kept walking until he came out the other side of the forest and found himself looking at the back of his parents' house.

When he entered the forest, he didn't think of it being the same forest that his parents' house backed up to. His neighborhood was over twenty miles away from the city. He ran twenty miles like it was nothing, and he would have bet in world record time too. He looked down at his muddy, bare feet.

As long as I am here, I might as well grab a few things, he thought.

The house had security alarm signs all over, but they were just to scare off burglars. His father was much too cheap to put in a real security system. Brian jumped the fence into his backyard. He grabbed the hose and rinsed off his feet. He didn't want to leave muddy footprints when he was trying to hide from his parents. Afterward, he tried the back door. Locked. In frustration he gave it a sharp tug. He heard the lock break, and the door slid open. *Oops,* he thought. He was surprised by his strength. He walked into the house hoping no one else was there

Something smelled really good. The aroma was mesmerizing. It must have been something Brian's mother cooked. Brian looked and there was nothing on the counters or on the stove. The aroma was making his mouth water. Brian followed his nose, making his way around the island in the kitchen and finding on the floor what smelled so wonderful.

Dog food? Really? I'm enticed by dog food now.

Embarrassed, he went to the fridge and found a stack of rib eye steaks. Brian didn't notice his teeth changing to resemble the teeth of a wolf. His stomach growled yelling at him to eat. Brian grabbed a steak and sank his teeth into the raw meat. With the sharp canine teeth, it took no effort to rip chunk after chunk away. He devoured the steak and grabbed another, then another. He held a steak in each hand, biting one and then the other. He continued until there was none left. Brian came out of his trance realizing that he was licking the blood from his hands. He went to the sink and rinsed off his hands.

A little bark echoed through the house. It must have been his sister's Chihuahua, Pom-Pom. He didn't hear his sister yell at the dog to be quiet. No one was home. He let out a sigh of relief as he walked out of the kitchen. His sister's dog ran up to him barking, then it started to cower. The dog peed on the floor before turning and running away.

That was weird.

Quickly, he went to his room and put on a pair of shoes. It was amazing how much tighter he could tie his laces now that he had lost all that weight. He went to grab some clothes but stopped himself, realizing that nothing would fit him now. His brother's clothes would have been too small for him, and he would rather kill himself than take anything his father owned. Brian waved it off. *Forget the clothes,* he thought. He went to the garage and grabbed the tent and sleeping bag his family hadn't used since he was little. Then he grabbed some matches and lighter fluid.

With camping gear in hand, Brian made his way back to the woods. He made sure to walk in far enough so no one would be able to see him if he made a fire. He found a nice dark spot by a fallen tree. It took a little time to set up camp. He hadn't set up a tent since he was eight. With his hands he dug out a pit and gathered wood to drop into the pit. He squirted lighter fluid on the wood and lit a match. Brian smiled as a flame shot into the air and thought, *What is it about guys and fire?*

Brian sat on the fallen tree, holding his hands up to the fire. He stared into the golden flames as they danced. He was now homeless and all alone, but for the first time in his life, he didn't feel hopeless.

Chapter Five

Chris pushed himself off the wet sticky floor and looked around. Where was he? He tried rubbing his hands on his pants, but that didn't take off whatever he was lying in. He was soaked in the dark, sticky substance. The smell of the small room was terrible, and the only light was coming through a vent in the bottom of the door. With what little light there was, Chris could see that the walls were made of concrete. He felt along the door; it was cold metal and had no handle to open it. He pushed against it, but it wouldn't budge. There was no bed, sink, or toilet, just a drain in the middle of the floor. Chris had a sick feeling in his stomach that most people who came to this room didn't stay here long enough to need a bathroom. His shoes stuck to the dark substance covering the floor as he went and sat down in the corner, feeling defeated.

After sitting for what felt like an eternity, Chris heard voices and footsteps coming toward him. He continued to sit on the floor with his arms wrapped around his knees, listening. The footsteps ended in front of the door. Chris could see the shadows of feet coming under the door. He heard what sounded like metal scraping against metal. The door flung open, and a bright light blinded Chris for a moment. A large man that looked like a body builder walked toward Chris. The man had a shaved head with a spiked collar around his neck. He wore a black tank top and leather pants. Chris thought he looked like a gothic bouncer. The man grabbed Chris and effortlessly picked him up off the ground by his neck.

"Don't hurt him, Donovan…at least not yet," a familiar voice said from behind the large man. As the woman walked around the large man, Chris recognized her immediately. It was the woman who had attacked him. Chris thought she could be very beautiful if he wasn't so terrified of her.

Another man entered behind the woman. This man was a tall, slender man. He was dressed in an expensive suit with shined shoes and a brilliant red tie that also looked very expensive. The man had thick black hair slicked back like Chris had seen in some of the old mobster movies.

"This is the boy?" the man asked in a pompous voice.

"Yes, Jaden, this is the boy," the woman said.

"Delilah, dear," Jaden started, "you always do this. You always want to turn the young, strong men. Did you not learn your lesson with Samson?"

"This will be different, my lord," Delilah said in defense. "This boy is not religious."

"You said the same thing about Samson, and he brought down a building on top of us," Jaden retorted.

"My lord, our mistake with Samson was that we tried to trick him into becoming one of us. He brought the house down on top of us because he knew that if he didn't, he would be ours. This boy is not Samson. He has no faith to turn to. I will give him my blood to turn him. Then he will want to drink," Delilah explained.

"Ah, you want him counted with us. You know better than anyone that he must drink human blood of his own free will," Jaden responded. "And you want to give him your own blood?"

"Yes, my lord," Delilah said proudly.

"You know that is forbidden. Vampires of your age are not allowed to turn humans," Jaden explained. "You know we get stronger as we age. Tell me, what would happen if you turned him and he became our enemy? Think how much damage he could do against us when he would be nearly your equal." Jaden stepped closer to Delilah until his nose almost touched hers. "We are the most powerful vampires, and our company, our family, cannot take you making another Samson—not at a time when we rule all we see. I will not allow you to destroy our family again." Jaden turned and walked for the door, stopping in the doorway without looking back. "I do not find him worthy to be counted with us, but if you want him turned, have one of the servants do it. You may make him into a half-breed."

Donovan dropped Chris to the ground and followed Jaden out the door. Once the two men were gone, Delilah turned her attention to Chris, who was coughing and gagging for air on the floor. She picked Chris up by the throat and slammed him against the wall. Chris watched as fangs slowly grew from the corners of her upper teeth.

"You are not allowed," Chris choked out in a desperate attempt to save himself.

"Tell him if you want. Then you can watch as he rips your heart out of your chest," Delilah said.

Delilah moved so fast Chris couldn't even react. She drove her fangs into his neck so hard he felt his neck break. In a matter of seconds, he began to feel light-headed. The already-dim room was beginning to grow darker. Delilah stopped sucking and let Chris fall to the floor. He was so weak from the loss of blood that he couldn't resist her when she pulled his mouth open. She pulled out his tongue and sliced it with her sharp fingernail. The pain was dulled by his weakened state. He could taste his own blood in his mouth. Delilah bit her wrist, causing blood to pour from her veins. She held it against Chris's open mouth, filling his mouth with her blood and mixing with his.

Chris was so weak he didn't realize what he was doing. His natural instincts took over. His mouth was full; his instincts told him to swallow. He swallowed a copper taste. The second time he swallowed, the copper taste wasn't as prominent. The third and final time he swallowed, the copper taste was replaced with a sweet taste.

Delilah stood and watched as Chris began to convulse. "This happens to everyone. Your body is trying to fight the change," Delilah explained. "You will die, but you will return again, reborn as one of us."

Chris stopped convulsing and felt the world spin. He could barely keep his eyes open. He could barely see Delilah walk out the door and a minute later return with a girl bound and gagged.

"This is for you when you wake up," Delilah said. "After you feed your change will be complete, and you will be free to leave your cell." She watched as Chris's eyes rolled back in his head and lost consciousness. She closed the metal door, locking the girl in with the soon-to-be predator.

When Chris awoke he didn't know how long he was unconscious. He could feel that he was different. He couldn't explain how he just felt different somehow. He opened his eyes and found the room was not as dim as it was before. He sat up and felt his neck. There were no punctures in his neck from being bitten. His neck didn't even hurt, and he was sure that it had been broken. The only evidence that he was attacked last night was the blood that now stained his shirt. With his new eyes, he looked on the floor as he saw that it was dark red. The sticky, dark substance was the blood from the victims that formerly occupied these rooms. He could hear a rhythmic beating in his ears. He looked straight to the source of the sound.

In the corner sat the girl that Delilah brought in. Her heartbeat sang to Chris like an invitation to come and feed. Chris recognized her as the girl that had been his girlfriend his sophomore year. Her name was Amy Thompson. Amy was a cute redhead with blue eyes. Chris liked the dimples that formed in her cheeks every time she smiled. She was on the cheerleading team and always made sure she looked her best no matter where she went. Now she wasn't smiling at all. She sat in the corner disheveled and dirty. Her blue jeans and purple sweatshirt were dirty and torn, as if she had been dragged. As Chris moved he could hear her heart beat faster. He could feel the ground vibrate with every beat of her heart. If he stared long enough, he could see the warmth of her blood travel through her body. The temptation was strong and pulled at Chris. He wanted nothing more than to attack Amy and drink her life away. He had to resist.

"Amy," Chris called to her.

Amy started crying again. Chris untied her and pulled the gag from her mouth "Are you going to kill me, Chris?"

"No, I'm not going to kill you," Chris answered. He stepped back to show he meant no harm. He felt ashamed that he wanted nothing more than to drain the life from her. "How did you get into this mess?"

Amy stopped crying and wiped her nose with the sleeve of her sweatshirt. Her heartbeat began to slow. "I was at a dance club and this bouncer was flirting with me. I never liked the gothic, bad boy type, but I couldn't take my eyes off him. I was drawn to him like I have never been drawn to anyone. He asked me to come with him outside. When we got outside, he grabbed me and tied me up and threw me in his car. Next thing I know I'm being dragged down here," Amy explained. "How did you get here?"

"Bad timing. I was picking on Brian, and we ended up walking into a house with some bad people," Chris told her.

"This wouldn't have happened to you if you stopped picking on him like I told you to," Amy said. "That's why I broke up with you. I couldn't stand how much of a jerk you were."

"I swear if I can get out of this…" Chris started but didn't finish.

"It might be too little too late," Amy said. "Did you see where they took Brian?"

"I don't know what happened to Brian. I know he tried to save me, but then I woke up here," Chris said. "I don't think he's alive, or I am sure he would be here with us. I hope he is dead. Death would be better than this." He sat down next to Amy and put his arm around her.

"Even after everything you did to him, he tried to save you?" Amy asked.

"I know," Chris said. "He's better than I am, always has been. If our roles were reversed, he would have never traded his friendship with me for a chance to be popular." Chris couldn't meet Amy's eyes. He was ashamed of himself. He quickly changed the subject. "Any ideas on how we are going to get out of this?"

Amy shook her head and then leaned her head against Chris's shoulder. "I don't think we are ever getting out of here." They sat like that for a few hours. They talked about school and friends. Amy talked about how she was going to miss her family. Chris sure wasn't going to miss his.

As they talked Chris's stomach started cramping. It felt as if someone was stabbing him repeatedly in the stomach. It was too painful to bear. He looked at Amy and could sense her pulse beating stronger. It was like a drum banging in his ears. He couldn't see her anymore, only the blood traveling through her body. It was so warm and inviting. He needed the blood that was inside of her. Chris had never wanted anything more. Fangs grew from the corners of his upper teeth. He could feel as they slid into position.

When he looked at Amy, he saw her lifeless body on the floor with her neck torn open and blood all over her. Chris shook his head. He knew that he had to fight this feeling. He had already turned his back on one friend and made his life a living hell; he would not condemn another. He pushed the feeling away. Never was there anything as hard as refusing the urge to drink Amy's blood. He stood up and walked to the back of the room to distance himself from her. When he did, he could feel his fangs retract, leaving his teeth looking normal once again.

"What's wrong?" Amy asked.

"Nothing," Chris said. "I just needed to stretch."

The door to the cell opened suddenly, startling Chris and Amy. Delilah walked in and looked at Chris. She then looked down at Amy, and Chris could see the anger form on her face.

"You're a disappointment," Delilah said sternly, the anger evident in every syllable. "I am starting to wonder if I should have killed you instead of your fat friend."

Shock was evident on Chris's face. "You did kill Brian?" he mumbled. He had hoped that Brian would be dead instead of being trapped in this place. The knowledge that he was dead weighed on him more than just the hope that he was. Chris wanted to be grateful that Brian would never see the inside of a cell like this. The guilt that this was all his fault and Brian would be alive if it wasn't for his bullying was too great to feel grateful. Tears fell down Chris's cheeks.

Delilah delighted in the pain Chris was now inflicted with. "I stabbed him in the heart and left him for werewolf chow."

Anger replaced shock. Chris was angry at himself, but at that moment he wanted nothing more than to rip Delilah limb from limb. He charged Delilah with fists clenched tight. He swung, and Delilah stepped out of the way with superhuman speed. Delilah swung at Chris's face in retaliation, nails like claws. The nails ripped into his face and tore the flesh. Chris fell back against the wall, grabbing his face. Blood dripped between his fingers.

"You're pathetic," Delilah spat out in disgust.

Chris saw his stepfather in that moment standing over his twelve-year-old body. "You're pathetic," his stepfather would say after he beat him to the floor. "No wonder your father left. I would leave too if I had a weak, pathetic son like you." Chris continued to get beat every time his stepfather was displeased with him. If he lost a game, he would get beat. If he forgot to pick something up at the store, he would get beat. Chris couldn't remember a time where his stepfather was ever pleased with anything he did. His mother would sit there and let it happen, too afraid to stop it. Chris was just happy that his stepfather took his anger out on him and not his mother. After she died the beatings from his stepfather were endless.

Chris looked up at Delilah and saw her for who she truly was. She was no better than his stepfather, the man he hated more than anything else in the world. He swore to himself in that moment that he would never do anything this woman ever told him to do, even if it meant dying a painful death.

Delilah grabbed Amy by the back of the shirt and lifted her to her feet. She pushed Amy toward Chris. "Drink," Delilah ordered.

"I won't hurt her," Chris yelled back.

A devilish grin came across Delilah's face. She ran her finger gently down Amy's cheek. "Perhaps I should just show you how this is done," Delilah said.

Amy's whole body started shaking with fear. She was so scared that she even wet herself. Chris didn't like seeing her this scared. "Chris," Amy begged, "help me."

"Oh, you know each other? How delicious," Delilah said.

He rushed Delilah, hoping to knock her down so the two of them could escape. Before he could get close enough to Delilah, Donovan stepped into the room with an iron bar. Donovan swung it like a baseball bat, striking Chris in the head. Chris flew against the wall and hit his head again. He fell to the floor, amazed he stayed conscious.

Delilah laughed at Chris's misfortune. "Here's your first lesson, Chris. I always win," Delilah said smugly. Chris's stepfather also used to tell him that. "Now watch as I drink the life from your friend." Amy's face went pale with fear. "I love the fear. It makes the adrenaline dump into the bloodstream and make the blood taste so much sweeter."

Amy screamed as Delilah bit into her neck. The scream died down the more Delilah drank. Delilah then threw Amy in front of Chris. Amy's blood spilled onto the ground. Chris stared at the blood. His heart was pounding. He wanted so badly to partake. He moved away from Amy's body. He was not going to become like these people. He was not going to become his stepfather.

"Pity," Delilah said. "I thought for sure that would get you to drink. No one has ever refused to drink before. You have a strong will that I am looking forward to breaking. In time…you will drink." Delilah put her hand on Donovan's shoulder. "Let's not let this one go to waste. She might be able to persuade her friend here to join us. Turn her."

"But Jaden—" Donovan began

"Is not here," Delilah cut him off. "You really think your hundred years means anything to me? To me you are just as weak as they are. Now do as I say."

Donovan took out a knife and cut his wrist. He then cut Amy's tongue and put his wrist to her mouth. Amy immediately began to drink. After she gulped down the blood, she began to convulse. Donovan stood up and walked out of the room with Delilah following.

"Perhaps this one will show you how to behave properly," Delilah said as she closed the door.

Chris sat across from Amy, watching over her for what he could only guess was all night. He noticed that Amy was growing paler as the time went by. Chris wondered if he appeared that white. He looked at his hands and arms and couldn't tell. By morning Amy looked like a porcelain doll. Every scar and blemish she had was now erased.

When Amy awoke she sat up, feeling her neck much the same way Chris had. She looked around the room and then at Chris. "Did last night really—" she started to ask.

"Happen?" Chris cut her off. "Yes, it did." Chris scooted himself across the floor until he was right next to Amy. He put an arm around her and held her close.

Once again the door to their cell was open, and Delilah glided into the room haughtily. Behind Delilah walked Donovan with a bound and gagged old man. He was dressed in rags and smelled like garbage. Chris knew that they had just grabbed a homeless man off the street.

"There is only enough for one of you. Which one is it going to be?" Delilah stated.

Chris looked at the man and could feel his pulse beating. He wanted so badly to tear into the man and drain him of his life-giving blood. His stomach cramped with want for blood. The pain was intense. He thought of his stepfather again. Killing this man would make him just like his stepfather. The thought gave Chris enough motivation to resist his hunger and the pain that came with it. With effort, he backed up until he felt his back against the wall.

Looking at Amy, Chris could tell she was feeling the same thing. Amy, on the other hand, didn't resist. She raced forward, jerking the man's head to the side so fast that Chris could hear the neck break. With no hesitation Amy bit into the man like she was biting an apple and began to drink. She didn't let go until there was not one drop left in the man. She let go of him, letting the man drop lifelessly to the floor. After she was done feeding, Chris noticed that Amy wasn't porcelain-white anymore. Feeding made the pigment come back into her skin again. She looked like she had before, a normal girl.

"That's a good girl," Delilah said, like she was praising a pet. "You drank until the heart stopped beating. Most vampires need to be told to do this. Not you. You will make a great pupil. Before we leave tell your friend how it felt to drink."

"It felt incredible, Chris," Amy said. "I could feel energy race to every part of my body. I could feel the warmth of his blood fill my body. I feel more alive than I ever have before. I feel as if I can do anything. You need to try it."

Chris looked at Amy with disgust. "I will never," he said defiantly.

Delilah looked like she was going to kill Chris that instant. "I don't know how you are resisting. You are going to stay in this cell until you drink, and believe me you will drink. It's just a matter of time." Delilah turned to Amy. "Come dear."

Amy followed Delilah out of the cell. Amy blew Chris a kiss before Donovan closed the door. At that moment Chris realized that she was no longer the Amy he knew. She was now one of them.

He pushed his back against the wall and slid down the wall until his butt hit the floor. Chris knew if he ever let go of his hate for his stepfather, then he would kill and be just like the rest of them. He needed to hold on to that hate, hold on to anything that kept him from becoming like them.

Chapter Six

Delilah led Amy up a metal staircase and through a long cement tunnel that ended at a large metal door. Through the door two rows of benches sat in the middle of the room facing a stone stage with thick metal chains bolted to the ground. The stones of the stage were stained dark red with the blood of the victims they had held.

The two women walked through the room to a hallway with large metal doors every hundred feet. The metal doors were elaborate in their workmanship and very beautiful, unlike the prison doors. Delilah stopped at the fourth door on her left. Roses with large thorns were engraved into the door. Inside was a large bedroom with a single bed in the far corner. A desk sat to one side with a bottle of what looked to be red wine sitting on top. To the other end sat a bookshelf filled with dusty books older than Amy. Crimson tapestries covered every wall hiding the cement behind it. It reminded Amy of blood that she would have found unsettling before her transformation but found strangely comforting now.

"This will be your room, Amy," Delilah said. She walked into the middle of the room. "Do you like it?" she asked.

"Oh yes," Amy replied. "It's wonderful. I had to share my old room with my sister. It was much smaller than this."

"That old life of yours is over now, Amy," Delilah stated bitterly. "I never want to hear you mention it again."

"Yes, Delilah," Amy answered.

"I will leave you for now, my dear," Delilah said. "Drink some wine and get some rest. Tomorrow you have a whole new life to look forward to."

Amy closed the door behind Delilah and looked around her new room. She went to her desk and uncorked the bottle of wine. She had never drank before. She pulled the cork from the bottle and smelled it, imitating what she had seen her father do many times. Amy could smell a little alcohol in the bottle, but what caught her attention was the smell of blood. She took a long drink from the bottle, tasting the blood-mixed wine in her mouth. She closed her eyes and enjoyed the euphoria she felt. Amy walked to the bed with bottle in hand and sat down on the edge. She looked around her room and drank to her new life.

It wasn't long before the bottle was empty. Amy set the bottle on the floor and laid herself down on the bed. Her head was spinning from the wine. As soon as her head hit the pillow, she was asleep. Dreams of ancient ceremonies with dark motives came to her. Everyone she saw stood around a stone stage like the one she had seen earlier. Each person had on black robes. She didn't feel scared as she normally would have dreaming of anything like this. She felt at ease within this dream. She felt the urge to participate. The ceremony went on for hours with vampires sacrificing humans on the stage and drinking their blood. Amy dreamt that she sacrificed a handsome young man and shared him with her fellow vampires. The vampires all welcomed her and embraced her as one of their own.

A loud roar broke the elation of the party. The vampires screamed and yelled out, "Warriors." The Vampires scattered into the darkness. Again a roar was heard, and a few bodies were thrown from the darkness back into the circle of light. Those thrown got to their feet and stared into the darkness, waiting. Their faces were torn and bleeding from whatever was out there.

Another roar sounded, but this time it was from above. Amy looked up and saw a massive furry shape fall into the middle of the group of vampires. It's body was covered in soft, black fur. The beast had long ears and a massive snout with large white teeth and a tail that whipped back and forth behind it. The long fingers of the beast had razor-sharp black claws. Golden eyes glowed as it stared at her. The beast rose to full height on long feet. It stood, pointing a black claw at her.

Terror pounded in her heart. The beast opened its mouth and ran for her on all fours with its tail raised high in the air. Blood from its vampire victims dripped out of its mouth, making it look extremely vicious. Chains flew around the beast's limbs, pulling it down to the ground. Smoke rose from where the chains touched the werewolf. The werewolf howled in pain and shrank to the human form of a man.

Naked, the man sat in the middle of the room sobbing. His face was veiled by shadows concealing his identity. Amy stepped closer to see what this man looked like. A hand grabbed her shoulder and held her still. A young woman that looked Amy's age walked past her. Her face was also veiled by shadow. The young woman walked behind the werewolf now in human form. She grabbed the man by the hair and jerked his head to the side. He did not fight in any way. He sobbed and accepted what he knew was coming. The young woman bit into his neck. The man whispered, "I love you."

The woman looked up at Amy, shadows still concealing most of her face. Blood dripped from her mouth. "Now it's your turn."

Amy sat up in bed, breathing hard. She was surprised to see that at the end of her bed, sat Delilah. "What did you see, my dear?" Delilah asked.

Still breathing hard from the dream, Amy tried her best to calm herself before she answered. She described her whole dream from beginning to end. Delilah listened intently.

Delilah picked up the wine bottle and turned it in her hands. "Everyone sees something different," Delilah said. "This wine you drank had the blood of what you call a werewolf inside. Their blood enhances our strengths and abilities for a short period. If one drinks for the first time, it acts as a conduit to the master. He will speak to you in your dream of a prophecy meant only for you. The blood will no longer bring you such messages."

"So what I saw wasn't real?" Amy asked.

"It was very real. What you saw was what our master wanted you to see. Our master wants you to lure a werewolf to us," Delilah explained.

"Who is our master?" Amy asked.

"Who do you think our master is?" Delilah asked sarcastically.

"The devil?" Amy asked.

"Yes, and he wants us as his most elite to cleanse this world of all humanity. To enslave mortals and usher in his reign," Delilah stated.

Amy welcomed the idea of destroying all humanity. All of her humanity was destroyed the minute she drank the homeless man's blood. There was nothing left inside her that cared for this world or anyone in it.

"What do the werewolves have to do with this?" Amy wondered. "Wouldn't they be playing on the same team."

"Everything in this world has its opposite: pleasure and pain, sickness and health, love and hate. As we were created to destroy this world, warriors were created to protect it. They are our enemies," Delilah explained.

"Warriors?" Amy asked.

"That is the real name for what you call werewolves," Delilah stated. "Now enough of this talk. I have a present for you." Delilah walked to the bedroom door and opened it.

Donovan stepped inside, leading a thirteen-year-old girl and her parents. It was Amy's family. When Amy's father saw his daughter, he smiled and ran for her, only to be stopped by Donovan. Donovan pushed Amy's father to the ground so that he was kneeling and looking up at Delilah. Her mother and sister were forced to kneel beside her father.

Delilah smiled and looked back at Amy. "I sent for your family so that you can show them your new life here and prove to us where your loyalties lie."

Amy walked forward until she was standing in front of her mother. She looked down at the redheaded woman that she resembled. "Oh, Mother," Amy said, helping her mother up. She wrapped her arms around her mother, and her mother embraced her daughter, weeping. Amy's mother then started to gasp, and her body began to jerk. Amy let her mother's lifeless body fall to the floor. She wiped her mother's blood from her chin. Amy smiled down at her father with long fangs still red with her mother's blood. Tears fell down his cheeks as he realized what his daughter had become.

"Would you care for some, Delilah?" Amy asked, still staring down at her father.

"Thank you, child," Delilah said. She walked over to Amy's father and picked him up by the throat. She bit into Amy's father, draining him of his life.

"Donovan, my creator," Amy said, "I give my sister to you."

Donovan smiled and grabbed Amy's sister by the hair and lifted her into the air. Amy's sister looked at her with pleading eyes as Donovan bit into her with brutal force. Amy met her sister's stare and felt nothing as she watched her sister scream with fear and die in front of her.

"Welcome to our fold," Delilah said, embracing Amy.

"Donovan, get someone to clean up these bodies," Delilah ordered. As Donovan left the room, Delilah turned her attention toward Amy.

"Now, my dear, it is time for me to teach you how to hunt, especially if you are to return to school."

"Do I have to go back to school?" Amy whined.

"It's not for learning, my dear," Delilah responded. "You'll find that school is the best place to lure prey. Young men's hormones make it almost impossible for them to think straight. Before they know it, they are a meal on your table."

Delilah laughed and led Amy out of the room. As they walked Amy asked Delilah, "What vision did you see when you drank the wine your first time?"

"I saw that I would turn a young man into a very powerful vampire."

Chapter Seven

Delilah and Amy walked past Donovan and into the bar. Amy had to use a fake ID the last time she came here. Now Donovan just winked at her as she walked in. The music was loud, and everyone inside had a hidden agenda: who could they relate to, who could they take home, who could they exploit, and for the ones inside like her, who would be their meal? The first time Amy was here, it was to have a good time. Now her agenda was to find someone to eat. She remembered how she was so intimidated by all the people. When she saw their faces, she wanted to hide her own. Now she looked at their faces and didn't see people. She saw empty vessels holding on to the blood she so desperately wanted. They were pathetic humans whose only purpose in life was to feed her desires. They were nothing better than cattle, allowed to live until a higher being wanted food.

Amy followed Delilah to the bar and stood looking at the crowd. "Which one would you like tonight, dear?" Delilah asked.

Amy looked at the dance floor and then everyone at the bar. One man stood out to her. He looked down at his drink and nowhere else. His shoulders were slumped, and he looked as if he had the worst day in his life. His dark hair was messy like he didn't care what he looked like.

"I want that one," Amy said.

Delilah looked at the man. "Oh, that one does look yummy. He looks as though he would not care if you took his life. Perfect for your first time. Me, myself, I like one that is vibrant and full of life. It makes it that much more rewarding when I kill them." Delilah turned to look Amy in the eyes. "Now remember what I taught you. Our venom can also work as drug to influence their mind. It only has to touch the tongue, then they will be open to anything you suggest."

"What if I can't get them to ingest the venom?" Amy asked.

"Then you have to do what nature intended for you to do when you were made a woman: seduce him," Delilah said.

"I can't force him to take it?" Amy asked.

"You can, but they will be more likely to try and resist the effects," Delilah answered.

Amy got off her stool and walked over to the man. The new clothes Delilah had bought her were tight and uncomfortable. Her leather skirt didn't give much room for walking, and her tight shirt didn't leave anything for the imagination. Delilah had told her that it was part of hunting. "One must entice her victim," Delilah had said. "Use your body and bring them to you, much like a Venus flytrap. Look like the innocent flower to your meal, and then snap on them when it is too late. If the meal comes to you, then all that is left for you to do is snap the trap shut."

The poor man didn't notice as Amy grabbed the seat next to him. Sitting this close to him, Amy noticed how lean and almost starved the man looked. She ordered herself a drink and looked at the man. "You look like you've had a hard day," she said, feeling so stupid. She had heard that line in so many movies and thought it was so cliché and now here she was saying the same stupid line.

The man looked at her with deep blue eyes. They were pretty but sad. "You could say I had a hard day," the man replied.

Amy tried to look him in the eyes, but he looked back at his drink. How was she supposed to seduce him if he wouldn't even look at her? The bartender came with her drink, and she took a sip. Delilah had told her alcohol didn't affect vampires, but it was good to keep appearances and blend in. "Tell me about your hard day," she said after sipping her drink.

"Let's see, I lost my job. I went home and told my wife, and she left me and took my kids with her. Now I am sitting at this bar drinking for the first time in my life. How does that sound for a hard day?"

"That sounds more like a crappy day," Amy said with a sympathetic tone, even though she couldn't have cared less. "But I have good news for you. Your day is about to get better." Amy leaned forward, trying to show as much cleavage as possible, but the man wasn't even looking.

"Thanks for the offer, but I would rather just sit here drowning myself slowly," the man responded.

Amy looked to Delilah for help, but she was on the dance floor working a web of her own. Amy looked back to the man and tried to improvise the best she could. "At least let me buy you a drink and give you a little something on such a bad day." She motioned to the bartender to get a drink for the man next to her. As the bartender was fixing the drink, Amy put her finger in her mouth and gently bit her fingertip. To anyone looking they would think it was very seductive. In reality she was extending her fangs just enough so she could wipe some venom off her fang onto her fingertip. When the bartender brought the drink, she grabbed it from him. She ran her finger around the rim, smearing the clear venom around the glass.

The man grabbed the glass from her and thanked her. He took a sip, and Amy could see the venom take effect immediately. The man's head started to hang a little more, and his shoulders drooped. Amy looked up from the man to see Delilah walk by with a young woman motioning for Amy to meet her out back.

"Follow me," Amy said. The man stood up and followed Amy through the bar and out the back.

Delilah stood with the young woman, who looked like she was in the middle of a bachelorette party. She had on a tiara and a sash that read: BRIDE TO BE. The young woman stood in a trance. Amy guessed she was drugged, too.

"You did well," Delilah said, looking at Amy's catch. "You're a natural at this." She walked over to stand beside Amy with her victim in tow. "Now I want you to watch what I do." Delilah's fangs extended as she pulled the woman's head to the side at a painful angle. "It doesn't matter where you bite them. I enjoy the neck myself. I feel that I can get more blood flow. Your fangs will inject venom just like a snake into your prey that will keep their blood from clotting. It will also make the heart beat faster, pumping more blood to you. You may have already noticed this with your first few meals. The faster the heart pumps, the faster we can finish off our victims."

Delilah bit the woman, but she seemed not to even notice that her life was being drained from her. When she was finished, she continued the lesson. "You will notice that the bite will seal itself up after a few seconds. That is another result from the venom, and it will keep anyone from knowing that vampires killed her. With no blood in the body, the venom dissolves and with it the last trace that we killed this person. If you don't drink until the heart stops beating, the venom will eventually change their blood."

"Change their blood? To what?" Amy asked.

"That is what I am about to show you, dear. Watch the young woman."

Amy watched as the young woman's whole body convulsed like she was having a seizure, and then she stopped as if dead. The young woman's eyes opened and looked around as if realizing where she was for the first time. She got to her feet and wrapped her arms around herself nervously. The young woman was very pale.

"This is what happens when you don't finish your meal," Delilah stated.

"What is she?" Amy asked.

"She's a vampire," Delilah stated. "Not a full blood vampire like us but a half-breed. These are merely bitten vampires. They still have some semblance of their old lives left in them but not enough to want to go back to them. They are more like us now than they are like humans. The difference is it doesn't make them look human as it does for us, and sunlight is deadly for them. With us it's more of a nuisance."

"Then why make them?" Amy asked.

"Why for subjects, my dear. You can't rule without subjects. Some make wonderful servants. We let them live like this as long as they don't reveal who they really are to the world. Think of this as chess, dear. Every war needs pawns. If they prove themselves loyal over time, then we might change them fully into one of us," Delilah explained.

"They can still become like us?"

"Of course they can. Just ask Donovan. He was a servant before joining our ranks. He served Jaden very well, and thus he was allowed to become one of us. All it takes is blood from a full vampire to complete the change."

Delilah walked forward, stopping in front of the young woman. Extending her fangs once again, she bit into the woman and drained her of whatever was left in her body. This time the woman did scream, but it was weak and muffled. There wasn't much blood left, and Delilah finished quickly. The woman fell to the ground, convulsing again and then went still, this time never to get up again. "You see, a full vampire's venom is deadly the second time to half-breeds. If they don't get our blood in time, they die. Now it is your turn," Delilah instructed Amy.

Amy turned to the man still standing beside her. Without hesitation she bit into his neck, holding his head by the hair with her right hand. Amy had to remind herself to stop drinking early. It was hard to do, but with effort she was able to make herself quit. The man fell to the ground, lifeless. Amy stood over him. His bite wounds healed, and he started to convulse. After a minute his eyes opened, and he got to his feet, looking at Amy.

Delilah walked up beside Amy. "What is your name," Delilah asked.

"Eric," the man replied.

"Well, Eric, you belong to Amy now. Do you understand?"

Eric nodded his head slowly

"Good," Delilah said.

"Are they always like this, like a zombie?" Amy asked.

"He is newly born, dear. He is just low on blood. Once he feeds he will be much better."

Donovan walked out of the back door holding the arms of two young men. The two men didn't look like they were under the influence of any venom. No, these men looked more like they had passed out at the bar. Donovan walked the two men to stand in front of Eric.

"Ah, right on time, Donovan," Delilah said.

"Wherz zee pwize wee won?" one of the drunk men said. Pointing up at Donovan's face, he continued, "You tell wee won."

"You, gentlemen, surely did win," Delilah said. Then she turned to the new half-breed. "Eric, your first meal is served.

Eric, who looked dead before now, looked very much alive. He jumped onto the first drunken man, knocking him to the ground and ripping into his throat. The second man tried to run, but Eric grabbed him by the leg and held him in place with his new strength while he finished his first meal. Afterward, he pulled the second man to the ground, biting and ripping his neck apart.

"I love watching a half-breed's first time. It's so primal," Delilah said, clapping her hands together. "It almost makes you forget what pathetic creatures they are."

The half-breed finished his meal and stood, looking at the two women as if seeing them for the first time.

"Just like children," Delilah pointed out. "Did any of your meal actually make into your mouth?"

Eric wiped the blood off his chin and looked at his blood-covered hand. "Am I a vampire?"

"What else would you be," Delilah said in a mocking tone. "You are no longer human. We have saved you from that existence. If you want to become a full vampire, you must do as I say."

"Yeah, OK," Eric said, as if he wasn't paying attention.

Delilah stared at him with a look of anger on her face that made even Amy nervous.

"Yes, ma'am," Eric said, looking very much afraid.

"Better," Delilah said. The look of anger left her face as quick as it came. "I will tell you the rules as you follow me."

Eric answered, "Yes, ma'am," not wanting the wrath of Delilah.

As they walked Delilah spoke about the rules. Amy wasn't sure if it was Delilah's rules or the general rules for all vampires, but she now knew better than to question.

"There are a few rules we live by," Delilah started. "For you half-breeds, you must not go into the daylight, or you will die. You will heal quickly, and anything that does not heal on its own will be healed with blood, except your pale skin. You will remain as pale as you are now until the day you are made into a full vampire. You will not show up in mirrors. You only half exist in this world, and mirrors will only show someone who fully exists. For every vampire, full or half-breed, these next rules are the same. You must not feed in public or have any witnesses left alive who have seen you feed. We have worked for centuries to have the humans believe us as myth and to esteem to be like the vampires they see in the movies. All it takes is to be spied on once and centuries of work would be for nothing. If you see a warrior—to you it would be a werewolf—run. They are our enemies and will kill us on sight. Only a full vampire can hope to win a fight against a warrior, and even then the chance is slim. Vampires have woven into the fabric of every society around the world. Most of the media you hear, see, or read belongs to us. After media, politicians are not far behind. They sought us out for help. Politicians hunger for power, and they don't care how they get it. The mortals that are with us we will make into a shining knight. The mortals who are not with us we will crucify. Mortals don't suspect a thing. They will believe anything we tell them to believe. Because of the media and politics, we have seized hold of every government and population. The key is not to do everything at once but to work a little at a time. Big changes mortals will fight against, but little changes they will accept until they have swallowed all the poison. We work in secret, and we must stay in secret until we are told otherwise. Everyone understand?"

Amy and Eric both said, "Yes, ma'am."

"Now, I am going to give you an example of a man who has broken these rules. This man I found doing stage performances. He would do anything from magic shows to Shakespeare. He loved the limelight. He was a very good entertainer, and that's what attracted me. One night I stalked him and changed him into a half-breed. He was very enthusiastic about his new life. He learned the rules, and accepted them, just as you did. The problem came from his need for attention. He couldn't stand living in secret; he needed to be famous. He found a writer and followed him for a time before revealing himself. That alone would have meant a death sentence. This half-breed told this writer wondrous tales about himself. He called himself the king of the vampires. He used his sleight of hand to make this human believe that he could turn into a bat, or a wolf, or even fog. With his vampire speed, it would have been no challenge to fool any human. He told the human that he was from a royal lineage. This human wrote everything that he was told and then published the book he wrote under the title *Dracula*. All this half-breed dreamt of became a reality, or so he thought. He was the most famous person in all the world. He was also feared and despised. Whomever he revealed himself to tried to kill him. He thought he would be loved. He was now the most hated creature in the world."

Amy interrupted, "You're telling me that Count Dracula is real?"

"He is real, my dear," Delilah responded, "in a way. He is not what you have seen in the movies. Luckily for us the mortals eventually loved Dracula. Some even wanted to become like him. That is where we discovered how powerful media really could be. It was what humans today call a happy accident. It still didn't change the fact that this half-breed broke the rules. No matter what came of it, he still had to be punished."

Delilah led the small group underground just as daylight was starting to break. They were led to the room that held the cells where Amy was held. Delilah went to the only door across from the cells. In the room were tables and devices that looked like they could only be used for torture. One table held tools that didn't look like they were used for anything pleasant—a lot of silver tools with hooks and blades.

No table was occupied except for one in the corner. The table sat at an incline facing a slowly spinning fan. The fan blades were large, blocking the sunlight that was trying to poor in behind it. In between the rotation of the large blades, the sunlight would poor in for a few seconds. The person on the table would scream with pain when the sunlight hit him and then cry tears of pain when the shade covered him. This would repeat every few seconds.

The group followed Delilah to the table in the corner. "Everyone, I would like for you to meet Dracula," she said, waving a hand toward the poor man. As she waved her hand, sunlight hit Dracula. It was almost as if she planned for the timing of the fan for a more dramatic affect.

Amy watched as the sun hit Dracula. He grunted, trying not to scream, but eventually he did. His skin smoked and then caught fire.

When the shade covered him, the flame died and his skin was left black and ashen. To Amy it looked like a marshmallow that had been on fire and the flames had been blown out.

"But Dracula isn't your real name, is it? Your real name wasn't good enough to immortalize you in books. Why don't you tell these good vampires what your real name is," Delilah demanded.

The man screamed with the sunlight burning him. When he was in the shade, he laughed and said, "Vlad the Impaler."

"That isn't your real name either," Delilah said. Her face became angry like Amy had seen with Eric. Delilah walked toward the fan and held it in place so the sunlight poured in. Her arm didn't burn with the sunlight. Instead, where the sun touched her arm, it looked like rotting flesh. "No, your real name is Vincent. But, alas, who would give any esteem to Count Vincent? Oh no, watch out. Here comes Vincent to eat you!" Delilah laughed a sinister laugh.

The whole time Vincent was burning and screaming. His whole body was now in flames.

"This pathetic excuse for a half-breed reinvented himself into Dracula. I have to say the name was a nice touch. It really does sound better than Vincent." Delilah turned her attention to the others in the room. "Let this pathetic excuse for a vampire be an example to you all. Break the rules, reveal yourself to anyone, show our true nature, and you will share his fate. Delilah then turned the fan so the shade hit Vincent.

Vincent sat on the table with no more skin or hair on his body. Some muscle was burnt away to show the bone underneath. His cheeks had burnt away, revealing the teeth inside his mouth.

"Amy, my dear," Delilah said, "would you please take a ladle of blood from that bucket next to you and give it to Vincent?"

Amy did as she was asked. She ladled blood from the bucket and slowly poured it into the mouth of Vincent. Instantly he began to heal. His muscles reformed, followed by his pale skin wrapping itself around the muscles, and then his hair grew back to what it was before. His mouth even grew his cheeks back. Within half a minute, he looked like he had never been hurt at all.

As soon as he was healed, Delilah let go of the fan, and the torture began anew. As he began to scream again, Delilah led Amy and Eric toward the exit as if nothing could be more normal.

Delilah stopped before going out the door. "Disappoint me in any way, and either of you can have the table next to Vincent. Sunlight wouldn't hurt you, Amy, my dear. For you it would come down to classic, painful torture with dull instruments. I find the classics to work the best. You two wait for me here. I have one more torture to oversee."

Chapter Eight

Nighttime had set upon Brian, and the only change he recognized was that the light was a little less bright with his sunglasses on. The pain in his eyes had left with the light. He took off his glasses and found that he could see better than he could during a noonday. The colors seemed to be more vibrant and alive. The pine needles on the tree seemed greener than they normally would, while its trunk, a mixture of brown and white, stood out to him like never before. No detail escaped his eyes. Every curve and crevice revealed itself to him like never before. The ground was a darker brown than it was before. Each dip and mound that would otherwise be hidden was now showing itself to Brian. He could make out each ant marching across the dark canvas of earth searching for food. Never before could he see each leg of an ant move unless he was close to the ground. Now he just stood there in awe at the new world that was revealed to him through his new eyes.

"I can now see in HD," Brian joked.

The night sky had completely changed to his new eyes. The black night sky was no longer there, nor was it a blue sky. It was a light gray sky instead. It looked odd to Brian. His whole life the sky was either black or blue. Now he stood there looking at a gray sky. The stars were still shining, but not as brightly as they had before. To Brian it looked like someone covered the sky with a gray blanket and poked holes in it to let a little bit of light through. It was at this moment that it occurred to Brian that he would never see darkness again. This was what night would look like to him for the rest of his life, however long that would be.

Werewolf genes rock, he thought, smiling to himself.

Gurgling noises broke the silence. He was hungry again, and he knew of only once place that had food. He just hoped they didn't notice the broken door. He ran through the woods, enjoying his speed and strength. His new eyes picked out obstacles to avoid, and his new body reacted with ease. He ducked under limbs and jumped over stumps. Dips in the earth were no longer hidden and easy to avoid. In a moment's time, he was at the edge of the forest and looking at the back of his parent's house.

As he got closer to the house, he could hear his parents yelling. They were loud, which was unusual. His father was much too worried about his appearance to let the neighbors hear him yell.

Brian jumped the fence and reached the back door, holding his breath as he tried to slide the door. He let out his air in relief. It was still broken. He stopped when he heard his sister yell.

"Pom-Pom is freaked out. What did you do to her, Craig?" she yelled.

"Nothing, Janet. I don't care about your stupid dog," Craig yelled back. They were both upstairs.

"Well, it had to be you. Who else would do this?"

"Maybe Brian did it," Craig yelled, mocking his sister.

"Yeah right. Dad said Brian's still at the hospital."

Brian's father told his siblings that he was still in the hospital. The man didn't even care enough about Brian to tell Janet and Craig that their brother ran away. Brian felt his anger rise. He clenched his fists and breathed slowly. His father was no longer his concern. He was here for food, and then he was gone. He promised himself this was the last time he would see this house.

Bedroom doors slammed upstairs, signaling that Janet and Craig had reached the end of their yelling match.

Brian slowly walked into the kitchen and over to the fridge. He opened the fridge door and wanted to do a little dance. The steaks were replaced. He looked in the freezer and found a few more pounds. He licked his lips and loaded his arms up with meat. He started to make his way outside when his heard his father yell. It sounded like they were yelling by the front door. Odd, they usually fight in his father's office where no one could hear them. His father had his office soundproofed for when he met clients so no one could eavesdrop.

"I don't understand why you are so angry," his father yelled.

"How can you not see?" his mother yelled back. "This was all your idea. You thought it would be bad for business to have your clients see you with our son. Dinners were planned at restaurants where you knew your clients would be so they could see you with your loving family, vacations so they could see what a wonderful father you were. What's worse is you made me start believing it, too. Brian was stuck in his room with no one to care for him. He went to school with no friends to talk to. It took me losing my son to see what kind of mother you turned me into."

"What do you want me to do about it now? He's gone, April. The boy ran away."

"Because of you, Charles. He ran away because of you. We need to go look for him. I need to go look for him. I'm going to call the police."

"You can't. It might get out that he is our son, and I cannot risk that."

"Of course you can't. It's all about you and how you look to your clients. I don't care anymore. You are done controlling me. I am calling the police."

"If you do, they will not believe you. I will just tell them that I enrolled Brian in military school and that you are taking it hard."

Brian's mother started to cry, and his heart went out to her. He never heard his mother care about him before. He moved cautiously to the hallway so he could see his mother. He wanted to look at her and see what it looked like when a mother cared. The only problem was his parents were not in the hallway. He could still hear his mother crying. The sound was coming from his father's office. A scent flowed to him from under the office door. It smelled almost like it does during a rainstorm. Brian wondered if his father got a spray for his office. The smell was quickly covered up by something spicy, almost like a hot pepper.

"I don't have time to worry about this anymore. My client is going to be here any minute!" his father yelled. Brian could hear the anger in his voice.

"Of course I wouldn't want to ruin your reputation," his mother responded sarcastically. She opened the door and said in a hate-filled tone, "I will never forgive you for this."

She slammed the door behind her and turned. Brian hesitated too long, and she caught sight of him. Brian made his way for the door with his mother following behind. "Brian," she yelled out. He stopped despite himself. He didn't know why. He couldn't find the strength to run when he heard his mother's plea.

He stood there with his arms full of meat while his mother circled around him. Tears flowed down her cheeks as she looked upon her son. She held her hand against his cheek. The warmth of her touch felt good. She smelled of freshly picked flowers. It was so fragrant and sweet. Brian didn't know she wore perfume that smelled like that. He thought she wore a little too much, then he attributed it to his strong sense of smell.

"I'm sorry," his mother said with tears in her eyes. "I am so sorry. Please forgive me."

Brian felt tears trickling down his cheeks. The hate he felt for her began melting away. In a way she was just as much a victim as he was.

"You are not the one who needs to be sorry, Mother." He was surprised at his response. He hoped his new voice didn't frighten her.

His mother stood her ground, looking into Brian's golden-yellow eyes. "What happened to you? How did you change into…this?"

"I can't tell you."

"Your eyes, your hair, your voice…everything is different. I don't understand how this could happen. If I didn't see your eyes at the hospital, I wouldn't have recognized you."

"You can't tell anyone I look like this." He looked his mother in the eyes. "Please."

"I won't. I promise." She looked at the meat in his arms. "You're hungry. Let me cook you something."

"I can't. I have to go. Please, don't tell anyone I was here."

"At least let me give you some money for a hotel."

Brian bent down to kiss his mother on the cheek. He seemed to have grown a few inches. He felt like he towered over his five-foot-four-inch mother.

Brian moved past his mother, and she made no attempt to stop him. She started crying again, and her fragrance immediately changed to that of a rainstorm. Brian turned to look at her again, thinking it odd.

"If you need anything, Brian…"

He nodded his understanding.

"It doesn't matter what you look like. You will always be my son."

A car door shut in front of the house, and Brian knew he really needed to leave. He shut the door and stood there looking into the house as his mother turned and left the room.

A putrid smell came to Brian, and he almost vomited. He heard his father greet his client and usher the man into the office.

"We have a problem," Brian's father said.

"What kind of problem?" the client asked. The voice belonged to a man.

"One judge would not cooperate," his father announced.

"Only one judge? I thought there would be a handful more with some morals, but one? I can take care of one judge. You needn't worry about him any longer."

"What do you plan on doing?"

"Fifty judges is a massacre, but one judge is only an accident."

Brian wanted to get closer and hear what his father was involving himself in. Whatever it was didn't sound good. Brian turned the corner and saw a tall man with a crooked nose standing in front of the house with his arms folded. The man wore a leather jacket over a polo shirt with blue jeans and what looked like military boots. The man must have stepped in something because the stench coming from him was unbearable. It smelled like something rotting, almost like spoiled meat. The man turned and saw Brian and became immediately irate.

The man reached into his jacket, pulled out a knife, slipped something over his knuckles, and sprinted toward Brian. Brian didn't know what to do; he was like a deer caught in the headlights. He told his legs to move, but they wouldn't. Brian just stood there as the man came full sprint, hitting him with the metal he slipped over his knuckles. Brian flew against the fence, knocking it down. His face burned where he was hit.

"I'm going to drink your blood, warrior," the man hissed as vampire fangs extended out of his mouth. The man stood over Brian, lifting his knife and driving it toward Brian's chest.

This time Brian did react and kicked the man in the crotch. It might not have been the most manly of moves, but it was effective. The man fell to the ground howling in pain. Brian got to his feet and made his way to the forest as quickly as his legs would take him.

The man didn't waste any time chasing Brian. He was right behind him and gaining ground. Brian knew the reason the man was gaining on him so quickly.

Why am I still holding on to this meat, Brian thought. Even though it was slowing him down, he couldn't make himself drop it because he was so afraid. He made it to the edge of the forest.

Suddenly a sharp pain came from the back of Brian's leg. It burned so badly. Brian fell to the ground, and his pile of meat scattered around him. He rolled over it in time to see the vampire open his mouth and dropping on Brian. Brian held the man by his shoulders, doing his best not to be a vampire snack. The man pushed down hard, his saliva dripping from the ends of his fangs. Brian had an idea that he had seen in a movie. He hoped it would work. He let the vampire fall toward him while he head-butted the vampire in the nose with all of his might. Brian saw stars immediately, but the vampire rolled off Brian, holding his nose.

Growling came from behind him. Farther in the forest, Brian saw two massive werewolves with gray fur and golden-yellow eyes. The vampire must have heard the growling too because he started to scramble toward Brian's house on his hand and knees. Brian grabbed the man by the ankle, dragging him backward. The vampire rolled over and pulled the knife out of the back of Brian's leg. The pain was intense. In a fit of rage and pain, he pulled as hard as he could. Instead of pulling the vampire closer to him, he sent the vampire flying over his head toward the warriors.

"Whoa," Brian said, looking at his hands, not believing what he had just done. He let out some laughter. "I guess you won't like me when I'm angry."

The laughter stopped when he heard the vampire yelling and screaming as tearing and crunching sounds echoed through the woods. Brian closed his eyes and tried to block out the sounds, hoping that he would not vomit. When the night became silent again, Brian got to his feet and stood there, looking at the two pairs of golden eyes looking back at him. Golden eyes meeting golden eyes.

For a long moment, they just stood there looking at each other. Finally Brian couldn't stand the silence anymore.

"Um, hi," he said. This was odd talking to two massive beasts. Most people would run in terror right now, but Brian didn't feel like he needed to fear them. "I'm not sure what I'm supposed to do. Do I go with you? Do I ask you questions? Can either of you talk? The ones I saw before were able to talk."

"Don't be stupid," one of the warriors said. His voice was very deep and terrifying.

Brian had to shake his head. Not only did the warrior speak, it insulted him. *That's something they don't put in horror movies,* Brian thought. "Well, what do you expect me to do?" Brian didn't hide the irritation in his voice.

"We need to leave before this one's master comes looking," the other warrior said with a voice as deep as the first.

"I have a camp set up deeper in the forest," Brian responded.

"Lead the way," the first warrior said.

Brian gathered his fallen steaks before limping toward the two massive beasts. Each step he took shot a ripple of pain up his leg. When he was a few feet away from the warriors he got to see their handy work. There wasn't much left of the vampire that attacked him. It was a bloody pile of ripped flesh and dismembered body parts. It was truly a grotesque scene and too much for Brian to behold. He vomited on the forest floor. He knew it wasn't a very good first impression he was making. At least he missed his armful of meat.

"What did I tell you?" the second warrior said to the first. "He is truly innocent."

"I can see that," the first responded. "Let's hope the next time he can hold down his food. Let's leave this here for his master to find."

The warrior threw a hairy, clawed hand on top of the broken carcass that used to be a vampire. It didn't look like a hand that belonged to the vampire. He looked at the warrior who threw it, and there was only a stump where his hand should be. His forearm was dripping blood. Brian then vomited once again. The first warrior rolled his eyes and let out a sigh. Brian thought it was a funny sight to see such a scary monster act in a ridiculous way.

"Lead on," the second warrior said.

Chapter Nine

The forest was eerily quiet as Brian led the two warriors. Not one sound came from them as they walked. For creatures that big, Brian thought he would have heard their feet hit the ground, or even a twig snapping. There was no way they could avoid making any noise, but no, there was not one sound. They weren't even breathing heavily. It was enough to creep Brian out, if he didn't know that these were the good guys.

Brian led them to his campsite. He was thankful that it was deep enough into the woods that no one would come across it, at least that's what Brian hoped. As he dropped his armful of steaks into his tent, he watched as the two warriors slowly walked around the camp, sniffing the air.

They came into the camp and one said to the other, "Nothing."

"Nothing," the other echoed in reply.

"Would you like to pee around the camp, too?" Brian immediately bit his lip. When he was a child, he had a problem of saying things before his brain could catch up and let him know not to say that. When he became obese, he learned the hard way not to say anything or it would catch unwanted attention. It seemed that this childhood problem had returned.

The warriors did not reply to Brian's comment, which he was very grateful for. They began to shrink in front of Brian. He had to rub his eyes to make sure that he was sure of what he was seeing. They were shrinking. It was amazing for him to watch. How many people out there could say that they have seen a werewolf change forms? Brian watched carefully, wondering if he would learn to do the same.

The change started with shrinking. For every part of their body that moved and shrank it let off a small popping noise. The sound was similar to someone popping their knuckles repeatedly. As they were shrinking down their ears moved to the side of their heads and formed normal human ears. Their massive snouts pushed back into their faces until a human nose and mouth were formed. The fur on their bodies shriveled and pulled back into the skin as if someone had attached a vacuum to their bodies and sucked their fur back inside. The black, razor-sharp claws turned white and became human fingernails and toenails. Their feet and hands shrank until they looked like human hands, except for the one who lost one. Their teeth flattened into normal human teeth. A popping sound was being echoed from their bodies until they were in human form. The last part of them to change was their golden eyes. One's eyes changed from golden to gray and the other to brown. That's when Brian realized that they were both completely naked.

"You're naked," Brian announced, looking to the sky.

"Just think of it as being in a gym locker room," one of the newly formed humans said.

Brian recognized that voice. He brought his eyes down making sure not to bring them down further than their faces. In front of him stood his new teachers, Mr. Aurelius and Mr. Samuel. Mr. Aurelius was the warrior that had lost his hand in Brian's defense.

"Mr. Aurelius, I can understand, but Mr. Samuel, you are a werewolf?"

"Why does everyone say that?" Mr. Aurelius complained, causing Mr. Samuel to let out a small laugh.

Mr. Samuel turned his attention to Brian. "You can call me Samuel, and this is Marcus."

"Right, like the Marcus Aurelius." Brian waited for them to tell him it wasn't *the* Marcus Aurelius, but they never did. "You mean he is?"

Samuel answered his question. "We are immortal, Brian, just like you are now. Some of us might be people that you recognize out of history, like Marcus here."

Brian had always heard the word *immortal* and knew its meaning, but it never really meant anything to him until that moment. That's when immortality hit him right in the face and the realization of what it really was to be immortal.

Excitement washed over Brian, and he wanted to ask Marcus lots of questions about his timeline and what it was like way back then. That's when he saw Marcus's bloody stump dripping. Guilt replaced the excitement, and he quickly ran into his tent, ripping some of the fabric from his sleeping bag.

"I am so sorry about your hand," Brian said, handing the piece of fabric to Marcus.

"I appreciate your sincerity," Marcus responded, grabbing the fabric. "And thank you for the dressing." Marcus handed the piece of fabric to Samuel, who helped him wrap his wounded arm.

"Is it going to grow back? I'm not sure how this whole thing works," Brian said both nervously and curiously.

Samuel answered the question as he finished helping Marcus. "Normally we would have kept Marcus's hand and bound it to his arm until it healed. But he was cut with a silver blade. Warriors cannot heal from silver. Just touching silver feels like we are sticking our hands into a furnace."

"So that's what he hit me and stabbed me with," Brian rubbed his cheek where he was hit with the vampire's silver knuckles.

Samuel saw the mark on Brian's cheek and stepped closer to investigate. "This is curious," Samuel announced to Marcus as he looked at Brian's cheek. "Brian has singe marks on his cheek as if he was literally burned."

"Didn't you just say that silver burns you?"

"I said that it feels like it is burning us. To you it actually does burn." Samuel sniffed the air around Brian. "You even smell different. Can you change your eyes back to normal?"

Brian shook his head. "I don't believe so. I woke up in the hospital like this. I think for me this is my new normal."

"What are you thinking, Samuel?" Marcus asked.

"I think he is a new breed of wolf, Marcus. Just like my sister informed me he would be."

"You're Almira's twin brother?"

"I am. How did you know her name?"

"When we adopted her, that name just felt right."

"Interesting," Samuel said. "We only spoke a few times in my dreams, but I knew how fond she was of you. I thought it was just a dream at first because my sister hated all humans, but she came to me again and told me the same message."

"That's when you came looking for me?"

"We were already here; we just had to get jobs at your school to find you."

"You were already here?"

Marcus answered Brian's question this time. "Your father has been under our surveillance for some time. He has been meeting with vampires a couple times a week. We were trying to find out what they were plotting."

"Wouldn't they just eat my father?"

"Not necessarily," Samuel replied. "Vampires' end game is the destruction of this world. They can't just turn all mortals to do that. Mortals would just fight back. They need to coerce the mortals to give up their own freedoms and welcome destruction freely. They work in the shadow of the world while their puppets work in the open. That's why some mortals are so important to them. They can put the mortals into positions of leadership where they can make laws to slowly take away the freedoms and moral liberties. Before mortals realize that they have been tricked, it is too late."

"Mortals can see what is happening, can't they?"

"Did you?" Marcus asked. "Mortals are nothing more than cattle. It is easier to be told how to think or how to feel instead of learning on their own."

"The vampires have their fangs in everything from politics to television," Samuel answered. "Every mortal has a television in their homes. That means that every mortal has a tool of the vampires in their homes. Through movies and television, they can slowly introduce new ideas. The mortals don't even know that it's happening."

"This is a little hard to accept," Brian said skeptically.

"All right, I understand it can be a little hard to accept when you have been raised in the middle of the problem. Let's see if I can explain it in a way that you might understand." Samuel paced for half a second before continuing. "Many years ago the movies showed the vampires as evil and bad, correct?"

Brian nodded.

"Now vampires are heroes and looked at as sex symbols."

Marcus cut in. "Vampires are now seen as mysterious and misunderstood. They show themselves as the caring beings that just want to be loved by humans, while they show us as brain-dead monsters that only need to be destroyed."

"My point is," Samuel continued, "they started out with a truth: vampires are evil. Then they twisted the truth until it became accepted that only a select group of vampires are evil but the majority is good in nature."

Brian thought about some of the movies that he had seen growing up and remembered the old movies that his parents had shown him that scared the crap out of him. Now when he watched television, it was the vampires that were the victims. What Samuel was saying did make sense.

"Do people like my father realize who the vampires are?"

Marcus answered, "They do, but they do not care. People like your father will do whatever is asked of them for the promise of power or money, or both. They do not know the vampires' end game, and they do not care. As long as they think they can get what they want, they will sell their soul to get it."

"So everything that I have seen on television or in the movies is wrong?"

"More or less," Samuel said.

"So the full moon?"

"Does nothing," Marcus said as he went to the fire and moved some of the ashes around with a stick. The fire burst back to life, and he threw in a few branches that were next to the fire.

"But silver is a truth they put in all movies?"

"They wanted all mortals to know how to kill us if they ever discovered us. The most effective lies always have a little bit of truth mixed in," Samuel said, taking a seat next to Brian on the fallen tree.

Brian was uncomfortable with how comfortable they were with their nudity. "Is there anything else that can hurt us, or is it just silver?"

Marcus spoke up. "There are many things that can hurt us. There are a few that can kill us. Removing our head always works. Then there is vampire venom. A little stings, but get enough in your bloodstream, and it will cause your heart to explode. The easiest and most painful way is to use silver."

"Great. Vampire venom, heart explosions, and removing my head. This all sounds so comforting. And why silver? It doesn't make sense. It seems so random that out of everything in this world, silver is the thing that hurts us the most."

Samuel held up his hand for Marcus to be quiet. He could see that Marcus's not-so-subtle way of explaining things was causing a panic in their new warrior.

"It wasn't always silver, Brian. The moment Judas betrayed Christ for twenty pieces of silver was the moment it became our enemy's greatest weapon. It took the enemy some time before they discovered it, but they finally did. We have lost many warriors since then—faster than we could replace them. We are losing this war, Brian. Now that our enemy controls the media and politicians, it has become increasingly faster. Mortals are slipping faster than I have ever witnessed before."

"Almira said that the order was failing, too."

"What all did my sister tell you, if you don't mind?"

Brian told the two warriors everything Almira had said to him before he woke up in the hospital. Samuel was listening intently, nodding every few words. Marcus kept gathering wood for the fire but still listened to every word.

"Samuel, what he speaks makes sense," Marcus said as he stood up from the fire.

"It is what I have been suspecting for some time. The order is falling into disrepair."

Marcus came forward until he stood in front of Samuel. As he came forward, Brian noticed that his bandages were soaked with blood and dripping. He went to the tent and ripped some more fabric from his sleeping bag. He thought a couple of steaks might help Marcus feel better. He grabbed a couple of steaks and handed them to Marcus.

"If he is to change the order, he needs to be part of the order," Marcus said as he took the piece of fabric and the steaks from Brian with a thank-you.

"You are right, Marcus. Brian does need to be part of our order to change it."

"Samuel, you know the law. If we take him there, then—"

"They will carry out the law. I know."

Brian didn't like when people were talking about him like he wasn't there. "What do you mean carry out the law?"

Marcus wrapped the new fabric around the old as he answered. "Our leader has made a law that if any warrior is created without permission, they are executed."

"Oh, is that all?" Brian joked sarcastically. "What were you planning on doing with me before now?"

"I wasn't planning on you becoming a warrior until after I had taken you before the council. After I kept you from dying, I was planning on keeping you from the council. Now, I don't see any other choice but to plead for the council's mercy."

Marcus used his teeth to rip through the plastic of the steaks. "You know Cyrus will not hesitate to terminate him."

"Who's Cyrus?" Brian asked.

Samuel ignored Brain. "The whole council is gathered together this week. If we can get Brian in front of the council, Cyrus will have a harder time carrying out punishment."

"He can't exclude the council from judgment like he always does if they are sitting right there," Marcus added with a mouth full of meat.

"Plus the council will be more willing to side with me since I am, after all, the oldest living warrior."

Brian gave up asking questions since they were both ignoring him. He sat down on the fallen tree and listened to them talk about him, even though he was only a few feet away.

"If the council is there, then Jaya will be there and will help our cause," Marcus said as he pushed the last of the steak in his mouth.

"We can hope," Samuel replied. "She can't appear to make her husband look weak."

Brian was going to ask who Jaya was and who she was married to, but they were just going to ignore him anyway. He watched Marcus as he licked his fingers and then started pulling the bandages off his injury. The wound was already scabbed over, and it looked like new skin was starting to cover it up.

Marcus noticed him looking and answered his question before he could ask. "We heal quicker when we eat. What could take days or hours would take hours or minutes if we eat. Raw meat usually works the best."

Samuel stood up from the fallen tree. "Brian, stay in the camp. We are going to get transportation and be back sometime tomorrow. I can't stress the importance of staying away from your house."

"I don't care if the forest burns down around you, stay here until we come back," Marcus added.

The eyes of the two men changed to a golden-yellow, and then the change happened so quickly that if Brian would have blinked, he might have missed it. They grew taller and shifted form until two massive beasts stood in front of him. Changing into wolf form appeared to happen much faster than changing out of it.

The two warriors got down on all fours and took off running. Brian was impressed by how fast they moved. On all fours they were able to run twice as fast. The warriors dodged trees and ducked branches and were soon out of sight.

Once they were out of sight, Brian went to the tent and grabbed the rest of the meat. He sat by the fire thinking of the warriors' transformation and wondered if it hurt to change forms. He thought about becoming a tall werewolf and scaring all the kids that had picked on him in school. He would never do that, but it was fun to think about. Brian laughed at the thought as he bit into another steak. The thought then came to him that he was a different breed. He might not be able to change into another form. His human form might be the only form he had. He didn't like that thought. If he could change, he didn't like the thought of having a tail either.

Brian sat staring at the fire until he finished all the steaks. He kicked dirt on the fire and then turned in for the night. If he knew the nightmare that was going to follow, he would have stayed awake the entire night.

Chapter Ten

As he slept, Brian dreamt that he was in a small room. A small pit of fire sat in the middle of the room with long metal shafts protruding from the flames. Brian half expected to see a blacksmith hammering away next to the fire.

Chains hung from the ceiling just behind the pit. From those chains a man hung off the ground by his wrists. Brian quickly realized that it wasn't just any man…it was Chris. The closer he got to Chris, the worse he looked. His clothes were torn and bloodied. He was covered in bruises. Brian was no doctor, but it looked like his ribs might be broken. Brian called out to him, but Chris did not react.

The door opened and in walked a large man with a shaved head and a mesh shirt and a dog collar. He looked like some kind of bouncer for a goth club. The large man carried a cup over to Chris. "If you drink this, all your pain will disappear," the man promised.

Chris looked at the man the best he could with one eye. The other eye was swollen shut. He spit in the man's face, which brought a quick jab to Chris's ribs. Chris let out a silent cry of pain as his ribs cracked.

"Drink this and I will stop," the man said. He lifted the cup to Chris's mouth. Chris turned his head. This brought another quick jab to his ribs. Brian could hear the crack of Chris's ribs with the impact of the man's punch. Tears rolled down Chris's cheeks from the pain.

Chris kicked the man's hands, sending the cup across the room and crashing onto the floor. Brian looked at the broken cup and saw the red liquid spreading across the floor. *Blood,* Brian realized. He looked at Chris and saw the fangs sticking out of his mouth slowly retract. *He's a vampire,* Brian thought. *If he's one of them, then why are they torturing him?* He looked at the blood spreading across the floor. *He's refusing to drink.*

The man was about to hit Chris again when the door opened and in walked a woman that Brian recognized immediately. It was the one who stabbed him and dragged Chris away. Past her Brian could see another man lying on an angled table. The man looked to be in as much pain as Chris. In the same room, Brian thought he saw Amy Thompson. She was a redhead with blue eyes that was on the cheerleading team. She wasn't ever mean to Brian, but she wasn't exactly nice either. She looked different somehow, but Brian didn't exactly know how. Next to her stood a man that looked just like his uncle, Eric. The door slammed shut, blocking both of them from his view.

"Has he drank yet, Donovan?" she asked.

"No," Donovan answered.

Delilah walked over to Chris and grabbed him by the hair, pulling his face up to meet hers. "How can you be resisting?" she screamed. Chris didn't say a word, which made Delilah more angry. She spun on her heels. "Burn him," she yelled at Donovan.

Delilah moved to stand behind Chris. Donovan pulled a metal shaft from the fire. Half of the rod glowed white from the heat. Donovan first swung the shaft like a baseball bat, striking Chris across the chest. Chris's scream echoed around the room. The sizzle of his skin was sickening. When Donovan pulled the rod away, pieces of Chris's burnt skin clung to it before tearing off his body.

"Are you willing to drink, or do you want Donovan to continue?" Delilah asked, but again Chris was silent. "Donovan's been gentle with you thus far because of me. Don't make me unleash him." Delilah nodded to Donovan, who smiled eerily. She pulled Chris's head back by his hair again. "Did you know that your eyes don't burn with intense heat? No, they burst inside your skull."

Donovan held the glowing metal shaft against Chris's left eye, while Delilah held his head still by his hair. Chris screamed and writhed with pain. His horrific screams echoed all around them. The sizzle of Chris's flesh made Brian want to vomit. Tears flowed freely from Brian's eyes. He looked down at the floor, unable to watch anymore.

When Brian looked back at Chris, they started on his other eye. Chris kicked and writhed with pain. His mouth opened, but screams didn't come out anymore.

He had to do something, anything. He reached out for Chris and found himself sitting up in his sleeping bag. The burning sunlight lit up his tent, causing intense pain. He wiped the tears from his eyes as he felt around for his sunglasses.

That was the most realistic dream I have ever had, he thought. *Was it a dream? It had to be. I couldn't touch anything and couldn't smell anything. Chris couldn't hear me. It was definitely a dream. No, a nightmare—the most horrible nightmare I have ever had, more than likely caused by the sun burning my own eyes.*

Finally, Brian had found his sunglasses when he heard a scream for help. The voice was his mother's. He didn't care about Samuel's orders at that moment. All he cared about was helping his mother. He burst out of his tent running as fast as he could. He couldn't be sure, but it felt like he was running just as fast as he saw the warriors run on four legs. Brian dodged tree limbs and roots with ease. It was like he was created just for this. He didn't even have to think about moving; his body reacted for him.

Brian slowed at the edge of the forest. He jogged up to the back of the house and edged his way around the side until he stood at the front corner. There he saw a balding man with a bad comb-over. His hair was dark brown with some streaks of gray. He had a giant beer belly sticking out from under his shirt. He looked and smelled like he hadn't showered in a week. On top of that was the smell of alcohol. The man was saturated with it. Every time he spoke, it carried in the air. As he spoke Brian could see teeth missing in his mouth. It was Chris's stepfather. The man beat Chris whenever he got the chance. He was the biggest waste of skin that ever walked the earth in Brian's opinion. This man, Brian believed, was the reason that Chris acted the way he did.

Chris's stepfather pushed Brian's mother to the ground. "My son is missing, and it is your son's fault. You owe me money for my pain and suffering!" he yelled.

That is the reason right there. You don't care about Chris. You see a way to get some money. Brian watched, not wanting to reveal himself unless the situation got worse.

Brian's father answered from the front door out of Brian's view. "The police have already investigated and found that your son was the one at fault. If anyone needs restitution, it is us." When Chris's stepfather looked confused, Brian's father used different words. "We would be the ones getting money, not you. Now I have already called the police. If you touch my wife one more time, you will go to prison. I will make sure that you will lose everything you own."

Piece of crap won't even come outside to defend his own wife. He watched his wife get pushed to the ground and won't do anything but threaten a lawsuit. Brian had to resist the urge to run out and club his father over the head with Chris's stepfather.

Chris's stepfather slurred unintelligible words and walked away. Brian's mother turned her head with tears in her eyes and found Brian hiding against the side of the house. He looked at her, and she shook her head. She knew that he wanted to come help, but she didn't want Brian to reveal himself. It was better if Brian's father didn't know where he was.

"Come inside, dear, before the neighbors actually do call the police," Brian's father said.

That piece of unflushable crap didn't even call the cops! Brian wanted to break through that door and rip his father apart limb by limb. He looked at Chris's stepfather stumbling up the sidewalk. *Well, if my father won't do anything, I will.*

Brian ran to the back of his house and made his way around the back of his neighbors'. The tall fences weren't even a hindrance to him. He hurdled the fences as if they were just little hedges. After he jumped six fences, he made his way to the side of the third house down from his. He waited until Chris's stepfather was in view and shot out of hiding, grabbing the drunken man and pulling him out of view. He lifted the man with one hand by his throat. Brian was impressed with how easy it was for him. This man was by no means a skinny man.

The side of the house was shaded, which allowed Brian to take off his sunglasses and look at the man with his golden-yellow eyes. If it wasn't for the shade, he wouldn't look very terrifying with tears in his eyes. Chris's stepfather looked terrified, which was Brian's goal. A sweet smell started to overpower the alcohol. That smell was followed by the smell of urine pouring down the man's leg. Brian wanted to laugh, but that would have ruined his threat.

Brian yelled at the man, his new deep voice pushing his message across in a way that his old voice never could. "You leave Mrs. Porter alone from now on. Do you understand me!" Chris's stepfather began to cry and nodded his head. "If I even hear that you came back here, I will rip you in half."

Brian dropped Chris's stepfather to the ground and let out a low growl. He didn't realize it was coming from him at first. It was such a natural thing to do. He growled and stooped down until he met the man's eyes. Chris's stepfather took off running, bumping into everything on his way. Brian knew that if he told anyone what happened, no one would believe a drunk.

Feeling like he had done something to help his mother, Brian turned and ran back into the forest. He didn't run as fast as he could. He wasn't looking forward to sitting at the campsite all day without anything to do. It turned out he didn't have to.

By the time he got back to camp, Marcus and Samuel were already there. Brian was happy to see that they were wearing clothing. Both had a light jacket on—Samuel in red, and Marcus in green—and both wore blue jeans and hiking boots. They had broken down Brian's tent and threw it on the fire with his sleeping bag on top.

"What are you guys doing?" Brian yelled.

"We need to remove all evidence that you were here," Samuel answered. "Where were you? I told you to stay here."

"I…had…a situation with my mother." He was hesitant to answer. He didn't know how Samuel would react. He was hoping it wasn't even close to how he just acted with Chris's stepfather.

Samuel wasn't upset at all. "Was she in danger?"

"Yes."

"Did anyone see you?" Samuel asked.

"Just my mother, who won't tell anyone about me, and one drunk man who tried to hurt her."

"Did you put the fear of God into the man?"

"I sure did."

"Good," Samuel said, smiling.

"Good," Marcus repeated, nodding his approval to Brian.

They stood around the fire, watching Brian's stuff burn while asking Brian to recount for them what he had done. He made sure to include his father and how useless he was. When he got to the part about Chris's stepfather urinating himself, Marcus and Samuel burst out laughing, which made Brian laugh.

"Nothing says you got your point across more than when some-one urinates themselves," Marcus laughed, wiping the tears from his eyes.

Samuel finished laughing and breathed a few times, calming himself down before talking. "Well, it seems you have done good toward your mother this day. You should be pleased with yourself. How did you send him on his way?"

Brian told them that he had dropped him and then starting growling at the man until he ran away. He described how he just started growling without realizing what he was doing. Brian even described how the scent of the man had changed and smelled sweet. He described how it had happened a few times with smells he couldn't identify. "Is it because my sense of smell is heightened?"

This time Marcus and Samuel didn't laugh. Samuel spoke very seriously to Brian. "You must not reveal this to anyone. I feel that you are more wolf than you are human. You are more wolf than any warrior, even me. Growling is what we do in wolf form, but it never comes on in human form. Also, that smell you describe is something no living warrior can do. My father was the only one I knew of that could do that, and he taught himself how to do it. It wasn't something that came easily to him, as it seems it does for you."

"What am I smelling?"

"Emotions, Brian. You smell what people are feeling. And I am afraid that there is no one that can teach you what it is that you smell. You are going to have to figure that one out on your own. Again, I can't stress this enough: this is something you must keep secret. No one can know that you can do this. Also, you need to fight to keep control. You can't let anyone see you growl in human form, especially other warriors. It could get back to the council, and that would solidify your death."

"I try not to do anything that makes me stand out. But I didn't even know that I was doing it."

"Marcus and I will keep an eye on you. We have sworn to protect you, even if that means turning against our own order to do so. Now, let us be off. We have to be in front of the council as soon as we can."

They buried the remains of what used to be Brian's camp. Dirt was cast on the fire pit until it was level with the ground. Marcus put a few branches on top to look as if they had fallen there. When finished no one would have guessed this spot was used for a campsite unless they were really looking.

Chapter Eleven

Samuel drove the black SUV away from the forest and down through the city. The SUV made Brian feel like he was being escorted by the secret service. As they sat in silence, Brian looked over the vehicle, admiring the leather seats and every upgrade a person could possibly want. "Is this standard issue for warriors?" Brian asked, hoping he would get something similar when he was given a vehicle. He could just imagine all the kids at school being jealous when he pulled up in something like this.

"If you can find it," Marcus replied, looking out the window of the passenger seat.

"What do you mean, 'if I can find it'?" Brian got the feeling that the vehicle was not issued at all. "Did you guys steal this from a vampire or something?"

"If it makes you feel better, then yes," Marcus said, making himself smile.

"As a warrior sometimes you need to do things that you normally wouldn't like doing," Samuel explained. "For example, stealing a car to make sure your newest warrior isn't put to death."

Brian replied, "Touché." He could see their point. He was living in a different world now, and the normal rules were no longer applicable. If he needed to steal a car, then he would have to. He would do whatever it took to make sure they won and the vampires lost.

As he looked out the window, he recognized the part of town they were in. He escaped from the hospital not too far down the road. He looked for Mr. Duncan as they passed the restaurant. He wasn't there.

"Pull over," Brian demanded.

The car wasn't fully stopped before Brian jumped out and ran to the spot where Jack Duncan was supposed to be. He ran up to a waiter who was serving on the pavilion outside the restaurant.

"What happened to the homeless man that was lying there?" The words flew out of Brian's mouth faster than he expected them to.

It took the waiter a second to process what Brian had asked. "Oh, the homeless dude? The cops came by this morning and made him move. We needed to open the pavilion this morning, and he was making our costumers uncomfortable."

Brian wanted to push the waiter's "dude" down his throat. What was he going to do now? How was he going to find him? An instinct nagged at him that he could find Jack easily if he were to catch his scent. He went to were Jack last was and started sniffing the air. If a homeless man made the patrons uncomfortable, he didn't know how a guy sniffing around the air made them feel. They probably thought he was on drugs or something. It was about this time that Marcus and Samuel jumped out of the car to join him.

"What is going on, Brian? We don't have time for this," Marcus complained.

Brian ignored them and kept sniffing the air. There it was, the scent he was looking for. It was faint, but he thought he could follow it. He followed the scent as best he could. He continued to sniff the air as he walked. Anyone who passed by looked at him like he was crazy. It didn't help that Marcus kept telling everyone that they were taking him to the hospital to be tested.

A few times Brian went the wrong direction and had to backtrack until he picked up the scent again. He felt like a hound dog looking for a fox; he was sure he resembled it, too. As Brian went along, he found it easier and easier to track Mr. Duncan. He could tell what direction the scent was carried and was soon sniffing the air every few steps instead of the entire time. It wasn't long before Brian was jogging and following the scent.

After half an hour of searching, Brian finally came to the end. Under a bridge in the park laid Mr. Duncan. He was wrapped in a blanket to keep warm from the breeze sweeping under the bridge. When Mr. Duncan saw Brian coming, he smiled.

"Well, if it isn't the runaway," he called out.

"Hello, Mr. Duncan," Brian said in return. He bent down to look Jack in his brown eyes. "You weren't where you said you would be. I got worried."

"Ah, those good people were getting a bit uncomfortable with me around. I can't say I blame 'em. I came down here where it's quiet and no one bothers me." He looked past Brain and saw Samuel and Marcus. "Did you bring bodyguards, kid?"

"These guys are good guys. You don't look good, Mr. Duncan. When was the last time you got something to eat?"

Jack looked into the air as if he was doing the math. "I think a few days ago. But you shouldn't worry about me, kid. I am fine. Go live your life and stop worrying about this old man."

Brian stood up and took a couple of steps to talk to Samuel and Marcus without Jack hearing. "I would like for him to come with us."

"What? No, we are not a charity," Marcus replied.

"He helped me when I needed it. He is a good man. He helped people in the war, and I believe he would be a great addition to the warriors. Besides, wouldn't it help to show the council that you can follow their rules by brining Mr. Duncan before you show them me?"

Samuel looked at Marcus. Brian could see a whole conversation go between them without a word being said aloud. Only people who have worked together a long time could do that.

"I can't leave him like this; he deserves better."

Marcus shook his head like a father telling his son he couldn't have a toy. "You don't know anything about him."

"I know that he was a medic in the military because he liked to help people. Now he is out here and every person treats him like a second-class citizen. For a man who only wanted to help people, this is a crappy way to end up."

Marcus and Samuel looked at each other in another silent conversation. Finally Samuel broke the silence. "This seems very close to the situation we had with you and Jeremiah, Marcus."

"It does have some similarity. Let's bring the man before the council, if that's what Brian wishes," Marcus replied. "It couldn't hurt to show the council that we can follow the rules. Besides, with the council there, it will be more than likely that he will be accepted."

Brian cut in, "What's the worst that could happen, they say no?"

"The worst that could happen is the council says no and he is put to death. But that hasn't happened for a few hundred years. I like your chances." Marcus laughed while he turned and walked away.

"He's going to get the car started. Let's grab your friend," Samuel said.

Brian ran over to Jack with a smile on his face. "Mr. Duncan, how would you like a job where you can help people every day?"

"Depends on what it is," Jack said, a little hesitant to agree.

Brian thought someone might have played a cruel prank on Jack and that was why he was a little hesitant. He could smell a sweet, sugary smell coming from Jack. From the look on Jack's face, Brian could tell that he was smelling was fear. It was the same smell Chris's stepfather had when Brian literally scared the piss out of him. He didn't want to scare Jack, but he couldn't exactly tell him the truth out in the open like this.

"I can tell you in the car on our way to the office we'll be working from. Those nice gentlemen I am with gave me a job and said that I can offer you one too."

"All right, Runaway. You have always seemed like an honest kid to me. I am trusting you. Don't let me down."

"Mr. Duncan, you'll find that a whole new world is about to open for you," Brian said, helping Jack to his feet. It took some convincing by Samuel for Jack to leave his things where they were.

Jack walked in between Samuel and Brian back to the car, and then they were on their way again. Jack sat in the backseat with Brain, while Marcus drove with Samuel in the passenger seat. Samuel gave Brian permission to tell Jack the true story about werewolves and vampires and how it was an eternal struggle between good and evil. Samuel filled in gaps that Brian didn't know. Jack didn't believe a word of their story until Samuel changed his eyes and then grew his claws out. Brian was happy to see that Jack wasn't freaked out like he would have been and wanted to know in what way he could help.

Marcus looked at Samuel and nodded as if to say, "Brian was right about this guy." At least Brian hoped that's what the nod meant.

They drove the rest of the way with small chitchat. Brian wanted to get Jack some food, but Marcus said, "We can get him some food—and a *shower*—when we get there."

Four hours later Marcus drove the vehicle into a downtown city. Tall buildings surrounded them and seemed to swallow them up the further into the city they drove. Brian had never been into a city this big before, and it was overwhelming. He started longing for the forest and wondered which side of himself felt that way, the human side or the wolf side.

Marcus stopped the vehicle in front of a tall bank building. They all followed Samuel inside the building and past the lobby inside the bank. It was just a boring bank. Brian wondered why they were here. He was about to ask if they were getting money so they could get something to eat. The security guard at the front of the bank turned and looked at Samuel. His eyes flashed golden and then back to normal. It was so quick Brian almost thought he was seeing things. Any mortal would never have noticed anything, and if they had, they more than likely would have thought they were seeing things, like Brian just had.

Samuel looked at the security guard, and his eyes flashed golden. The security guard went back to staring straight ahead as if nothing happened. Brian realized that this was how the warriors signaled each other in human form.

"Keep your glasses on, Brian, and do not say a word until I tell you to," Samuel whispered as he led the small group through the bank.

Mortals were filling out deposit slips and talking to tellers as they made withdrawals. The bank had many mortals walking around. All the while the eyes of tellers and bank managers would flash golden. Samuel would flash his eyes golden back. Not one mortal noticed, even when they were looking right at one of the warriors when their eyes flashed.

At the back of the bank stood a security guard by a solitary door. Samuel flashed his eyes first this time. The guard flashed his eyes and opened the door for them. They walked into a small hallway that led to an elevator. There were sixteen buttons for the building's sixteen floors.

"How far up are we going?" Brian asked curiously.

"We are going down," Samuel replied.

"But we are on the ground floor. There is no down button."

Samuel waited for the elevator doors to close. He stuck out his index finger, and his fingernail grew until it was a dark black claw. He stuck it into a hole under the control panel that read: MAINTENANCE KEY. Samuel moved his claw until there was a click. The elevator started to move down.

"We are going down," Samuel said again, looking at Brian.

The elevator travelled on for a long while before finally coming to a rest. Brian didn't know what he was expecting, but it definitely wasn't what he first saw. When the elevator doors opened, it revealed what looked like a normal office reception area. The walls surrounding the reception area were made of polished stone. Brian realized that it wasn't stone brought in to decorate the office, but that the office was dug deep into the earth. The walls were earth polished to a brilliant shine. There was a half-circular oak reception desk with granite counter tops in the middle of the room. Behind the desk sat a woman with bleach-blond hair and olive skin. Her brown eyes watched them get off the elevator. Brian thought she was quite beautiful, but there was something about her that was quite frightening as well. Behind her was a tall set of oak doors, and above the doors were the letters *HW*.

"HW?" Brian asked.

"Holy Warriors," Samuel answered.

Brian hit his forehead in a "duh" moment.

The woman behind the desk looked at each of them one by one, but when she got to Marcus, her stern face changed to one of concern. She ran around the desk, kissed him on the lips, and then took his forearm in her hands. The injury was completely skinned over and looked like it had been a year since he lost his hand.

"What happened?" she asked, a tear forming in the corner of her eye and dripping down her cheek.

"We were saving this recruit from a vampire who was armed with silver," Marcus responded, sounding like a schoolboy who had been caught stealing by his teacher.

The woman turned on Brian. "You are the reason my husband misses a hand."

She lunged at Brian, but Marcus caught her with one hand, and Samuel held her back with both of his.

"It was not his fault," Samuel said, the strain noticeable in his voice. Brian didn't think he could hold her back much longer.

The woman's fingernails became claws, and her eyes changed golden. A spicy, peppery smell came from her. Brian didn't need time to figure out this emotional scent. He knew he was smelling anger.

"Ahmose, my love, it was in defense of an innocent. It could not be helped. It was not the boy's fault," Marcus kissed Ahmose on the forehead and held her head to his chest.

Ahmose relaxed into Marcus, accepting his embrace. Her emotional scent changed immediately to a sweet smell, almost like a field of the sweetest-smelling flowers. Brian recognized the smell as similar to the one he smelled from his mother. He would bet anything that this was the scent of love. It made him feel good to know that his mother actually did love him.

"Ahmose, I do not want to interrupt you and Marcus, but I need to know if they are in there," Samuel said.

"They are, Samuel, but they asked me to keep you out." Ahmose wiped tears from her cheek as she spoke.

"Are you going to?" Samuel asked, almost like it was a joke between them.

"How can I when my handsome husband distracted me?"

"I should go in with Samuel," Marcus told his wife.

"No need," Samuel interrupted before there was an argument. By the look on Ahmose's face, there wasn't going to be one. "It would be better if I just went in. If Cyrus sees you, he might kill Brian right there to show that he is in charge. He's used to me disobeying. I am older by a few hundred years, after all."

Ahmose led Marcus around her desk where he sat on the edge, while she sat in her desk chair. Samuel led the two new recruits through the double doors and into the hallway behind Ahmose's desk.

Portraits lined both sides of the hallway. Each portrait was a painting of a warrior in their wolf form held by a golden frame with a nameplate. The portraits seemed to go on forever, only broken up by an oak door here and there. Brian looked at each warrior in wolf form. They each had gray fur, but some had darker gray fur and some lighter gray. Other than that Brian couldn't tell one warrior from the other. He was sure that Samuel would be able to tell him if he asked. After they passed through one of the sets of doors, the portraits changed from warriors in wolf form to warriors in human form.

"Why are these portraits different?" Brian asked.

Samuel stopped walking and looked at the portraits on the wall. "These are the warriors who gave their life in battle to keep this world safe. The portraits that are in human form started when we could take human form. We don't know what the warriors before would have looked like in human form. Each sanctuary around the world has a hall dedicated to their fallen warriors." Samuel walked over to the first human portrait. The name plate in the frame said *Vidar*. "This is Vidar, the first human I recruited, and the first human warrior to die. The vampires killed him three weeks after I recruited him. We found him drained of his blood. His heart had exploded in his chest from the vampire venom."

"Marcus already mentioned that vampire venom could make our hearts explode, but I didn't know they could drink our blood, too. That hardly seems fair," Brian complained.

"War isn't fair, Brian. Don't ever expect the enemy to play fair. Not only can they drink our blood, but it makes them just as fast and just as strong as we are in wolf form."

"So the moral of the story is not to get bit," Brian said half sarcastically.

"The moral is not to get bit, not to get caught, and especially not to let vampires know what you look like in human form," Samuel said as they continued down the hallway again.

"I hope you'll teach us how to avoid that kind of death," Mr. Duncan said.

"Not to worry, Jack. We will train you the best we can to keep you alive."

Brian tried to look at each portrait as he walked. He couldn't believe how many lives were lost and how no mortal would ever know the sacrifice on their behalf. This invisible world protected them, and they would never know it.

The hallway ended at a set of double doors. They weren't as tall as in the reception area, but they were more beautiful. They had a wolf howling at the moon carved into each door.

"My father made these doors," Samuel explained. "He carved them soon after Almira had left with the other wolves refusing to take human form. He carved her howling at the moon. Whenever we move to a new sanctuary, we take these doors with us. My father said that seeing her every day would help remind him of her strength and, in kind, give him strength to lead the warriors. Let's hope they can bless us with luck."

Samuel breathed deeply before pushing the doors open. He led Brian and Mr. Duncan into the room and stood before a long conference table. There were seven men and women on one side of the table and six on the other. Each man wore a dark suit and a designer tie. The women wore different styles of black dresses, each one as elegant and beautiful as the women wearing them. Brian was starting to wonder if there was such a thing as an unattractive female warrior. At the end of the table sat a skinny man in a dark suit and red tie. His hair was brown with streaks of gray at the temples. He had a trimmed beard that matched his hair, brown with streaks of gray. Just behind him sat a thin woman with gray hair. She also wore a black dress, but it looked more expensive than the other women's dresses.

The man at the end of the table stood up and addressed Samuel, not bothering to hide his irritation. "This is an outrage, Samuel. This is a closed meeting. You must leave, or I'll have you thrown out." The man bent over and spoke into an intercom. "Ahmose…Ahmose!" He was the first warrior Brian heard that did not have a deep voice.

"She is attending her injured husband, Cyrus," Samuel interrupted.

Cyrus quit pressing the button and looked at them with a face reddened by anger. Brian could smell the spicy scent drifting across the room from him. It was strong and potent. *This guy must really hate, Samuel,* Brian thought.

The woman just behind Cyrus arose and stepped up to the long conference table. "Samuel knows that this is a meeting with the heads of every sanctuary around the world. He would not interrupt if he didn't think it was important. I say we hear him out."

"Thank you, Jaya," Samuel said.

Cyrus flopped down in his chair while Jaya continued to stand. "Fine, let's hear what is so important that you interrupt this important meeting," Cyrus said, looking at the three of them with his gray eyes becoming daggers.

"I have brought these two for initiation into our order," Samuel began, but he was immediately cut off.

"That is not important enough business to bring before the council," Cyrus said with a devilish grin. "For wasting our time, I say no. Put them to death and let's continue on."

The scent of ash and smoke now washed over Samuel. His eyes raged at Cyrus, and Brian could tell that he was smelling the scent of rage. Looking around the room, Brian knew he was the only one that could tell how angry Samuel was. When Samuel spoke it was calm and collected. "I am not finished yet, Cyrus. Please allow me to finish before you pass judgment. I ask that the whole council be allowed to judge and not to have their leadership taken from them. They are the smartest, most capable warriors. That's why they are the leaders of their chapters. Don't push their judgment aside as if they are not."

Every person at the table began to nod and speak in agreement that they should have a voice in the matter. Brian could see that Cyrus did not like to look bad, especially in front of the council.

"Fine," Cyrus said, "finish."

"Thank you, Council," Samuel began again, obviously making a jab at Cyrus by not thanking him. "I come before you to ask that the Humanis clause be rendered in judgment of Brian Porter." Samuel wasn't allowed to finish again.

"You have already turned him!" Cyrus yelled as he rose to his feet. "You know that means immediate death." Then Cyrus yelled something in a language Brian had never heard before. As he looked around the table, he found that the rest of the council didn't understand either.

Samuel understood it, but when he spoke, he did so for everyone to understand. "I know that you are the leader of all the warriors and what you say is law, but they are all leaders too. You must judge as a council and not on your own."

A man that sat closest to Brian spoke up. "I ask that you not use the original language again. We cannot do what is necessary if we do not understand what is being said."

"Robin, you have no judgment here," Cyrus said defiantly. "You are in charge of training and are only here as a formality to report on training and new recruits…if we have any."

A woman spoke up from the middle of the table; her accent sounded French. "This does not make his statement less true. You will refrain from speaking in the original language."

"Fine," Cyrus said. "Council, what would you have us do?"

The French woman spoke again. "Samuel, please tell us why we must invoke the Humanis clause."

"I have found this young man to be worthy of becoming a warrior. The laws set forth by Cyrus forbid me from bringing him before you until he has lived his full life."

"So you admit that he has not lived a full life," Cyrus interrupted.

The French woman again spoke up. "Cyrus, please do not interrupt. He is asking for the Humanis clause. This clause implies that he has not lived a full life. Continue please, Samuel."

"I will cut to the end to save Cyrus's patience." It was another remark to sway the council away from Cyrus. "This young man had been stabbed and lay dying. If I did not act, we would have lost a great man to death. He is worthy, and I believe he will be a great warrior."

Cyrus didn't seem to care about Samuel's story. "Who is this other man that stands with you?"

"This is Jack Duncan, a former medic that fought for his country and wants nothing more than to help whomever he can. I find him also to be worthy. He has lived a full life. He has been brought to my attention by the young man before you."

Cyrus stood up, out of his chair, and placed his hands on the table. He stared at Samuel as he said, "I find it interesting that your new recruit can follow the rules where you cannot. The mortal doesn't need to be here while we talk about your transgressions. What does the council decide on the mortal?"

They decided the matter in seconds. Robin spoke when they decided. "We have always trusted the judgment of Samuel. He will be accepted." It seemed like Robin was speaking more to remind the council to trust Samuel.

"Fine, take the mortal, Robin. You should not be here for the rest of the judgment," Cyrus said, beginning to pace back and forth behind the table.

Jaya stepped around the table and approached Brian. "You saved his life, but I wonder: Why does this young man wear sunglasses inside?"

As she reached up to take off his sunglass, Brian jerked his head back defensively. It was only after Samuel nodded for Brian to consent that he allowed Jaya to remove his glasses. His eyes burned immediately with the light, and tears trickled down his cheeks.

"His eyes do not change," Samuel said, answering the question before it was asked.

"It will make it difficult for him to blend in with mortals," Jaya stated, putting Brian's sunglasses back on. "Any other changes?"

"Yes, his hair has turned black, and he has lost a considerable amount of weight," Samuel added.

Brian thought Samuel was telling everyone too much but dared not open his mouth and make things worse. His life was on the line. Jaya walked back to the other side of the table while the council talked back and forth about Brian's appearance.

Cyrus seemed really concerned about Brian's eyes. "He cannot blend in. His eyes will give him away. Our success comes from anonymity. He is too different from the rest of us."

Jaya spoke up. "I respect your judgment, Husband, but it was Samuel's father who turned the first human into a warrior. Afterward, we were able to take human form. Others were angry then and said that it was too different. Some warriors even left to become mortal wolves. I think it is fitting that Samuel created a different warrior like his father did. I welcome the change and say that he becomes a warrior."

Cyrus breathed deeply and sat down once again. "I see this is going to be up for debate. Samuel, have your young recruit wait outside. I will call Robin to come meet him."

The walk back to the reception felt longer than the walk in. He didn't know if he was going to live or die. He was scared about what his future held, if he had a future. For all he knew, he would be dead before the day was over. It brought him some comfort to know that at least Jack was not going to be killed. If Brian was killed, he knew that he helped one person while he was a warrior. He looked back at the closed conference doors. Behind the doors Samuel was arguing for

Brian's life. He looked at the carved picture of Almira and wished that she could help right now.

Out in the reception area, Marcus and Ahmose were still making eyes at each other. "How did it go?" Marcus asked as soon as he saw Brian.

"I don't know. Cyrus seems to have his mind set to kill me," Brian said, walking to the edge of the desk.

"Not to worry. The council has much respect for Samuel. He will sway them. Do not worry yourself until it becomes time to worry."

Ahmose got out of her seat and hugged Brian. He was a little taken aback by her sudden niceness. "Sorry we got off on the wrong foot. I am really protective of my love. I don't like to see him hurt."

"I am just sorry that he got hurt," Brian replied.

"That means a great deal," Ahmose said. She reached up and took off his sunglasses and looked at his eyes. "Marcus told me all about you." Brian looked at Marcus, who only shrugged like it wasn't a big deal. Then he shook his head as if to say, "Not everything."

"Your eyes will never change?"

"Not that I know of."

"Marcus said that you will be a great warrior. There is a sickness in our order. No one knows what it is, but everyone can feel it. I tell you now that we don't need another great warrior. We need a champion."

Chapter Twelve

Robin led Brian to a hidden elevator beside the reception desk. The doors to the elevator were made out of the same polished earth as the walls around them. When the doors were shut, the elevator was invisible to everyone. Ahmose hit a hidden button under the reception desk that opened the doors to the elevator. Once inside there was only two buttons to push, up or down. Robin pushed the down button, and the elevator began to descend. Brian wondered how far below the surface he was and how much further he would descend. He wondered if this was the only elevator to escape if Samuel didn't succeed.

As if reading Brian's thoughts, Robin turned to him. "I wouldn't worry too much. Samuel has never had the council go against him. They trust him, and he is the oldest living warrior. That carries some weight."

That eased Brian's mind some, but he still wondered if he was going to be the first thing Samuel and the council didn't agree on.

When the doors opened, a cool, damp feeling rushed into the elevator. The elevator opened up to a wide, long hallway. It was similar in appearance to the floor above, but the walls were not polished. The hall was so wide that columns were cut from the earth down the middle of the hallway. As they walked their footsteps echoed off the floor.

"Here is where you will learn what it means to be a warrior," Robin began. "Here you will learn our history, what we do, and how to blah, blah, blah." Robin stopped walking and looked at Brian. "Cyrus wrote down a whole speech for me to give. If you want to know what it is, you can ask your friend, Jack. Since you are not a normal 'new recruit,' I will forgo the normal litany and just speak with you as friends should."

Robin continued walking, again stopping at different doors. Each door they stopped at looked like a high school classroom door. The door was a normal wooden door with glass framed in the upper half so anyone could look in. Most of the rooms had desks inside, but no one was sitting in them.

The first door they stopped at Robin said, "This is where you will learn our history. And over here," Robin walked to the other side of the hallway, "this is where you will learn how to use your warrior body. If you so desire, you can also learn sword fighting in the same room from our resident Viking." Robin continued down the hallway. "If you have an accent, we can help you get rid of it, or create one, whichever is better for you to blend in. We don't have language classes. If you are assigned to a different sanctuary, you will learn the language there before you are put in the field. We have classes to help keep up with the current phrases. With the advanced media, the language has been changing quicker than ever. Every other year it seems we have to get the warriors back to a sanctuary to learn the newest phrases all over again."

Robin passed a few dark and empty classrooms before coming to a solid door. "You'll like this room, if you like movies."

Robin cracked the door enough for Brian to see a movie playing on a big screen. The room was designed to look like a theater with stadium seating and a projector. The room even smelled like butter-flavored popcorn. The movie playing was the newest vampire flick that hadn't even come out in theaters yet. Brian had seen some of the commercials, and when he was a dumb mortal, he had wanted to see it.

"All warriors are required to come back here and watch movies that our implants in Hollywood send to us. This way we can keep up with trends and know what propaganda vampires are selling mortals so we are not caught off guard. This is another way we can find out how far the world has fallen around us. In other words: how much we will be fighting against."

Brian could hear the woman on the screen profess her love to the vampire. From the back of the theater, he heard one of the male warriors yell out, impersonating a female, "Oh, you are so sexy and sensitive; I can't resist you. You must torture me, and when I can't take it anymore, eat me." Everyone in the theater then broke into laughter. Even Robin giggled a bit as he shut the door.

"When you have been fighting this same nonsense for as long as we have, you can get tired of how mortals view vampires. It helps to laugh when you can," Robin explained, leading Brian to another classroom.

The next room had a group of warriors sitting in a circle with a stereo in the middle of them. "This is where we listen to the newest and most popular music so we can talk to mortals and not seem out of place."

One of the warriors inside the classroom yelled, "This isn't music! I can't believe they call this music. They might as well bang rocks together."

"Obviously, we are old and don't like any of the music that you young people like. But we still have to pretend." Robin listened to the song through the door and looked as if nails were scraping a chalkboard.

Brian wanted to laugh. "This song is popular, but with twelve-year-old girls. No one from my high school would be caught dead listening to this song."

"You see, this is why I agree with Samuel that a warrior should be recruited when they are found to be worthy regardless of age. We could blend in better if we had a warrior from this timeline helping us. With the rules now, we have to wait until they have lived a full life, and by doing so we take recruits who don't relate to younger mortals."

"When was the last time you had a new recruit?"

"As you can see from the classrooms, they are empty. We have had one here and there, but it has been at least a few hundred years since Cyrus has let us fill these rooms with new warriors."

"How are you supposed to fight a war if you don't have any new recruits?"

"We can't." Robin's face showed his frustration, and the smell of anger washed over him. "Don't say a word of this conversation to Cyrus. I have a feeling that he already wants to kill me, and this would give him a reason."

"I don't know what you're talking about. We just had a boring tour," Brian said with a sarcastic grin.

Robin laughed, "I can tell that we are going to get along great." He led Brian to the last door in the hallway. The room had many long tables with computers on them. Very expensive printers lined the tables in the back of the room. "This is where you would come to change your identity if the enemy ever learns of it. You would get assigned a new name, birth certificate, identification, passport, and anything else that would be needed with a new identity. We can do security clearance here as well, but it takes some time. In some cases, if the need is great enough, you would get assigned to a new area, sometimes in a different country."

In the back of the room, a man stood but was hidden by the computer. He was shorter than most of the warriors he had seen walking around. He looked to be about five foot six. He might have looked shorter, but what he lacked in height he made up for in size. He looked like a professional weight lifter. He wore a white T-shirt and black sweat pants. The man had blond hair cut short enough to look like he was in the military. A long scar ran from under his eye to his chin. If this guy came up to Brian on the street to say hi, Brian thought he would have peed himself.

The man wrote on something and then stuck it to his shirt. The man grabbed some things off the printer and then came out of the room. As he got closer, Brian saw that it was a nametag that read: HELLO, MY NAME IS…DENNIS.

"Hello…Dennis," Robin said, making sure to read his nametag. Robin looked at Brian. "Once a person changes their identity, all of us have to stop calling them by their old name. Dennis here will have to memorize every detail of his new life in case he gets questions about it from mortals."

"That's right," Dennis said. "It's good to see a new recruit again. Make sure he makes it to my class, Robin Hood."

"You know I don't like to be called that," Robin complained.

Dennis only laughed as he walked to the end of the hall and down some stairs out of sight.

Robin saw the question on Brian's face and blew out air in frustration. "Yes, I am that Robin Hood and don't believe what you have read or seen in the movies. The story has been blown way out of proportion."

"Then what is the story?" Brian was intrigued. He had always loved the story of Robin Hood growing up. He saw the Disney version so many times his mother got sick of it. He could still recite the whole movie from beginning to end.

"In England, there was this horrible vampire. He enslaved most of the townsfolk and took the title of sheriff. When a vampire is in a political office, we cannot just kill him. It would bring too many questions from mortals. We have to do it subtly. We make it look like an accident, or we make the vampire disappear and blame it on a horrible mortal. That's what I was planning on doing. I was keeping an eye on him and figuring out a plan until I was forced to kill his vampire lackeys. They were burning down a mortal family's home. I couldn't just stand by. Unfortunately, the sheriff saw me transform and knew who I was in human form. He posted wanted posters all over town. The poster only said 'Robin' underneath a crude portrait of me. The townsfolk referred to me as Robin Hood.

"With the posters up, I had to kill the vampire before he was able to tell any other vampires about me. I broke into his office and killed him by shooting an arrow through his neck, head, and chest." Robin shrugged. "I wanted to be thorough. After I killed him, there was a stockpile of money and crops that he had taken from the townsfolk. I told them where they could find it and that they could have it all back. The townsfolk I guess told the tale about what happened, and it blew up from there."

"What about Maid Marian?" Brian asked.

"The sheriff had a young woman in the jail cell that he kept to feed on. He was careful not to bite her or she would turn. He would cut her and poor her blood into a cup. The sheriff would like to make his victims suffer as long as possible. She was weak when I found her, and I carried her away and was granted permission to make her a warrior. I don't know where they got the name Marian. Her name is Madelyn. Maybe they thought Marian sounded better, or maybe it just got twisted over time. That's the whole story, kid."

"That's it?" Brian was a little disappointed. "What happened to Madelyn? Did you guys ever get married? Is that part of the story true?"

"That's it. Madelyn is still alive and well. We did get married, but almost fifty years later. She has been a great warrior and is now our history teacher. She is also a professor at the mortal university. We place warriors all over the mortal world to keep an eye out for enemy activity. Unfortunately, being undermanned, all we can do is monitor and report."

Robin saw the disappointed face Brain was wearing and said, "Didn't anyone ever tell you not to meet your heroes? They never are what you imagine them to be. Imagination is always better."

Robin turned and led Brian down the set of stairs at the end of the hallway. They descended for what seemed like forever, and when Brian thought they were at the end, they turned and descended more. By the time they were done, Brian wondered if they were on the other side of the planet.

The hallway they walked into was similar to the one they had just come from—same light, same floors, and same walls. This one had different doors that were spread out much farther on the left side of the hallway. On the right side was only one set of wide doors.

"This is the cafeteria," Robin said as they walked past the set of wide doors on the right. Not far from the cafeteria, Robin stopped and pointed to a door on the left. "This will be your new home if Samuel is successful. You won't be having a roommate with so few of us now. Go in and relax the best you can. I need to report to the council that the tour is over." Robin squeezed Brian's shoulder. "I am glad to have met you, Brian."

Chapter Thirteen

Brian went into his new home, and it was nothing like he expected. He was expecting maybe a cot and a desk. Instead it looked like an entryway to a real house. The floor was white marble leading to white carpet. Stairs led up to four bedrooms, each with its own bathroom. Each bedroom had soft beds made up with blankets and pillows so soft that Brian thought he could sleep for a week, even if he wasn't tired. Each bathroom was stocked with soap, shampoo, and towels. In every bedroom was a desk with a reading lamp. Brian wondered if he was going to have homework if he wasn't killed. Across from the desk stood a large dresser. He looked inside to find nothing. It appeared he would have to wear the same clothing every day.

Downstairs Brian found a giant flat-screen television with every channel he could possibly want. A large sofa sat in front of the television that Brian thought could hold an entire basketball team. The kitchen had everything a kitchen should have with a large refrigerator and gas stove. Granite countertops spread out through the kitchen, and a large dining table sat off to the side. Brian looked inside the fridge and cupboards. They both were fully stocked with food and drinks.

"Why do they have a cafeteria if there is all this food here?" Brian wondered.

Seeing all the food made his stomach yell at him. He grabbed an armful of food and some soda from the fridge. He sat on his new couch and turned the television on to the first sports channel he could find. He gorged himself, discarding empty wrappers and boxes on the floor. Mindlessly he watched television while cramming food into his mouth. He ate and ate and never felt satisfied. Empty wrappers and boxes swam around his feet as he went back to the kitchen time and time again to retrieve an arm full of food.

Eventually there was no more food to get. He searched every cupboard and found nothing, not even a crumb. Looking at all the empty containers and wrappers on the floor, he couldn't believe that he was still hungry. His stomach still grumbled with hunger. The cafeteria across the hall came to his mind, and Brian figured there was never a better time to go and have a look.

Quickly he left his apartment, and as he shut the door behind him, he heard someone call his name. Samuel came walking toward him with a thick packet in his hands.

"Where are you headed?" Samuel asked.

"Cafeteria. I'm starving," Brian answered.

"Your home is stocked with all the food you could want."

Brian looked at Samuel, embarrassed. "I already ate all of that."

"All of it?" Samuel was shocked, but he could hear Brian's stomach grumble and complain. "You need to feed more than just your human side right now. I need to talk to you, but it can wait until after you have fed." Samuel led Brian to the cafeteria.

The cafeteria looked more like a giant cave than a cafeteria. The ceiling looked like it had been carved with a pick ax. Lights hung down from the ceiling over round tables that were scattered throughout the room. The tables were wooden round tables with creaky wooden chairs. The floor was rough and wavy like it was also carved out with a pick ax. As they walked their footsteps echoed throughout the cafeteria. Brian was led to the far right where there was a short line. They would walk in through a door and come out a door on the other side with a tray full of raw meat. Brian unconsciously licked his lips.

A woman came up behind them and said, "Samuel, I heard you were back and that you had brought a new recruit."

Brian turned to stare directly into perfectly red lips. They were hypnotic as they moved, especially when she spoke in her British accent. The woman was tall and thin with brilliant green eyes that Brian couldn't look away from. She tucked her long brunette hair behind one ear, and Brian almost fell over. She was absolutely beautiful. He tried to say, "Hi, my name is Brian," but all that squeaked out was, "Ha…"

Samuel saved Brian by clapping him on the back. "This is my new recruit. I'll introduce you two later after we have all eaten." Then he quickly changed the subject, though Brian didn't understand why. "How has Robin been?"

"Cyrus has him running all over doing more than a trainer in charge should be doing. With no recruits Robin has become more of an errand boy than a trainer in charge."

Hearing her talk, her name came to Brian as if someone had slapped him in the back of the head. "You're Madelyn," he blurted out.

She smiled, and even that made Brian want to fall over. "I am. Has Robin been talking about me?"

Brian was about to tell her the whole story of how he knew about her. Now that he could talk around her, he didn't know how to shut up. Luckily he didn't have to worry about that, as someone from the other side of the door yelled out, "Next!"

"You may go before us, Madelyn. It's his first time and might take a little longer," Samuel said.

Madelyn thanked him and went through the door.

"That settles it," Brian told Samuel. "There are no ugly warrior women."

Samuel squeezed Brian's shoulder in a way that reminded him of something he had seen a kind father do. "Maybe on the outside," Samuel said, before it was their turn to go in.

Through the door looked like a butcher shop. There was a glass counter with chunks of meat from different parts of different animals. Behind the counter stood a short, fat man wearing a white apron stained with blood. He held a cleaver in his hand with his arms crossed. He took off his New York Jets hat to scratch his bald head. He had some gray hair left but not much.

"Samuel, it's good to see you again," the man said with a Bronx accent.

"Mick," Samuel greeted in return, "how's your great-great-grandfather?"

"He's good. He was in here a couple of days ago. I'll tell him you were asking about him."

"Thanks," Samuel said, before he turned to Brian. "Mick's great-great-grandfather was recruited, but he wouldn't join while his family was in danger. So we made a deal. If he joined, we would protect his family and they could live here with us and stay mortal. Everything they could possibly want would be taken care of. We also employ the family in different tasks. Mick, his father, and his father's father have been our resident butchers. Mick's sons travel around hunting with their uncles and a warrior to get the meat you see here. His daughter is, I think, in law school."

"Medical school," Mick corrected.

"Medical school, thank you. She is attending where Madelyn teaches."

"Do they have to stay here, or can they leave whenever they want?" Brian asked.

"They are not prisoners, Brian. We don't want to keep them here if they don't want to be. Any member of the family can quit and lead a normal life if they want. If they do that, then they cannot return. Mick has family that has left to lead a normal life, but Mick has chosen to stay here with us. His daughter, I believe, will choose to leave once she is done with her schooling. Even if she does leave, she will always be under our protection."

"That pretty much sums it up, kid, and any friend of Samuel's is a friend of mine," Mick said. "Now, what will it be for you?" Mick hit a button on the wall, and hooks on a motorized chain started coming out from a refrigerated section and stopped behind Mick.

Brian thought it looked like the bloodiest dry cleaner he had ever seen. Each carcass had chunks cut out of it except for one near the back. Brian sniffed the air out of sheer instinct, and the aroma from the meat filled his lungs.

"Since you are a friend of Samuel's, I'll let you have your pick of our freshest stock."

"I would like that one," Brian said, pointing to the one in the back.

"That's a good one, kid. It's a bull elk from the Northwest that my kids brought me this morning. How much do you want, and from what section?"

"The whole thing."

It was clearly evident that nobody had ever made that request before. Mick looked to Samuel for direction. Samuel nodded for him to get the elk.

"I tell you what, kid. You go find a seat, and I will get a cart and wheel it out to you," Mick said.

As Samuel and Brian walked to a table, Brian asked, "Did I do something wrong?"

Samuel spoke like a concerned parent trying to comfort their child. "No warrior has ever asked for a whole carcass before. A few big chunks of meat, and we are good. This, I fear, is another sign that you are more different than the rest of us. I believe more than ever that you are more wolf than human."

They sat down at a table where a familiar face was sitting. "Brian, this is…" Samuel began to introduce Brian before reading the man's nametag. "Not again. What, is this four times in the last ten years? Brian, this is, I guess, Dennis."

"I don't know how they keep finding out who I am. I have been more careful than ever and still they seem to find me."

"Brian, Dennis here is one of the few people I can trust. Anything you want to tell me can also be told to Dennis."

Dennis looked at Brian. "You were the guy Hood was showing around."

"That was me. He said he didn't like to be called Robin Hood," Brian said, trying to defend Robin.

"I know, that's why I call him that," Dennis said, laughing at his own joke.

Samuel began to tell the story of how he met Dennis. "Brian, Dennis here was second in command to Leif Ericsson. I met him here in America just outside of what is now Baltimore. I was here getting reports from warriors and scouting for new locations for sanctuaries. Dennis caught a disease and would not survive long. He told his fellow Vikings to leave without him so they too wouldn't get sick. I found him lying against a tree, watching the ocean where his friends had left him. I introduced myself and offered to save his life if he would join our ranks. I am very glad that he accepted my offer. Our order has been better because of him and could use more men like him. It was after I recruited him that Cyrus came up with new rules for recruiting. At first Cyrus wanted it to be only his decision on who was recruited. The council argued until he conceded that the council could vote on recruits. When the council isn't here, Cyrus still takes it upon himself to deny all requests. The council has been furious with him about it, but they are powerless to do anything when they are not here."

"That's when we started losing numbers and couldn't replenish our ranks," Dennis added.

Samuel said to Dennis, "I need your word you will help to protect this young man. He is a new breed of warrior, and I fear, if discovered, his life will be in danger."

"How different is he?"

"I don't know all the ways yet," Samuel began to explain when he was interrupted by Mick, who was bringing the cart with the bull elk carcass on it.

Brian forgot about everything and everyone else in the room. His attention was now on the elk in front of him. It was almost as if he was in a trance. His teeth elongated and became sharp like a wolf, and he sank his teeth into the carcass, tearing chunks out. Blood dripped from his face as he tore bite after bite. Brian then picked up the eight-hundred-pound carcass like it was paper weight and began devouring the animal. He began to growl as he ate.

Samuel looked at Dennis. "See what I mean…different? We need to get all the people out of here, now. They can't see this; otherwise it will get back to Cyrus." He spoke to both Mick and Dennis.

"I'll tell everyone Cyrus's shipment came early, and I need to shut down for half an hour. It's pretty much true. His shipment came this morning," Mick said.

Mick went from table to table apologizing and motioning for everyone to leave. As they walked out, Dennis and Samuel were careful to block their view. Mick closed the doors, telling everyone that if they had a problem, they could take it up with Cyrus. He then locked the doors and came back to stand with Samuel and Dennis.

"I'm pretty sure that everyone was too upset to see what this kid was doing. What's wrong with him anyways?" Mick felt unsettled by what he was watching Brian do. It was like watching a wild animal feeding right before they attacked the human who fed them.

"No one can know about this, Mick," Samuel said very seriously.

"You know me, Samuel. I won't tell no one," Mick promised.

"I know I can trust you, Mick. I just want to stress how important this is. This stays here. You can't even tell your family."

"You got it," Mick promised again.

"I would like to ask Mick's question again," Dennis said. "What is wrong with this kid?"

"Like I told you before, he is different. There is nothing wrong with him; he is a new breed of warrior. The more I am around him, the more I see that he is more wolf than he is human."

They watched Brian eat in uncomfortable silence, accompanied only by the sounds of Brian's chewing and growling. Bones were broken, cleaned, and piled on the cart as Brian devoured every bite of meat and fat. Not once did Brian slow in his eating. It was as if his hunger would never be satiated. The last bite was eaten with as much enthusiasm as the first bite. Brian licked his fingers of the blood and turned, looking at the three men staring at him.

"Did I do something wrong?" Brian asked again. His teeth were now back to normal.

"Brian, do you realize what you have done?" Samuel asked.

"Yeah, I ate some meat. Why?"

"Yes, but do you remember how you ate?"

Brian looked confused for half a second. "I just…" Brian's eyes looked strained as he tried to remember. Then his eyes widened slightly with the memory. "I just tore right into the meat. I think I even picked it up. Was I growling?"

Samuel breathed a sigh of relief. "It is good that you remember. For a second I thought the wolf side of you was beyond your control. Brian, I fear it will not be easy, but you will have to keep control of your wolf side, especially while you are in view of others. It will bring unwanted attention from those that might mean to do you harm. In the worst case, it might bring the attention of the vampires identifying you as a warrior."

"I'll try," Brian said, hanging his head low.

"Do not worry," Dennis said. "You are not alone. We will help you if we can."

His whole life he had been on his own. It felt different to have people that cared for him enough to look out for him. He knew in his heart that they could only help so much. Almira said he was a new breed, and that meant, even as much as these warriors wanted to help, he was still alone.

"I better get this cart back and get Cyrus's order ready before he gets here. I'm sure he's heard some complaints by now," Mick said, grabbing the cart and pushing it back to his work area.

"Do you still feel hungry?" Samuel asked.

"No, I feel great," he responded.

"Good, now let us discuss what I came down here to discuss. The council was split down the middle on you. It finally came down to their dislike for Cyrus more than their wariness of you. In the end, no matter how much I argued on your behalf, the council agreed that you must be killed."

Chapter Fourteen

Amy approached the door slowly. She had heard Chris talking, as if to someone, but there was no voice in return. She entered the room, closing the door behind her. There Chris hung like Delilah had described—from the ceiling, chained by his wrists in front of a fire pit full of sinister tools. He was so skinny that all of his bones could be seen through his skin. He looked like a he hadn't eaten in a year. His eyes were seared shut, and his ribs could easily be seen as broken through his pale skin. His blood-soaked jeans and shirt were torn, and some patches were burned into his flesh. He was hardly recognizable as human let alone Chris.

None of what Amy saw bothered her. Being a vampire had twisted her heart so much that things like this delighted instead of repulsed her. "How's it hanging, Chris?" Amy asked, laughing loudly.

"Get out of here, Amy!" Chris yelled, kicking his burnt feet in her direction.

Amy ignored him and scanned the room. It was empty except for Chris. "Did you think you were talking to someone?"

Chris was silent

"There is nobody here, Chris. Who did you think you were talking to?"

Chris held his tongue again but turned his head slightly as if listening to someone next to him. "She's not Amy anymore; she's a vampire. The Amy we knew is dead," Chris said, looking beside him and not at Amy.

"The Amy *we* knew?" Amy repeated. "Who is it that you think you are talking to?"

The door opened, and Delilah walked in with a short, fat man that reeked of alcohol. The man wept as he was tossed to the floor. Delilah shut the door. "This had better work, Amy."

"This is the man Chris hates most in the world, even though Chris has become just like him," Amy said, as much to Delilah as to Chris.

Chris turned his head again as if listening to an invisible man beside him.

Amy continued, "Chris, I have brought you a present." Amy walked to stand next to where Chris seemed to be listening to someone that no one else could see. "I have brought you the man that has humiliated you and demeaned you your whole life. If you haven't guessed already, I have brought you your stepfather. You can have your revenge, Chris. All you have to do is drink his blood."

Delilah dragged the weeping man and dropped him by Chris's feet. Chris's stepfather took one look at Chris and pushed himself back until he was up against the fire pit. He started to sob out of fear. Not fear of what they had done to Chris, but fear that he would end up with the same fate.

Delilah pulled a lever on the wall that loosened Chris's chains and dropped him hard to the ground. Chris blindly felt around the floor until he felt his stepfather's feet. He felt with his hands until he was touching his stepfather's shoulders. The whole time his stepfather would cry harder and harder the closer he got to his face.

Chris turned his head, listening to someone behind him. "I won't, Brian," Chris said, as if Brian was standing there with them.

Amy was getting irritated. "Brian is not here, Chris. Did Donovan crack your skull so hard that you hear dead people now? Brian is dead because of what you did to him. He is dead because of what this man turned you into. Get revenge for you and Brian. Bite him!"

Chris pulled his stepfather's head closer to him. Tears flowed down his stepfather's cheeks as he begged for his life. Chris kissed the top of his stepfather's head. "I forgive you," Chris whispered in his ear. Chris's stepfather wrapped his arms around Chris, holding him and thanking him.

"You forgive him!" Amy yelled. "He does not deserve forgiveness; he deserves death!"

Chris announced boldly, "And who gives me the right to decide that? Everyone deserves the chance to be forgiven."

Amy was so angry she grabbed a red piece of iron from the fire and was about to hit Chris across his back. Before she could the door to the room was thrown open, and Jaden walked in wearing another expensive suit. His hair was slicked back, and he was wearing a blood-red tie with his black pinstriped suit.

Jaden calmly walked to the wall and pulled Chris's chains until he was suspended off the floor again. He walked around Chris inspecting every mark. He finally grabbed Chris by the chin and pulled his face over until he could see his eyes seared shut.

"It looks like you have defied me once again, Delilah," Jaden said. Though his voice was low and calm, it still brought terror.

Amy dropped the piece of iron and backed up until her back was against the wall.

Delilah defended her actions. "He will be a strong vampire, Jaden. You will see. All we need is for him to drink. We have brought the person he hates to tempt him."

This time Jaden did not speak calmly. His voice echoed off the walls in the room. "You have defied my orders and created another Samson." Jaden picked up Chris's stepfather by the throat, squeezing until the man's necked popped and he went limp. Jaden then tossed the man's lifeless body into the pit, where he immediately burst into flames. "You will kill this boy before he kills all of us. Do I make myself clear?"

Delilah avoided Jaden's eyes and nodded.

Jaden then turned his attention toward Amy. His voice was calm once again. "I didn't give you permission to make this one either."

Delilah still avoided meeting Jaden's eyes. "She was to be an example to the boy. She has proven herself very useful."

"Who made her?"

"Donovan."

"I will have words with Donovan," Jaden said, making his way out of the room. Before he closed the door behind him, he added, "Send her to my room. I will see for myself how useful she is."

Anger flared in Delilah's eyes. She grabbed iron from the fire pit and rammed it through Chris's stomach. He screamed with fiery pain.

"I'm not going to kill you, but I am going to make you wish you were dead," Delilah yelled. She left the iron in Chris's body and grabbed another piece, and then another, and then another until Chris looked like a pincushion.

"I guess I had better go to Jaden's room," Amy said, making her way for the exit.

"You don't have to, Amy." Chris sounded weak as he spoke.

"Shut up, worm!" Delilah yelled. "You think she demeans herself if she does this. You are like every man. It doesn't matter the race or breed. A woman's body is a tool to get what we want. All a pretty woman has to do is smile at a man, giggle when he speaks, and we have him. After that it's easy. We walk a certain way, and we can get a car. Drop something in front of them, and we can get a mansion. Lay with a man, and we can get everything. We can get a man to leave his wife and children. I've even made a man jump to his death. It's so easy. Men really are weaker. Amy knows this and knows that Jaden is a man like any other." Delilah walked over to Amy and gently rubbed the back of her hand down Amy's face. "After Jaden is through with you, I want you to ask him to spare Chris."

"I will," Amy agreed.

"You best go now. He will be more pleasant if he doesn't have to wait."

***

Amy went as quickly as she could to the hallway that held everyone's quarters. She had already seen Jaden angry, and that was enough to never want to see him like that again. She walked a long way until she reached the last door in the hallway. She found the door opened and Jaden scolding Donovan for changing Amy without his permission.

Jaden was flushed red in the face. "Guard my door until I have finished with this girl. Her performance this night could save your life."

Donovan stomped out of the room, meeting Amy's eyes with anger and sympathy. He stood at the entry, closing the door after Amy had entered. Jaden's room was massive. Lantern light danced across expensive red draperies that hung from the walls. To one side was a giant bed that could sleep at least eight people side by side. Red silk sheets covered the bed. On the other side of the room stood a giant fireplace with a desk on one side and a wine shelf on the other. The flames of the fireplace somehow burned red. In front of the fireplace sat a single red leather lounge chair with an end table next to it. Down the middle of the room ran a red carpet, splitting the room in half. Amy thought Jaden was playing up the vampire angle a little too much with all the red. There was so much red that Amy's eyes hurt.

Jaden went to his wine shelf and pulled down a bottle and a couple of glasses. He took the cork out of the bottle and smelled it. "Ah," he said, "fourteen hundred BC. That was a good year for warriors. This came from the first human that became a warrior. It took some time to figure out that the warriors could take human form and that they were recruiting humans. We thought we had destroyed all the warriors, or they had simply given up and gone into hiding. Think of our surprise when we discovered that they learned to change form."

Jaden poured the blood-filled wine into a couple of glasses and handed one to Amy. Amy took a sip, feeling the alcohol going straight to her head while the blood of the warrior both electrified and excited her. She felt like there was nothing that could stop her at that moment.

"I know this isn't your first time drinking warrior blood. As the leader I am able to see the vision that every vampire sees. I have seen yours, and I thought it quite impressive. I am glad that Donovan and Delilah have turned you. I believe you will prove to be a great use to me."

"But I thought you were mad at Delilah?" Amy was very confused.

"Delilah needs to learn her place. She believes that she can hide things from me and tries to usurp my power. If need be I would have killed you to teach her a lesson."

Amy's face flushed with a look of, "Is he going to kill me now?"

"I am glad that it did not come to that. But you need to learn, girl, that a leader must do what is necessary…even if that means making an example out of someone."

"Why were you mad at Donovan?"

"He should have reported to me as soon as you were turned. He was supposed to report to me on everything that woman does or says. I believe he didn't tell me to protect you. He always had a weakness for a beautiful face, which leads me to a proposition for you. Now that Donovan has failed me, I would like you to report to me on everything Delilah says or does."

Amy didn't know if she should. She felt like she was betraying the woman. More than that, she was afraid of what Delilah would do to her if she found out.

Reading her expression, Jaden said, "You owe Delilah no loyalty. She might have had a hand in making you what you are, but it is I that let you live. If you are worried about retaliation, she will not harm you if she ever suspects you are spying for me. I can make you my second, and she will have to do whatever you command. I can make you more powerful than Delilah. I can give you the power she craves."

Jaden was right. Why should she be loyal to Delilah? She would probably betray her if given the chance, especially for a little bit of power. Amy was tempted by the whole idea of having power that even Delilah craved. The ability to command and be feared like Jaden was too much to pass up. The thought of making Delilah cower before her put a smile on her face.

"How can you give me more power? I am already a full vampire. I thought I couldn't be changed more than I already am."

"There are secrets and abilities that only the head vampire has and knows. If we have a deal, then you must not speak a word of it to anyone. If you betray me in any way or speak of our dealings here, I will make you suffer before I destroy you. Do as I say, and I promise you will have a place in our master's court by my side."

Amy couldn't contain her excitement. "We have a deal. What do I have to do?"

"First we have to get rid of the weaker blood inside of you."

Jaden grabbed Amy by the shoulders and bit into her neck, consuming all that was inside her. Amy couldn't stand anymore, and her vision faded. She felt the life draining from her. She had been betrayed and knew that she was going to die.

"Open your mouth and extend your fangs," Jaden called to her.

She did as she was told, and Jaden pulled her head to his neck. She felt his skin against her lips and did what was now instinctive to her by biting down. She pulled his blood into her mouth and gulped. Her strength began to return. After another gulp she could stand on her own, and after one more her vision returned. She drank as much as she could before Jaden pulled her off. Jaden stumbled a bit, reaching for his wine glasses and finished what was remaining.

Amy stood looking at him with blood dripping from her chin. She could feel new strength coursing through her body. "I already feel stronger," she exclaimed.

"Of course you do; you now have my blood inside you. You are stronger and more powerful than anyone here, besides myself. You are my new second. If at any time you betray me, I will reward you with pain you have never known."

Amy suddenly felt hot all over her body, as if she was on fire. Her head started to pound against her skull like it was trying to escape. She fell to the ground, clutching her head and screaming.

"My blood is inside you, girl," Jaden said, waiting for a second to let his words truly sink in. "When I became leader, I was granted a few gifts. One of those was being able to control my blood when it is in another. The catch is, I have to give my blood to a full vampire and not just make a vampire with my blood. It signifies a deal being struck between me and the recipient. The recipient has to be willing to let me drain their body of their old blood and replace it with mine. I have always wanted to try it, but I could never find the perfect candidate. I saw the way Delilah trusted you and thought you would make a perfect candidate. You are too new to realize that all deals come with a price. Any other vampire would have refused and walked out of here without letting me finish a single sentence. You, on the other hand, crave power. You don't want to remain scared and weak." Jaden stopped Amy's pain and helped her to her feet. "You might have given up your freedom, but isn't it better with what you have gained in return?"

Jaden poured another glass of blood wine for Amy. She gulped it down, breathing hard from her trial. She didn't like that she could be controlled so easily, but she did feel that it was worth it, no matter the cost. No one but Jaden would intimidate her now. She would be the one doing the intimidating.

Jaden poured her another glass before continuing. "I have known Delilah for some time and can guess most of her designs. For instance, I am guessing that Delilah wanted you to beg for the young man she has in the dungeon."

"She did," Amy answered.

"It's that stupid prophecy she received. The problem is, her prophecy can be seen more than one way. She can just as easily destroy all of us, which she has almost done once before. I do not believe she will ever create a powerful vampire to join us. I think she will fail time and time again, killing many of us with each attempt. I think the vision she received was to stand as a warning. You are my second, so what do you think we should do with the young man?"

Amy took a sip of wine and thought for a minute. He was asking her opinion, and she didn't want to appear weak. She wanted to prove herself worthy of the power and position she now held. "I think we should let her waste her time with him. It will occupy all of her attention so she isn't scheming something else. If the time comes that he does drink, then I say kill him."

Jaden laughed. "That is good, and I will put you in charge of it. Keep pretending to be her friend. Do not let her know you are my second yet. Let her think you have convinced me to change my mind. If he does drink, you can be the one to kill him. Keep close to Delilah, and if she makes even the smallest plan that doesn't have to do with this boy, I want to know about it. I am getting tired of her scheming, and if I find that she has carried it too far, then I will not hesitate to kill her."

Amy set her wine glass down on the end table. "I will." She headed toward the door before Jaden called after her. Her head ached painfully and then subsided.

"Did I give you leave? When I am finished with you, then you can leave."

When the morning came, Amy left the room to find Eric standing in the hallway with a large cup full of blood in one hand and a damp towel in the other. Eric saw her and handed her the cup. "Delilah thought you would need this." Amy was bruised and bloodied, feeling like a boxer who just left the ring. She snatched the cup from Eric's hand without so much as a thank-you.

"Where is Delilah now?"

"She is with that boy."

Amy gulped the blood down and immediately felt better. Her bruises faded, and her cuts healed. She handed the cup back to Eric and grabbed the towel, wiping the dried blood from her face.

"Something seems different about you," Eric said curiously.

Amy quickly angered by the statement and yelled, "Go tell Delilah that her pet is saved!"

Chapter Fifteen

"Not this again," Brian said as he found himself dreaming of Chris again.

"Who's there," Chris said, lifting his head up to hear. He looked far worse than the first time Brian had seen him. He looked much more starved, and his body seemed more broken. His pale, translucent skin was painted with bruises and blood. Parts of his torn clothing were burnt into his skin or stuck to him with dried blood.

"Wait, you can hear me?" Brian asked, astonished. The first dream he couldn't interact with Chris at all.

"You took my eyes, not my ears." Chris turned his head, and it was plain to see that his eyes were seared shut.

Brian wanted to pull Chris down and save him from this pain, but his hands passed through the chains. He still couldn't interact with anything in the room. It was his dream, and he couldn't do what he wanted. *Maybe,* he thought, *I can't save Chris because there is no more Chris to be saved. This might all be my brain's sick way of helping me realize that Chris is dead.*

"You still here?" Chris called out.

"Yeah, I'm still here," Brian answered.

"Why are you so quiet? Are you trying to figure out the best way to torture me?"

"Why would I do that? We used to be friends."

That peeked Chris's curiosity. "Who are you?"

"It's me, Brian."

"Nice try. Brian is dead, and I killed him. Here's a little tip for the future: if you are going to pretend to be someone else, try and get the voice right. You sound nothing like Brian."

Even in his own dream Brian felt like an idiot. He forgot that he sounded different. "It's me, and I can prove it. We were best friends until I got fat and you didn't want to look like a loser with me."

"Anyone could have figured that out."

"Could anyone figure out that my mother used to make you take a bath whenever you came to spend the night? She felt bad for you because your stepfather wouldn't take care of you."

"That is something only Brian would know. Even after everything I did to him, he kept his promise and didn't tell anyone. If you are Brian, then what happened to your voice?"

"A couple of werewolves saved my life, but the transformation had some side effects…one of those being my voice."

"So you are a werewolf?"

"Yep. But they like to be called warriors."

"So you are a warrior now?"

"Yep."

"You didn't die?"

"Nope."

"And you found your way down here to save me?"

"No. This is all a dream that I am having. None of this is real. You died."

"This is no dream. I wish it was, then I could wake up. Every second I pray for death, but I am still alive."

"Yeah, right. I am in my bed asleep right now. This is impossible."

Chris let out a laugh and then winced at the pain it caused. "You want to talk about impossible? You are a werewolf, I am a vampire, and you want to talk about things that are supposed to be impossible?"

"You have a point," Brian said, now more depressed that he knew this wasn't just a dream. "Do you know where you are?"

"I don't know. I woke up in a cell."

"I want to help you. How am I supposed to find you? I can't leave you like this."

"I deserve this for how I treated you. I turned my back on my best friend. I became the man I hated most in my life, my stepfather. I am so sorry."

Brian tried to put his hand on Chris's shoulder, but it passed right through him. "No one deserves this no matter what they have done, least of all you. You were a bully, not a murderer, not a thief, not a criminal of any kind, a bully. You made me miserable because of what you said, but at the end of the day, that's all they were—just words. You made a mistake. Everyone is entitled to make mistakes. That's what makes us human, but recognizing our mistakes and correcting them is what makes us something more. Everyone deserves the chance to be forgiven. I forgive you, Chris."

Chris began to weep. "Thank you, Brian."

"You know that you didn't have to go to such extremes to apologize. A plate of brownies would have been easier," Brian joked, wanting to lighten Chris's mood. He couldn't imagine being tortured day in and day out. What would that do to someone's sanity, to their soul? He hoped that he could lighten Chris's mood and give him some hope.

"I would have, but I don't think I could have made enough to fill up your plate," Chris laughed, wincing at the pain.

"There he is." Brian smiled. "Hold on to your sense of humor until I can find a way to come and save you. Don't let them take that away."

"Knowing that you forgive me is all the help I needed," Chris said, smiling.

The door to the room opened, and Amy Thompson walked in. Brian thought he saw her the first time he was here, and now he knew for sure that he did. She was Amy, but at the same time, she wasn't Amy.

"How's it hanging, Chris?" Amy laughed loudly.

Brian wanted to hit her so badly.

"Get out of here, Amy!" Chris yelled, kicking his feet. Brian could see how burnt and raw they looked.

Amy scanned the room, and even though she was looking right at Brian, she didn't see him. "Did you think you were talking to someone?"

"She can't see me, Chris," Brian informed him. "Don't let anyone know that I am alive."

Chris didn't say a word. Brian knew the silence was for Amy, but he hoped that Chris heard and understood him.

"There is nobody, Chris. Who did you think you were talking to?"

"What happened to Amy? She was always sort of nice," Brian said.

"She's not Amy anymore; she's a vampire. The Amy we knew is dead," Chris said to Brian.

"The Amy *we* knew?" Amy repeated. "Who is it that you think you are talking to?"

The door opened, and Delilah walked in with Chris's stepfather. Brian wanted to know what they planned to do with him. He looked scared out of his mind.

"This had better work, Amy," Delilah said, shutting the door behind her.

"This is the man Chris hates the most, even though Chris has become just like him," Amy explained.

Brian stepped closer to Chris. "It's your stepfather. I don't know what they plan on doing with him, but don't listen to them."

"Chris, I have brought you a present." Amy walked to stand next to Chris on the opposite side of Brian. "I have brought you the man that has humiliated you and demeaned you most of your life. If you haven't guessed already, I have brought you your stepfather. You can have your revenge, Chris. All you have to do is drink his blood."

Delilah dragged the weeping man and dropped him by Chris's feet. Chris's stepfather took one look at Chris and crawled until his back was against the fire pit. Brian could see that Chris's stepfather was terrified of what would happen to him. The man could care less about his stepson.

Delilah loosened Chris's chains, and he dropped to the floor. He was so weak that he collapsed under his own weight. He felt blindly around the floor until he felt his stepfather's feet. Chris felt up his stepfather's body until he got to his shoulders and eventually felt his face. The whole time his stepfather would cry harder and harder the closer Chris came to his face. The absolute terror and panic was evident.

Brian urged Chris as best he could. "You can't do this, Chris. If you do, you will be just like them. Don't do it."

Chris turned his head toward Brian. "I won't, Brian."

Brian cringed. He didn't want anyone, especially Delilah, to know he was still alive.

"Brian is not here, Chris. Did Donovan crack your skull so hard that you hear dead people now? Brian is dead because of what you did to him. He is dead because of what this man turned you into. Get revenge for you and Brian. Bite him and drink him dry."

Brian breathed a sigh of relief when he heard Amy refer to him as dead. He breathed even easier when he saw what Chris did next.

Chris kissed the top of his stepfather's baldhead and whispered in his ear, "I forgive you." Chris's stepfather wrapped his arms around Chris, repeatedly thanking him.

"Good man, Chris," Brian yelled out.

"You forgive him!" Amy yelled. She did not look happy at all. "He does not deserve forgiveness; he deserves death."

Chris boldly announced, "And who gives me the right to decide that? Everyone deserves the chance to be forgiven."

Brian had never seen anyone as angry as Amy was just then. She grabbed a piece of iron from the fire and was about to strike Chris across his back when the door to the room was thrown open. In walked a man wearing an expensive suit, and his dark hair was slicked back. He was tall and very slender, and when he moved, he seemed to command all the attention in the room.

The man walked to the wall and pulled Chris's chains until he was hanging once again. He proceeded to walk around Chris, inspecting him. He grabbed Chris by the chin and pulled his face over, looking at his eyes.

"It looks like you have defied me once again, Delilah," the man said. His tone was calm, but Brian felt terrified listening to him.

Amy dropped the piece of iron and backed up against the wall.

"Who is this guy?" Brian asked.

Delilah was the one to answer. "He will be a strong vampire, Jaden. You will see. All we need is for him to drink. We have brought the person he hates the most."

Brian watched as Jaden got angry. Brian thought Jaden's calm was terrifying, but his anger was even more so. "You have defied my orders and created another Samson!" Jaden yelled out in anger, his voice echoing around the room. Jaden picked up Chris's stepfather and squeezed the man by the throat until his neck popped. Then he tossed his body into the fire like discarded trash. "You will kill this boy before he kills all of us. Do I make myself clear?"

Brian saw how terrified Delilah was of this man, and for good reason. She wouldn't meet Jaden's eyes with her own. She only nodded in agreement.

Brian felt a sense of urgency for Chris. "I will find a way to save you, Chris. I promise.

Chris responded, but no one other than Brian noticed. "Don't worry about me. If they kill me, then it will be a sweet release. You forgave me; that's all that matters."

Brian was about to say more when suddenly everything went dark and he sat up in bed. He was covered in sweat, breathing hard, and his heart felt like it was going to jump out of his chest. He knew what he dreamt was more than a nightmare. He really did see Chris. He didn't know how, but he did. Brian got out of bed and started pacing his room. How was he going to find Chris? How was he going to save him? Would Chris even still be alive? That terrifying vampire was determined to have him killed. Something inside of Brian told him that Chris was not going to die. The best thing he could do for Chris was train so when he did find Chris, he could actually save him. Brian knew that he needed to tell Samuel about his dream. He needed as much help as possible if Chris was going to make it out alive.

As Brian sat on the edge of the bed, he saw the packet Samuel had given to him out of the corner of his eye. He had forgotten all about it. He was not in a good mood when he came back to his quarters. Samuel said that the council voted that he needed to be killed. That meant that Brian Porter would cease to exist, and the packet held his new identity. His mother would get a visit from a police officer notifying her that Brian had been killed. Last night he threw the packet on the desk, wanting to be Brian Porter for at least one more night and wishing he could do something to comfort his mother.

Brian sat at the desk and grabbed the packet. Samuel had said that the new identity was best, given all the changes that he had gone through. New name for a new look. He was warned not to contact his family or anyone else from Brian's old life. If he did bump into anyone, he was to act as if he had never met them before, and that included Sarah, too. He breathed out a long sigh with the thought of Sarah. He never thought there was a chance he would never see her again. Her beautiful blue eyes still burned at the forefront of his memory. He knew that he couldn't contact her, but Brian didn't know if he would ever stop thinking about her.

Breathing a heavy sigh with the memory of Sarah, Brian spilled out the contents of the packet across the desk. He let out another sigh. *Good-bye, Brian.* He picked up an official birth certificate. *OK, my new name is…Slade Aurelius? What the crap?* He had the last name of Marcus. This had to be some kind of joke. He scanned down and read that his parents were listed as Marcus and Ahmose.

The newly named Slade Aurelius got up from the desk and walked into his bathroom. There, in the mirror, he looked at the man with the golden-yellow eyes and black hair. "I don't look like a Slade, do I?"

A sudden movement caught the corner of his eye. He turned and saw nothing. Another movement out of the corner of his eye came again. When Slade turned, still there was nothing. Either he was seeing shadows, or whatever he was seeing was moving too fast for even him to see. He looked around the room but saw no other movement.

Passing it off as paranoia, Slade turned back to the mirror and was startled. He nearly fell to the floor when he saw a creature standing on the bathroom counter looking at him. The creature was a little over two feet tall and was standing on long feet that had two toes with long white claws and a long heel that also had a claw. The creature had long arms with two fingers and a thumb of equal length, each with long white claws. The creature was covered in green scales that resembled snake skin, and its stomach was a lighter shade of green than its body. Its head was more oval than round, and its mouth was wide with dozens of small, razor-sharp teeth. Instead of a nose, the creature had a couple of slits above its mouth. The creature studied Slade with long, oval eyes that were yellow with an elongated pupil like a snake's eyes. The creature had long, rigid ears that were the shade of its stomach on the inside and the shade of its body on the outside. Behind it, a small tail whipped back and forth, with a puff of brown fur on the end that resembled dried moss. It smelled faintly of sulfur and smoke. With everything that he had witnessed over the past few days, Slade didn't know why he was so surprised to see this creature.

The creature pointed up to the light with its little finger. Slade looked up at the light and back at the creature. "Do you want the light on?" he asked. The creature shook its head. It pointed again and then looked at Slade. "I don't want the light on. It hurts my eyes."

The creature motioned with its hand for Slade to come closer, and then it sniffed him like a dog. The creature grabbed his hand, sniffed it, and then bit it, leaving a dozen tiny teeth marks in his hand. Slade yelled as he pulled his hand back and saw that he was now bleeding. The creature pulled at Slade's elbow trying to get his hand back. Slade was hesitant and didn't know why he let the creature take his hand back. For all he knew, the creature would bite his thumb off. Instead the creature licked the bleeding wound with its pointed tongue. Slade's hand burned for half a second before the bleeding stopped and the wound healed, looking as if he had never been bitten at all.

"You hear now?" the creature asked with a raspy, snarled voice. It was the type of voice Slade imagined would come from lizards if they could talk.

Surprised, Slade answered, "Yeah, but why did you bite me?"

"Me bite, me lick, you hear," the creature said, pointing to its ear.

"I see. I wouldn't be able to understand you unless you bit me."

The creature nodded its head in approval of how quickly Slade understood. "You friend?"

"I guess so."

"You no like light. Me no like light. You eyes like me eyes. You smell not same. You friend."

"OK. My name's..." He almost said "Brian," but that wasn't who he was anymore. "Slade. What's yours?"

"No name," the creature said, looking sad. "We no have names."

"Well, if we are going to be friends, then I have to call you something. How about Stretch?" Slade thought it would be an ironic name

The creature shook its head.

"Daisy?" Slade asked, more to check if the creature was a boy or a girl. He really couldn't tell.

The creature shook its head again. "Me boy," it said, almost offended.

"OK, OK, I'm sorry." While Slade was thinking of the next name, the smell from the creature gave him and idea. The creature smelled faintly of sulfur and smoke. It made him think of the word *brimstone*. "I know. How about Brim?"

The creature nodded with excited approval.

"I'm glad you approve. They just assigned me my name. I don't look like a Slade, do I?"

Brim shook his head.

"Yeah, I didn't think so." Slade looked at himself in the mirror again. "I guess I had better get used to it. That name belongs to me now. What do you say we go downstairs and get something to eat?"

Brim jumped in the air with excitement and ran into the bathroom wall, disappearing. Slade shook his head with unbelief. Brim had just run through a solid wall. He quickly dressed and walked down stairs in shock, wondering if this was what it would take to make him snap. Maybe he already snapped and there was no Brim. Maybe he imagined the whole thing. It could have been the stress of seeing Chris and finding out his new name. Slade breathed a sigh of relief when he saw Brim bouncing up and down on the counter in excitement.

"At least I'm not crazy," Slade said to himself as he walked into the kitchen. "How did you get down here, Brim?"

Brim cocked his head sideways as if that was the weirdest question he had ever heard.

"Never mind," Slade said, turning to open the fridge. He stopped himself. "Wait, I already ate everything yesterday. Sorry, Brim. I don't have anything to eat."

Brim nodded his head as to say, "Slade did."

Slade opened the fridge, and it was completely stocked again, same with the cupboards. "How did all this food get here?" That's when Slade noticed that all the garbage he left on the floor was cleaned up. "I would have heard if anyone came in to clean. How did all this happen?"

"We," Brim said.

"You did this?"

Brim shook his head. "*We.*"

"You and others like you did this?"

Brim nodded his head. "Yes."

"Thanks, Brim," Slade said, impressed. "What would you like for breakfast?"

Brim pointed to the eggs in the opened refrigerator.

"Eggs it is."

Brim bounced happily as Slade found a pan and cracked eggs into it. He discarded the shells into the sink and watched as Brim jumped into the sink and gobbled down the shells.

"Did you just want the shells?"

Brim nodded joyfully, rubbing his belly.

"OK, I guess I am eating eggs for breakfast and you will get the shells."

Slade cracked a few more eggs, tossing the shells to Brim, who chewed them up happily. Slade cooked and ate his eggs while Brim watched curiously. It was as if he was asking Slade how he could eat the gross part of the egg. Slade finished and put his dishes in the sink but was still hungry. He looked into the cupboard until he found Pop-Tarts. Brim looked excited again. Slade unwrapped one and offered it to Brim. Brim turned his face and stuck his tongue out in disgust. If Brim didn't want it, it was no skin off Slade's back. He ate the Pop-Tart and watched as Brim grabbed the wrapper and shoved it into his mouth. Brim again rubbed his belly with delight.

"You eat garbage?" Slade asked, both shocked and curious.

Brim nodded his head. "Yum."

"Well, now I know how my floor got so clean."

Brim nodded proudly, which made Slade laugh.

A knock came to the door, and Brim disappeared through another wall. "I guess you are not the social type." Slade went and opened the door.

"Brian," Samuel said in greeting when the door opened.

Slade knew this was a test by the look Samuel had on this face. "I don't know who that is. My name is Slade."

"Well done," Samuel said proudly. "Put on your nametag or you will be rehearsing that line all day."

"Why Aurelius?" Slade asked as he bounded up the stairs to get his nametag. One great thing about being a warrior was that Samuel didn't have to yell his response for Slade to hear him.

"Ahmose and Marcus always wanted a son, and Ahmose asked me for a personal favor. She wanted to adopt you as her own. Since you are still just a child, she felt this would be her only chance. That and she really took a liking to you. She even picked out your name. It was one that she has been saving. If it isn't too awkward for you, she would like for you to think of her as your real mother."

As Slade looked at his nametag and listened to what Samuel was saying, he found that he no longer hated his new name. He never really had real parents, not in the sense that everyone else did. He was invisible to his family and always felt alone. He was the only kid that didn't have parents attend school functions or events. It was the worst feeling in the world when he looked around to see everyone's parents at a function taking pictures and he was all alone with no one to talk to. His family had disowned him and hid him away. Now there was someone that did want to be his family, and it brought a warm feeling to his heart. He now found a since of pride in his name and put on his nametag, honored to carry the name Slade.

"Don't forget your sunglasses," Samuel called up to Slade. "You will not have the luxury of having dark rooms today. We normal warriors can only keep our eyes golden for a few seconds without changing. Make sure you eat before we go. I don't know when you will break for lunch. With your metabolism, that might feel like a long time."

Slade ran downstairs with his sunglasses on. "Brim and I already had breakfast."

"Who's Brim?"

As Samuel and Slade walked to his first class, Slade filled him in on everything that had happened that morning. Slade gave every detail, from the way Brim looked, to him running through walls, to him eating garbage. Slade explained how he was bit and was then able to understand Brim.

"Amazing. You actually saw a gremlin," Samuel exclaimed.

"That's what Brim is, a gremlin?"

"Yes. Gremlins were slaves in hell ordered to cause all sorts of mischief to mortals. A barn door accidentally left open so horses ran away, or a gate left open so that livestock ran off—work of a gremlin.

Misplaced anything that you absolutely knew you left in a certain place—work of a gremlin. They would even carry out some of the punishments in hell. That was until my father freed them from their bondage. He killed their taskmaster. In return they keep our homes clean and our pantries stocked. No one has ever seen one since they were freed. They are frightened of us. Of course warriors would squish them into powder anytime we found one. But that was before they were freed. They are hard to catch. They travel through shadows to anywhere they wish to go."

"That's what Brim did? I thought I was seeing things at first."

"You weren't seeing things. Darkness and shadows are their best friends. Like you, they don't like the light. Since your place is so dark, they can move about freely here as if there were no walls. Light, it's the only way to trap them. I almost killed one long ago, but it was much too fast for me. That was the closest I have ever gotten to one. Now the warriors have all but forgotten about them and take for granted the work they do. Out of sight, out of mind, as you would say."

"Why would Brim show himself to me if they are scared of us?"

"They are scared of us, not you. You are different than us in so many ways—two of which, more than likely, caught the curiosity of your new friend. You don't like the light, and you carry a different scent."

Slade thought it was all very interesting, but his thoughts kept turning to Chris. "Samuel, I wanted to talk to you about something before class. You might think it's a dream, but it doesn't feel like it was a dream."

"Tell me what it is that concerns you, and I can judge better when I know the details."

Slade told Samuel everything that he had dreamt, not leaving out any detail. When he was finished, they walked in silence for a moment, and Slade was beginning to get worried that Samuel didn't think what he saw was real.

"We tried to save Chris after he was taken. The tunnel we found under the house was collapsed, and there was no way to clear the debris. We thought him dead or an enemy. If what you say is real, then Chris is stronger than I gave him credit for. The problem is that vampires are not known for their patience when it comes to turning a mortal. If Chris doesn't drink soon, they will more than likely kill him. If he does drink, then he will not be your friend anymore."

"I know he isn't going to drink. What if they force him to drink?"

"He must drink of his own free will. It has to be his choice. If they force him to drink and take away his free agency, then he will cease to exist. In other words, he must choose evil on his own or he will die."

"I just don't get the feeling that they are going to kill him. I don't know why, but I feel as if they want him for some bigger purpose."

"You focus on class the best you can today. Let me worry about Chris. I will put out word wherever I can to see if I can hear anything. While I am willing to do this for you, I want you to keep in mind that this could all be just a dream."

"I wish it was, but something tells me that it was more than just a dream."

Samuel stopped in front of a classroom where Madelyn was already writing something on a chalkboard. Two men and a woman were already sitting down talking to each other. All with a nametag on. Slade wasn't the only one with a new name today. Slade was about to head in when he heard an unfamiliar voice behind him.

"Hey, Runaway," the voice said.

Slade turned around to find a tall young man behind him. He was slender and had on a pair of worn jeans and a black AC/DC shirt. The young man had brown hair and brown eyes that Slade thought he recognized. It wasn't until Slade saw his old worn boots that he got an idea of who this young man was.

"Wait, Mr. Duncan?" Slade asked.

"Seeing as how I am no longer an old man, you might as well get used to calling me Jack."

Slade couldn't believe it. Jack had no gray in his hair, and he had all of his teeth. He looked healthy and strong. This is how Slade imagined Jack looked before going off to war when he was younger.

Samuel patted Jack on the back. "This is what happens when we recruit a warrior from somebody older. They return to the prime of their life. Jack will look like this until the end of time."

All Slade could get out was, "Amazing."

"I have to leave and report to the council again. You two learn as much as you can, and watch out for those three in the classroom. Cyrus recruited them himself, and I think not for a good purpose."

"I don't know what I can do, but I'll try," Slade said.

"Come on, Runaway, let's see what really happened in history," Jack said, leading Slade into the classroom.

Chapter Sixteen

"Since no one knew me, they said I could keep my name. All they had to do was roll back my birthdate to match the age I look," Jack explained to Slade as they walked to two empty seats.

Slade looked at Madelyn still writing things on the chalkboard. She was wearing a long black skirt and a silk blouse. It was an outfit he had seen a few teachers wear before but none looked half as good. He leaned over and whispered to Jack, "If my teachers in high school were half as beautiful, I think my grades would have been better."

"Mr. Aurelius," Madelyn said.

It took a moment for Slade to recognize his name. "Yeah?" he answered.

While still writing on the chalkboard, she said, "In the future, if you want to whisper something, make sure the one your whispering about isn't a warrior." She tapped a finger to her ear. "I can hear even the slightest whisper, too."

The other warriors in the room laughed as Slade slid down in his seat, red-faced with embarrassment.

Madelyn turned around and winked at Slade. "And thank you for the compliment." She looked at the rest of the group one by one before continuing. "I think we should start with introductions. We already met Slade. He's the one who doesn't know that we all have super hearing." The other warriors laughed again. "Next to Slade we have Jack."

Jack waved a hand forward. "Hi."

"On the other side of Slade, we have Rebecca."

Rebecca didn't say anything or look at anyone; she just sat there picking at her fingernails.

"Rebecca, I know the name is new to you, but you need to respond to it," Madelyn stressed.

Rebecca finally looked up and realized Madelyn was talking to her. She stood on her feet, saying, "Hello," to everyone.

Slade thought she was much shorter than the other warriors he had seen so far. She stood just a little taller than five feet. Her brunette hair fell just to her shoulders and mostly covered her dark brown eyes. Slade wondered how she could even see. He was sure that she was very pretty, if she didn't hide behind her hair. With her gray sweatshirt and blue jeans, she looked like a stressed-out college student.

Madelyn came to stand in front of Rebecca. "My dear, are you all right? The transformations sometimes take an emotional toll on us. If you need a day, you can go back to your house and rest."

A tear fell from Rebecca's left eye. "I just miss my mom and dad."

Madelyn looked at Slade, and he could see the same question he had on her face. *Her mom and dad?*

"Rebecca, what do you mean you miss your mom and dad?"

"I didn't get to say good-bye at the hospital. Mr. Cyrus said if I didn't want to die from cancer, I had to go with him. I didn't know I wouldn't be able to see my mom and dad again."

"Me too," said the young man next to her. He was tall with shaggy blond hair, blue eyes, and tan skin. He wore a white tank top and orange shorts. Slade thought he looked more like a surfer than a warrior. It didn't help that he was wearing flip-flops either.

Madelyn looked at the young man. "Brandon, what did Cyrus tell you?"

"That he could save my life. That my parents didn't have to be sad anymore," Brandon said, looking at Madelyn and then down at his hands as if he was trying to keep from crying.

"What about you, Clive?" Madelyn asked.

Clive was a slim black man just shy of six feet tall. He had short hair and light brown eyes. He looked like a businessman with his green polo shirt and tan slacks. He leaned forward when he answered Madelyn.

"I didn't care if I died. I lived a long, happy life. I watched my wife pass away last year, and I already said good-bye to my children. Cyrus told me that he could use a man like me and that I could make the world safer for my children. I just wish I could change the name I was given."

Madelyn smiled at Clive. "I am sure that you can make a difference. Changing your name this soon after you have been assigned one is almost impossible. I can ask, but I am sure the answer will be to wait fifty or sixty years." She turned her attention back to Rebecca and Brandon. "How old are you two?"

"Cyrus said we weren't supposed to tell," Rebecca said, not wanting to make eye contact with Madelyn.

"It's all right. You can tell me."

"I'm twelve," Rebecca told her.

Twelve, Slade thought. *No wonder she was hiding her face and wearing a baggy sweatshirt. She was hiding her new mature body.*

"I'm fourteen," Brandon added.

"If you two need to talk about anything, my door is always open to you," Madelyn said, squeezing Rebecca on the shoulder. Madelyn sounded calm, but Slade could smell the scent of anger wash over her. She was none too happy to hear how old Brandon and Rebecca were.

"You can all see how each warrior's human form is changed into their prime," Madelyn said, walking back to stand in front of the chalkboard. "Old will become young, and young will grow until they reach the age their bodies need to be at their peak. Mind will change with the body becoming sharper. They say that maturity also grows, but from what I have seen of the male warriors, it doesn't seem to be true."

Madelyn saw Robin walking by and excused herself for a moment. She closed the door behind her as she stepped into the hall. The others were talking among themselves about their backgrounds and didn't seem to be able to hear Madelyn and Robin talking. Slade, on the other hand, could hear every word. Madelyn was telling Robin the age of Rebecca and Brandon. She was so angry that her emotional scent could be detected through the closed door.

Robin calmed her down as best as he could. "Madelyn, I will take this to Samuel, but you must not bring this up again. The rest of the council left last night and that gives free reign for Cyrus to do as he wishes. I fear what he might do to you if you bring this complaint before him. Leave this to Samuel and forget that you ever came by this knowledge."

Robin walked away, and Madelyn came back into the room. She calmed herself as she walked back to the front of the class. The anger was still there, but it faded as she began teaching.

"This is not a class by any means. There are no tests or quizzes, and you may speak whenever you wish. Today we will go over history. Why should a person fight if they don't know why they fight or what they are fighting for? After history you will learn about our enemies and their weaknesses. Then you will learn how to blend into society. This becomes more important as you get older—or should I say, as the world changes around you and you stay the same as you are now?"

Madelyn paused for a moment before continuing. "Our history starts with the creation of the world. Warriors are as old as the world and are tasked with protecting it and humankind. We were to protect their freedom to choose. Warriors are a species to themselves. The warrior form that you have seen was their only form. It wasn't until later when humans were allowed to become warriors that warriors could take human form. Warriors were the only creatures alive that could descend into the depths of hell and withstand the environment there. To keep humans safe, warriors would often descend into hell to battle the evil trying to break out. Warriors were known by the humans then and interacted with us without fear. Many generations passed in peace before humans started to get greedy. They wanted to rule and enslave all those around them. They craved power."

"Warriors were standing in the way of anyone taking the freedom of another. If a human was to become a ruler over all, he needed a way to deal with the warriors. A human went and made a pact with the devil to become the first vampire. The vampire was strong and fast and fed off the blood of the humans he wanted to rule. He was even faster and stronger than us. Working in groups, we were able to kill that vampire, but not before he was able to create more. The other vampires were not as strong as the first, but they were still deadly. Warriors were stronger and faster than the newly created vampires, and they were easily dispatched. Out of desperation one vampire bit a warrior and learned that our blood made them just as fast and strong as us. After killing that warrior, the vampire spread what he had learned. Our offense now became a defense. They were hunting the warriors, killing us almost to extinction. Without the warriors' numerous armies, the humans became enslaved to those who made themselves kings. Word spread that warriors were monsters to be killed upon sight. Warriors have sworn never to harm a human, and many fell refusing to kill those they swore to protect.

"Years passed with warriors hiding from humans and vampires but still attacking where they could. One day a warrior came upon a human defending himself against a group of vampires. The human fought boldly, but it was obviously a losing battle. The warrior stepped in, aiding the human. The warrior killed every vampire that would harm the human. With the battle won, the warrior discovered that the human was gravely wounded and would die. Even though the warrior fought valiantly, it was not enough to save the human. As the warrior watched the human dying, a feeling came over him that if he bit the human, the bite would save him. The warrior did so, watching as the human was not only saved but was also able to take the warrior form. Now came a choice to each and every warrior. They could choose to continue the fight and gain the ability to take human form or live a mortal life, never taking human form. Many hated the humans for turning on them and chose to never take human form. They became the wolves we know today, still very much hating humans.

"Those that chose to take human form were now able to walk among humans and vampires without detection. Our ranks were refilled with the new ability of turning humans into warriors. The new ability came at a terrible price: warriors were no longer able to bear children of their own."

That's why Ahmose felt that I was her only chance at having a son, Slade thought.

"With ranks refilled, the warriors were able to drive the vampires into hell to live with their master. Not wanting humans to be used against them again, warriors decided to keep their existence a secret.

"Humans, however, are naturally greedy and crave power. They will seek evil means to get what they want if it is an easier path. The more evil the world gets, the stronger the forces of evil get, and it becomes harder for us to keep them where they belong. It is a constant battle that always involves the humans. When evil abounds, there are wars, slavery, and all manner of evils across the face of the earth. When good triumphs, there is peace.

"No matter how wicked the humans became, warriors have always found a way to push the vampires back and all those that fight with them. That is, until Christ was betrayed for thirty pieces of silver. Silver has become our greatest weakness. Even the touch of it can bring immense pain. A warning to all of you: if you get hurt or injured in any way by silver, you cannot heal from it."

Slade looked down at his hands, afraid that someone might read the reaction on his face. He had healed from silver, but the pain was worse than what any warrior would feel. It literally burned him.

Madelyn continued, "If you do not believe me about the dangers of silver, then you need to talk to Marcus. He is now missing a hand that silver removed. Our enemy may never have known about silver and our weakness to it, if not for some dissenters. Humans-turned-warriors left us and joined the vampires. They were the first true werewolves. They told the vampires of our weakness and, like the vampires, fed on humans. The older a warrior gets, the stronger he gets, so we sent out our oldest and strongest to deal with these werewolves. Afterward, our leaders came up with rules. New warriors had to be approved by the council; only young warriors could turn a human. If an older warrior changes a human, then that new warrior will gain almost all of the older warrior's strength and possibly become a danger to the rest of us. Humans were to be recruited after they had lived a long mortal life."

Rebecca and Brandon looked at each other, and though they didn't say a word, their expressions both said, "Why were we turned?"

"Lastly, the new recruit must have proved themselves to be of good moral fiber. The recruits are brought before a member of their council, and the council decides if they are worthy. With these rules came the hope that they would prevent warriors from joining our enemy.

"The rules worked and no other warrior dissented, but we have not been able to fill our ranks as quickly. Our enemy soon outnumbered us, making this war harder to fight. With the invention of the television, our enemy found a way into every home to sway every human. It became impossible for us to find new recruits. That is why you five sitting here are the first new warrior recruits we have seen in such a long time. With the enemy having their claws in every facet of media, they have slowly changed the opinion of the humans. You will find humans now have a love for vampires. No longer do humans reject ideas that could harm them, but they accept them with open arms. You might find yourselves getting discouraged, thinking all is lost. You must remember you are fighting on the right side, and hopefully in time the humans will wake up and realize what they are doing."

Madelyn looked at her watch. "That is close to our time. Tomorrow we will start learning about our enemies and how to fight them, starting with the vampires. Go across the hall where Dennis is waiting for you."

Being ushered from one class to another brought the feeling back to Slade of being in school again. But this time he wasn't being picked on by anyone. That was a nice change, but like before he didn't have a family to rely on again. Just outside the door, Ahmose waited for him. Maybe he did have family to rely on. Samuel had said that Ahmose wanted to adopt him. Seeing as he never really had a father or mother who cared about him, it might be good to have people in his life that did. Here stood a woman who desperately wanted him to be her family. It was an odd feeling to be wanted after so long of no one wanting anything to do with him. The lonely feeling Slade had every day was still fresh in his heart. By now his parents would think that he was dead and probably would never shed a tear. His father was probably drinking champagne to celebrate.

Ahmose stood just outside of class. She kept her eyes on the floor in front of her, fidgeting with her hands. This was not the same Ahmose who tried to attack him just the day before, and he knew why. She was not able to bear Marcus a child, and Slade was her last chance at having a family that she so desperately wanted. She was overwhelmed with fear that she was going to be rejected. Everyone in his life that was supposed to love him had rejected Slade. He couldn't do that to this woman. He didn't want to do that to this woman.

Slade looked on the woman with compassion. He grabbed her fidgeting hands to calm her. "I hope I'm not such a terrible son that you will want to change your mind."

Ahmose's countenance immediately changed. She looked at Slade with a tear in her eye. "You accept?"

"I accept," Slade said with a grin.

Ahmose wrapped her arms around Slade and kissed him on the cheek repeatedly. With tears in her eyes, Ahmose smoothed down Slade's shirt like a good mother would do for her son. "You go have a good class." She turned and made her way back to the elevator, humming a happy tune as she went, almost with a skip in her step.

Chapter Seventeen

Slade entered the room across the hall. This room was completely different from the rest of the classrooms. Neither the rock walls nor the rock floor were covered or polished in any way. Slade had the feeling of walking into a cave as he went into the class and joined the others sitting on the rock floor listening to Dennis. In a line in front of them were rubber mannequins bolted to the floor. They looked like the kind he saw on television that some fighters practiced on.

"I don't want to hear any more complaints about names," Dennis said, standing in front of the group wearing black sweat pants and a Minnesota Vikings T-shirt. It seemed that Slade missed Clive complaining about his name again. "You think I enjoy being called Dennis? I am a Viking for heaven's sake. How much fear does Dennis the Viking bring? None. The point of a name for us is not to stand out, but rather to blend in. I guarantee that no one will look twice at a Clive or a Dennis. Besides, if you don't like the name, you can go back to yours in a hundred years or so as long as there is no one from your past that can associate you with that name. Unfortunately, vampires have found out mine so often that I have had to change names and locations, and even my appearance."

Dennis stopped what he was saying and looked at Slade "Now that you are here, Slade, we can begin." He emphasized Slade in such a way that he must have had to remind himself not to say Brian. "I am going to teach you how to fight."

Brandon got really excited. "Are you going to teach us how to do kicks and punches? I want to know how to throw someone across the room."

"I am not going to teach you how to be ninjas," said Dennis, scolding Brandon like a teacher would do to a young student.

Brandon became red-faced and looked down at his feet, embarrassed. Slade thought he was showing his true age. What fourteen-year-old boy didn't love ninjas and martial arts? Every young boy wanted to be a ninja.

Dennis continued, "If you want to learn how to be a ninja, there are some great mortal instructors that can teach you all you want to know. Here you will learn how to fight like the warriors that you are. Don't worry, Brandon, ninjas will wish they could fight like you when you are done here."

Brandon, still red in the face, smiled. In his teenage world, anything that was better than a ninja was worth learning.

"When you fight you must be in your warrior form. Does anybody know why?"

Slade spoke up, "Our enemy won't know who is fighting them."

Dennis nodded. "That's right, Slade. Everybody hear that?" The rest of the class nodded. "Of course you heard that; you're warriors. You can hear everything now," Dennis joked, and the class laughed. "Your identity needs to stay safe. Our enemy controls everything topside. If they find your identity, they will use everything at their disposal to hunt you down." Dennis pointed at each of them as he spoke. "From personal experience I can tell you that it's not fun. If you are caught, we will change your identity and transfer you somewhere else. If that doesn't work, then you will go underground for thirty years or longer. So what must we do, everyone?"

The class answered, "Fight in warrior form."

"Good. Hopefully that is sunk in so we can move on. I will not only teach you to fight as warriors, but also to control your transformation."

Clive sat at the end of the line raising his hand.

"Clive, this isn't a formal class. If you have a question, you can just ask."

Clive got to his feet before he asked his question. "You keep saying warrior form, and now you said transformation. I'm not really sure what you mean. I was waiting for you to clarify, but it seems I'm the only one who doesn't know. Can you explain to me what you mean by transformation."

Jack and Slade looked at each other and then back to Dennis. They all silently had the same question. Dennis asked it aloud, "How can you be a warrior if you have never witnessed a transformation?"

"The man who came to me just had his eyes turn golden and his teeth became jagged and sharp."

"Me too," added Brandon.

"Me too," added Rebecca.

"And who turned you three?"

"Cyrus," they each replied.

Immediately Slade could smell the anger wash over Dennis. By how strong and spicy the scent of anger was, Slade thought that Dennis was a ticking time bomb. He wasn't. Instead Dennis blew out a deep breath and with it went the scent of anger. Slade was impressed by the control Dennis showed.

"I guess you three are going to be in for quite a surprise," Dennis said, laughing.

Clive looked at Dennis, and a scent washed over him. It was a new scent to Slade. The closest he could relate the scent to was maple syrup. It smelled similar to the syrup he would use on his waffles when he was little and his mother still made him waffles. Slade wanted to put an emotion to the scent so he could identify it later. Looking at Clive it wasn't hard to pinpoint. Clive was shaking as he sat back down. *"Thanks, Clive. I now know what nervous smells like,"* Slade thought.

Dennis came over to Rebecca, who had her hands if front of her face. Nervousness was pouring off her. She smelled like a syrup factory. "I am going to see if Madelyn is ready next door for you. She will be teaching you how to change so you don't have to undress in front of all these guys."

Dennis walked out of the room, and the scent coming from Rebecca got worse. She was breathing into her hands and shuffling her feet. Slade new something was wrong when the scent changed from a syrup smell to really sweet and sugary, the scent of fear. Once the scent changed, Slade could see the fear on her face.

Rebecca's eyes became golden, and she let out a blood-curdling scream that brought Dennis and Madelyn running over. Rebecca felt her teeth with her finger, as they became sharp wolf teeth. "No, no, no, no," Rebecca kept saying as she backed herself against the wall.

"Don't fight it," Dennis yelled as he came to her right side and put his hand on her shoulder.

"It will hurt if you fight it," Madelyn said, coming to the other side. "Relax, Rebecca. This will not hurt if you just relax. Breathe with me. In and out." Madelyn breathed in slowly and then out slowly.

Rebecca breathed with Madelyn and started to relax until gray fur started growing from every pore. She became more terrified, and her breathing became erratic once again.

Madelyn was quick to respond. "Keep your eyes on me, Rebecca, and breathe with me." Madelyn kept her voice calm and began to breathe again with Rebecca.

With every popping noise that came from her body, Rebecca would slam her eyes shut in fear. All the while Madelyn remained by her side speaking peace to her mind.

As Rebecca's body grew into her warrior form, her clothes began to rip and tear. The sugary smell of fear mixed with a smell Slade knew very well. It was the scent of his favorite candy when he was a boy. It was the scent of sour apple. Slade wasn't sure, but he guessed by the way the scent came when her clothes began to tear that it was the scent of embarrassment.

Rebecca tried hard hold her clothes to her body as she changed, but she couldn't as her hands grew. It didn't matter anymore anyway. With fur covering her entire body, it hid everything that made her a woman. When the transformation was complete, it was hard to tell Rebecca, a female warrior, from any other warrior. The only difference was Rebecca was slimmer than the male warriors. True identities were protected when in warrior from. No one could tell one from another or male from female.

As she stood before them in warrior form, Rebecca studied her hands and felt her body. She reached up and felt her face and snout. When she spoke, her voice was not as deep as the males, but it was just as menacing. "This is amazing," she said, looking at the whole room with her new eyes. "I can see everything so well." Slade had to hold back his laughter when he saw her tail wagging with her excitement.

Madelyn smiled and rubbed her back. "Yes, you can. You will be able to do so much more like this than you can in your human body. I want you to imagine yourself as human and concentrate. Imagine taking off your warrior form as you would a coat or a shirt."

Rebecca closed her eyes and concentrated. Immediately she began to shrink. Dennis ran to the corner where a duffel bag sat and pulled out a plain white robe. He ran back to Rebecca's side and draped the robe over her shoulders. Rebecca's body made popping noises as she shrank, but this time Slade could not smell any fear coming from her. When she was her normal height, Madelyn held the robe closed as Rebecca's fur receded. Within a few seconds, human Rebecca was standing before them holding her robe closed, covered in sweat.

"The first change is very taxing on your body," Dennis said to Rebecca, speaking loud enough for all to hear. "The more you change, the faster it will be and more your body will get used to it. Then you will not be covered in sweat when you change back."

Putting her arm around Rebecca, Madelyn ushered her out of the room. "Let's go next door, and we'll talk about this experience. Then you will be able to change again without having to worry about a bunch of men around you."

Dennis turned back to the rest of his class, seeing that Clive and Brandon looked like they were about to wet themselves. "Why do you two fear?"

Brandon couldn't speak, so Clive stammered for the both of them. "W-w-what was that?" His scent was a mixture of nervousness and fear.

"That was what a warrior looks like," Dennis informed them.

"She looked like a monster!" Clive screamed. "And what that poor girl went through looked painful. I do not want that happening to me."

"It is too late for you, Clive. You have already been bitten. Your warrior half is inside you waiting to come out. Do not worry about pain; there is no pain involved as long as you don't fight the transformation."

"So I don't have a choice? I am going to be a monster?"

"We are *not* monsters," Dennis said boldly. "We were chosen to fight monsters. You, like the rest of us, were given a choice. You chose to fight and protect this world from the ones that would destroy it. Those are the *real* monsters. This warrior body that you are so afraid of is the best tool we have against these monsters. If it were not so, your lineage would have been erased and you would never have been born. You better learn to love this form, because without it this world is lost."

Clive looked away from Dennis's gaze. His scent changed. It was no longer that of fear and nervousness; it was now embarrassment. Slade was bothered by how these scents were so familiar to him.

"I'm sorry. I didn't mean to offend," Clive said.

"You did," responded Dennis. "And I hope that you take offense one day, too. Now I want everyone in this room to disrobe and concentrate on transforming."

It reminded Slade of the first day of gym class. Everyone was uncomfortable and kept their eyes on the ground in front of them, not wanting to look around. Dennis stood in front of them, removing his clothing.

As he was undressing, he spoke to the group. "We undress for two reasons. First, our clothing will get destroyed. You saw what happened to Rebecca and can still see her tattered clothing on the floor still. Imagine someone, or our enemy, coming across her clothing. It is not hard to tell what happened. Second, if our enemy saw you wearing those clothes and then saw them destroyed, they will know your identity. Remember, your identity must remain hidden. Plus, this is my favorite shirt."

Dennis folded and set his clothes aside. "You will also need to hide your clothing until you can retrieve it. You don't want anyone coming across your discarded clothing." Dennis took a deep breath. "Now concentrate on transforming. The wolf in you wants to come out. Don't fight the change, accept it. Imagine putting on your wolf form as you would any other piece of clothing. It is your fighting form; you must put it on."

The transformation was faster than what the group had just witnessed with Rebecca. Within a few seconds, Dennis was standing before them in warrior form. He held his hands behind his back and walked to Clive. His tail swayed back and forth with each step. Slade thought it funny to see Dennis walk like a stuffy professor with his hands behind his back in warrior form.

Dennis leaned over to look Clive in the eyes. His voice was very deep as he spoke. "Your turn, Clive."

"What if I c-c-can't?" he stammered, the scent of fear back on him now that he was looking directly into the golden eyes of a warrior.

"You can just relax and concentrate. Don't fight the change." His voice sounded closer to a bear's growl than a human's voice.

Clive closed his eyes, shaking with fear.

"Relax and feel the change. You are doing nothing more than putting on your warrior clothing," Dennis said. Staying in his warrior form probably wasn't helping.

Clive breathed slowly like Madelyn was showing Rebecca. He opened his eyes, and they had now turned golden. "I can feel it," he exclaimed. His body changed quicker than Rebecca's did. Clive didn't panic but breathed calmly while his body changed for the first time. His warrior form was almost identical to Dennis's. The difference, if there was any, was that his gray fur was a slightly different shade of gray.

Dennis went to Brandon who had been too terrified to say anything the whole time. Dennis leaned over to look him in the eyes. "Your turn. Relax and breathe like Clive did. You'll be fine."

"What if I don't want to?" Brandon asked.

"Then you will be expelled from the warriors," Dennis answered. "Which means you will be put to death."

Brandon gulped even more terrified than before.

"Do not worry yourself," Dennis said. "You wanted to be better than a ninja didn't you? This is your chance."

Slade had to catch himself before he laughed out loud. He just heard a giant, terrifying werewolf bring up ninjas. On the other hand, it seemed to help Brandon. He was able to calm himself and change into his warrior form. He stood just as tall as Clive and Dennis. The difference with Brandon was he had a few specks of dark gray mixed with light.

"This feels awesome," Brandon said excitedly. His voice was just as deep as Dennis's.

Dennis came to Jack, who was already closing his eyes concentrating. Before Dennis could say anything, Jack had already turned into a hulking beast. Jack looked at his fur-covered hands with long black claws. He felt his face and ears. "I feel stronger, and I can see everything so much more clearly than before. The light hurts my eyes some but not too bad."

"I have never seen anyone do so well on their first transformation." Dennis couldn't keep how impressed he was out of his voice. "I think you are going to be a great warrior, Jack. And you are right; you are stronger, and the light will bother you some. I will turn the lights out as soon as Slade transforms."

Dennis came to Slade. "You might want to take off your sunglasses now."

Brandon mocked, "Yeah, wearing your sunglasses inside went out in the eighties."

Slade immediately became angry. He was mocked in his old life, but he wasn't going start being mocked at the beginning of his new one. Dennis looked at him with his warrior eyes. "You are not him. Do not bring his pain into this new life," Dennis said. Slade knew what he meant. He was no longer Brian. The mocking and pain that Brian suffered died with Brian's name. Slade was a fresh start, a new personage to live in. It would do him no good to bring his past into this new life.

Slade took off his glasses and threw them on his pile of clothes. His were not folded and stacked as nice as Dennis's or the others were. When Brandon saw his eyes, he called out, "He's changing already?" Brandon did not know that Slade's eyes would always be golden.

"Calm down," Dennis said, as much to Brandon as everyone. "While the virus that creates warriors seems to typically have the same effect on each of us, we are all different. Sometimes the virus can have a different effect. For instance, some warriors are slender, while some are muscular. Some become taller, while some stay the same height.

For Slade, his eyes will always be golden. He will be cursed to always see through the eyes that you see with now. Continue, Slade."

Closing his eyes Slade concentrated on his transformation. He pictured changing into a fur-covered beast like the others. He felt nothing. There was no stirring inside him whatsoever. Slade opened his eyes, clenched his fists until his knuckles were white, and closed his eyes again. He was trying to push something, anything, out that was supposed to be there. Nothing came. He pictured himself putting on the warrior body like it was a pair of pants or a coat like Dennis instructed, but there was still no change. The most that happened was his fingernails grew into razor-sharp, black claws.

"I feel nothing," Slade said. "I don't know what to do." He felt like he had just failed. Here in his new life, he was, once again, the odd one in the group. He was hoping against hope that this time would be different, that he would be able to be like everyone else and perhaps finally fit in and have friends. It seemed like it wasn't meant to be for him. Maybe it was his fate to never be like everyone else or have friends. Maybe he would always be the one that would be different.

Dennis let out a sigh that smelled like warm dog's breath. "Put your clothes back on; we will try again tomorrow."

As Slade was dressing, Dennis turned out the lights. Ten golden eyes glowed in the darkness looking around the room. Each new warrior was shocked and delighted that they could see in the dark, as if there was no darkness at all. They looked around the room and at each other, each exclaiming the wonder they felt.

Jack looked to Slade. "This is how you see all the time, isn't it?"

Slade nodded. "If you don't see any darkness, then it is."

"I couldn't imagine. This must be a headache to always see like this."

Dennis broke in before Slade could answer. Dennis instructed, "Each of you step up to a practice dummy. Each of you has claws and teeth. Each of them is sharp and deadly. Practice using them on these dummies. They are hard rubber, much harder than the flesh of our enemies. You will find that even these are no match for you. Begin."

Each of them stood before a practice dummy and began tearing away at the hard rubber with their claws. Even Slade, still in human form, swung his hands, raking his claws against the dummy. The hard rubber seemed more like warm butter being cut with a knife. Shredded rubber fell to the floor with each swipe until there was nothing left but the metal post. Dennis, still in warrior form, placed a new dummy onto each metal post, securing it with a few metal pins.

"Do not neglect to use your teeth. With the power of your jaw, it can take out an enemy quickly." Dennis went to Slade's dummy. He put his mouth over the head and bit down quickly, jerking his mouth to the side, severing the head of the dummy from its body. He spit out the head onto the floor. "See, now you try. Slade, you can just observe." As the others practiced, Slade's dummy was replaced.

All Slade could do was observe the others. He watched as each of the new warriors practiced biting and tearing the heads off the dummies in front of them. Brandon began to wipe his tongue frantically with his hands after spitting out the head.

"That tastes horrible," Brandon said in a half-muffled voice while wiping his tongue.

"Vampires do not taste better," Dennis replied.

"This isn't something we'll find ourselves doing often, is it?" Jack asked. "I mean in a real situation. Are we going to be using our mouths a lot?"

Dennis thought a demonstration would be better than an answer. On all fours he ran to Slade's dummy, since it was the only one untouched. As he rose to his hind legs, he sank his claws into the dummy's torso, breaking the bolts in the floor, and raised the dummy to his mouth. He bit down and tore the head clean off. He threw the dummy, still attached to the metal post, against the farthest wall. He spit out the head and looked down at Jack.

"A simple yes would have done, too," Jack joked.

Dennis laughed. "In my experience action is often better than words." Dennis shrank back down to being a human again and went to put on his clothes. "Everyone can go back to being human again. Tonight your skin might itch a little bit from the fur. This is normal for new warriors. Your bodies are not used to transforming. Take a hot shower, and the itch will go away. Don't scratch it, or you will get a rash."

Dennis went back to the duffel bag and pulled out three towels. He handed one to Clive, Brandon, and Jack as they transformed back into their human form. They were each covered in sweat, as though they had just finished running a marathon.

As he handed out the towels, Dennis began to explain, "Today was a short introduction day. Tomorrow will be much longer. You will be with Madelyn until lunch and then with me until supper. Tomorrow we will work on your fighting and fine motor skills until you are just as comfortable in your warrior bodies as you are in these. Now go get some lunch and enjoy the rest of your day."

Clive, Brandon, and Jack toweled off and dressed quickly, all the while talking about their transformation. Each one talked and laughed about how it felt to have their bodies change. Slade was the odd one out, not having experienced what the others had. He hoped this new life wouldn't have a repeat of what happened to him in his old one. He was tired of feeling alone with no one to talk to.

At first it seemed that his worrying was for nothing. "Come on, Runaway, let's go to the cafeteria," Jack said.

The small class was walking out the door when Dennis called, "Slade, stay behind for a second." Jack stopped and waited with Slade. Dennis looked at Slade with a question on his face that Slade could easily read.

"You can trust Jack," Slade said.

It eased Dennis's worry, and he continued, "Cyrus will most certainly hear about today, and I don't know how he will react. Be prepared for anything." Dennis turned to Jack. "Since you are a friend, I will trust you until proven otherwise. If Cyrus comes to you, you must do as he asks. But reveal to us what his plans are. Agreed?"

"I don't think he will trust me, but if he does, I will tell you whatever you need to know," Jack answered.

"He will come to you if you do not befriend Slade," Dennis said. Slade let out a disappointed sigh. "I know it is not an ideal situation. Right now you cannot afford friends when Cyrus is looking for any excuse to destroy you—later perhaps. But for now keeping you alive is my priority. That means that Jack needs to befriend the others while Slade goes straight home."

"This sucks," Slade exclaimed.

Jack slapped Slade's back. "Yeah, it sucks. Seeing you dead I think will suck even more. Let's do this and keep you safe. I will be your friend, Runaway. Even if I have to pretend not to be. If I say or do anything to you, I apologize now for it."

"That is settled," Dennis said. "Jack, catch up to the other two. Slade hang back for a second."

Jack ran out of the room to catch up to the others. Slade waited for a moment and then made his way out of the room. His old life was definitely repeating itself. It seemed that he was destined to lose friends and be alone.

Chapter Eighteen

This feeling was all too familiar to Slade. When he was Brian, he would have to keep his distance from the others at school to not draw attention to himself. He would hear them joke and laugh, and he craved to have that in his life. This time he thought it would be different. Brian was dead, but the curse of his life didn't die with Brian. Even at a distance, he could hear every word the others were saying as they befriended each other—Jack and Clive more so since they were closer in age. Jack made an effort to include Brandon in the conversation, and it looked as if Jack would have little trouble being included in the small group. Slade had to restrain himself from running up to the others to be included with the group.

He stayed back, watching as the others went into the cafeteria, and then Slade went to his quarters. If he hadn't been so consumed with self-pity, he would have smelled the wonderful aroma of meat coming through his door. Instead he was surprised to find Marcus and Samuel sitting at his kitchen table with a huge stack of sandwiches in front of them. They were talking about ways to keep Cyrus away from Slade. Slade could smell the meat on the sandwiches: ham, turkey, chicken, steak. The aroma made his mouth water. Ahmose poked her head out from around the corner to look at him. She was pouring a bag of potato chips into a bowl.

"How was your first day?" she asked, like a kind and loving mother would.

Slade was taken aback, not being used to having someone show that much interest in him. "Not very good, Mom." Slade wanted to try out calling Ahmose "mom." He thought it would feel weird, but it wasn't at all; it felt very natural.

Ahmose beamed from ear to ear being called "mom." The scent of fragrant flowers washed over the room. Ahmose gave off the strongest scent of love. "Come in here and tell me what happened."

Slade wanted to kick himself for feeling sorry for himself. Looking around the kitchen, he could see that he wasn't alone. He had more support now than he had his entire life. Who cares if he couldn't have friends at this point? Slade found that he had something better, a family.

"I couldn't transform today," Slade said, walking into the kitchen. Marcus and Samuel stopped their conversation and turned their attention toward Slade. A wave of aromas washed over the room. Each person was having a different emotion. Marcus smelled angry, while Ahmose had a scent he hadn't smelled before. It was like the scent after a lawn had just been mowed. From the look on her face and the way she set down the bowl of chips on the table, Slade could only guess that it was concern.

"You don't have to be concerned, Mom," Slade said, taking a shot in the dark that he was correct about the emotion he was smelling.

Ahmose spun around, shocked. "How did you...I wasn't concerned. I was—"

Samuel interjected, "Your new son here can smell emotions, Ahmose. It's best just to be honest with him so he can learn what he is smelling."

"I can smell emotions, and they are very strong and sometimes overwhelming. I hope that I am not freaking anyone out and making you regret wanting me for a son."

Ahmose's scent changed to sweet, fragrant flowers. "Of course I still want you for a son. I just didn't want you to worry about anything. That's our job to worry as your mother and father."

Marcus quickly jumped in. "I am not really comfortable with being called father right now."

Ahmose ignored him. "Your father and I will do what we can to protect you from Cyrus."

"Did you hear what I said? I am not really comfortable..." Marcus breathed out his frustration and turned to Samuel. "Can you help me here?"

Samuel turned slightly away from Marcus. "I think it's best if I don't get involved in your family affairs."

Marcus, defeated, grabbed a sandwich and took a big bite eating in his frustration.

Slade's mischievous side took over. "Dad, don't eat angry." He was going to have fun with this. Marcus looked at him, and Slade could smell the annoyance come from him. It smelled like cinnamon gum.

"Yes, Marcus, don't start eating before we have a word of prayer," Ahmose added.

The smell of anger started to rise up in Marcus, but it quickly went back down as he set down his sandwich and just said, "Yes, dear."

Ahmose sat down across from her husband with Slade in between the two. She offered a prayer that humbled Slade. His family had never been religious, so prayer was something new to him, but to also hear someone offer up thanks for him in a prayer made him tear up. If he didn't know it before, he certainly knew it now: this was going to be a different family than he had before.

When Ahmose finished her prayer, she turned to Slade. "I knew you were special from the moment you stepped off that elevator. To smell emotions is something I have never heard of." The smell of freshly cut lumber came off her. Slade could only guess that she was proud.

Samuel swallowed a bite of his sandwich. "It is not uncommon. Before humans were even a part of the order, warriors would meditate and work hard to be able to discern emotions. It was a long and hard process and even when mastered emotions were very faint to pick up on. Any warrior can learn it with years of practice. Slade seems to be the first warrior ever to come by it naturally."

"How does it work?" Ahmose asked. "What do emotions smell like?"

Slade sat forward. "I find that the emotions can change quickly, one replacing the other. It's hard to know what emotion is what, so I take my best guess. Like the smell coming from Samuel is like maple syrup. He's fidgeting with his fingers, which I would barely notice, if not for the scent. I would have to guess that he his nervous."

"Very good," Samuel said. "It's going to be hard to hide anything from you."

Ahmose sniffed the air. "I don't smell any syrup, not even faintly."

Samuel answered, "You won't. Every warrior smells emotions differently. That's why they can't be taught. The scent is unique to the warrior smelling it, something that only the warrior would be able to identify. My father practiced for a century to pick up on emotions. He said the hardest part of mastering it was for someone to be honest about what they were feeling. No one wants to reveal what they are feeling. With Slade, the emotions are so strong that it looks to be easier for him to identify, which is another aspect of Slade we will have to keep a secret."

"Is that why you're nervous?" Slade asked.

"No, I am nervous because I don't know what Cyrus has planned. He broke his own rules to recruit new warriors. He said they were all part of the Humanis clause. He used our own defense against us. All

I know right now is he sees you as a threat. If he found out you can smell emotions, it might push him over the edge. We are going to have a tough enough time when he finds out you can't transform. Whatever he does you must not retaliate. Anything that makes you different from the rest of us we need to keep to ourselves. We will take you out of here in a couple of weeks and hopefully that will be the end of it. Out of sight, out of mind."

"What if he can never transform?" Marcus asked. "He is a new breed, you said it yourself. What if the new breed means he can't transform? Maybe that's why his eyes won't change."

"You might be right," Samuel responded. "We don't know anything at this point about Slade or what he is capable of. We can't afford to worry about that now. We'll worry about it after we are out of here."

"Yes, let us worry about it later. My son needs to eat," Ahmose said. "I heard you had an appetite, and I really didn't know what kind of sandwiches you liked, so I made a selection."

They ate in silence for a moment, watching awkwardly as Marcus kept reaching for his glass of water with his missing hand and grumbling in frustration. Ahmose's concern could be read on her face every time she watched her beloved try. Slade felt guilty every time Marcus tried. He was alive because of Marcus, and it wasn't his fault Marcus was hurt, but he couldn't help feeling guilty every time he looked at Marcus trying to use what was no longer there.

"I'm sorry you are missing your hand now because of me," Slade said.

Marcus set his sandwich down and looked Slade in his eyes, speaking very seriously and yet in a caring tone. "This had nothing to do with you. A vampire, not you, did this. The evil infecting this world took this hand from me, not you. I would willingly sacrifice this hand again to keep you alive. You are going to change this order and cure this infection that has spread."

Slade let out a nervous laugh. "No pressure."

"You are not going to be alone in this, Slade," Samuel added.

"I don't know what I am supposed to do. How am I supposed to change things and keep this world from being destroyed?"

"My father used to say, 'Every challenge is a mountain, and no mountain can be climbed by starting at the top.' Lose focus of where you are on the mountain, and you could fall back to the bottom. Start at the bottom, Slade. Worry about training right now and don't worry about the top of the mountain. Your next step will present itself."

Ahmose squeezed Slade's hand. "And we will be with you the whole way. Now eat; these sandwiches are not going to eat themselves."

And there was her first official statement as a mother, which made Slade smile. As he grabbed one sandwich after another, he felt something on his leg. Thinking it was a bug, he swatted at it, but it wouldn't go away. Frustrated, he looked under the table to see Brim poking at his leg gently with his claws.

"Is there any way that we can turn off the lights and you all could turn your warrior eyes on?"

"We can only keep our eyes golden for a few seconds outside of our warrior form," Ahmose answered.

"Then can we dim the lights or something? Is there another pair of sunglasses close?"

Ahmose went to the counter and pulled her sunglasses out of her purse. She handed them to Slade. "Why do you need another pair of sunglasses? What's going on?"

Slade thought it would be better to show her than to answer. He put the sunglasses on Brim. The fancy pair that Ahmose had fit Brim's large eyes better with the large lenses. Slade then pulled up a chair and grabbed some boxes of cereal to stack on top. Brim climbed to the top of the boxes and sat like a child in a booster seat.

Brim played with the glasses on his face. "Me like. Eyes no hurt."

"They work? Good," Slade responded. When he turned back to the table, he saw Marcus, Ahmose, and Samuel staring at Brim with their jaws hanging open. Slade loved the shock on their faces. "This is my new friend, Brim. He's a gremlin."

"I have never seen a gremlin before," Ahmose said.

"Neither have I," Marcus added. Both stared at Brim like he was a figment of their imagination.

"I've seen a few, but I could never catch them," Samuel said.

Brim pointed at Samuel and sniffed the air. "You try kill Brim."

"Samuel tried to kill you," Slade repeated. "I promise you that he will not try again."

"You can understand him?" Samuel asked in surprise.

"Yeah, he did something to me this morning to help me understand him. What do you hear when he speaks?"

"All I heard was growling noises."

Brim growled some more, pointing at Samuel. "What did he say?"

Slade translated, "He said he knew your father; you two smell alike. He went back to find your father before he died since he was the one that freed the gremlins."

Brim jumped off his chair and disappeared into the shadows, only to reappear a moment later holding a small book that smelled like it was pulled from a fire. He handed it to Slade before climbing back onto his makeshift seat. He spoke, growling and pointing at the book and then to Samuel.

"He said that he got your father a journal so he could add his last words for his son." More growling. "He was to keep it safe until he found you." He made a low growl and bowed his head, making his ears droop. "The gremlins were sorry he died. He was their friend, and they hid his body where their old master would never find it."

"You honor my father. Thank you," Samuel said with a tear in his eye.

Slade handed Samuel the book that smelled so much like Brim. He figured hell must smell so much like sulfur that it would be unbearable. The edges of the journal were singed as if it was thrown into a fire and pulled out again.

Samuel grabbed the journal and opened the cover. He read aloud, "Samuel, I regret that I will never be able to look on you again in this life. Know that I love you and am proud of the man you have become. Hide this journal and keep it safe. No one but you is allowed to look on it. As you read you will learn why. I go to be with your mother now. Do not weep for me. My death was honorable."

Samuel wiped the tears from his eyes, thanking Brim again for the gift he received. The rest of the meal Samuel ate with the journal on his lap. One hand was always on the book, as if it would disappear if he let go.

Brim pointed at the sandwiches. Slade handed him one and watched as Brim studied and sniffed the sandwich. He took a bite, and his ears perked up straighter than before. He continued to take bite after bite, kicking his legs and bobbing his head as he chewed. "Yum, yum," he said, pointing for another.

Ahmose looked at Slade, and he translated, "He likes your sandwiches. He said, 'Yum, yum.' I think this is the first time he is trying real food. He usually just eats garbage."

"Thank you, Brim," Ahmose said, smiling. Her first contact with a gremlin, and he liked her food.

Brim got down from the table and walked under it to Ahmose's chair. He pulled her hand and held it. Slade knew what was coming next. "Whatever you do, Mother, don't scream or move."

Ahmose looked at Slade with that question on her face that said, "Why, what's going on?"

Brim bit down on the side of Ahmose's hand. She bit her lip and held back the words that she wanted to yell out. She didn't move her hand, as her son had told her. Brim licked the wound, which sealed up and left a tiny scar with Brim's teeth pattern. Brim went back and climbed on his chair, taking another bite of a sandwich.

"These good," Brim said.

Ahmose looked to Slade in amazement. "I understood that."

"He did the same thing to me this morning. I think it's the only way we can understand them."

"Amazing," Marcus said.

"I think he liked your food so much that he wanted to tell you himself," Slade explained.

They ate lunch while Ahmose made small talk with Brim, who enjoyed that she could understand him. Slade wasn't able to eat like he did before. He ate only six sandwiches before he was full.

Samuel explained, "It's probably because of the elk you ate yesterday. Your body is finally caught up with the transformation you went through. I am just guessing, though."

Even with Slade full, the sandwiches did not go to waste. Brim ate every one and the entire bowl of chips, and the napkins they were all using. He let out a small burp and went to sit on the couch in the living room. They all watched the whole display in amusement.

Ahmose turned to Slade. "You're not allowed to leave until training is done. Your father and I are going shopping for some clothes for you. Is there anything you need or want?"

"I don't have anything to wear except what I have on," Slade answered. He looked at Brim sitting on the couch. "I think you might want to get another pair of sunglasses. I don't think you are going to get those back anytime soon."

Ahmose laughed as she stood up. "I figured as much. We'll see you tonight. We might bring back dinner. Anything in particular you want?"

"I can't think of anything," Slade answered.

"I got to go too," Samuel said. "I need to read this and check up on what Cyrus is doing."

They all left Slade's quarters, leaving him alone with Brim. Slade jumped onto the couch next to his little friend. "I am going to introduce you to a great game, Brim. It's called football." Slade turned on the television. "It's not the season right now, but they usually have some old games we could watch. I'll teach you everything you need to know so you can love the game as much as I do."

Chapter Nineteen

The couch is where Ahmose and Marcus found the two when they got back hours later. "Have you two been doing this since we left?" Ahmose asked. "Isn't there something else you could be doing?"

Slade enjoyed the motherly talk. "Not really anything else I can do. Don't want to risk a chance encounter with Cyrus."

"Smart," Marcus said as he carried in shopping bags with his one good hand.

Ahmose carried a lot more and set them on the table. Brim zipped to the table so fast it looked like he just appeared in the midst of the bags. It startled Ahmose. "I didn't know he could move that fast."

Slade laughed as he walked to the table. "I think he can when he wants to. When I first met him, I couldn't keep track of where he was moving. Maybe eating all that food earlier slowed him down."

Brim looked in each bag one by one. He pulled things out, grunting when he saw they weren't for him, and threw them behind him. "I'm sorry, Brim, I didn't get you anything. All this is for Slade." Brim disappeared and reappeared back on the couch, watching an old Super Bowl game. "I promise I'll get you something next time."

Brim didn't answer and kept watching the game, looking like a little child pouting for not getting what he wanted.

Marcus rubbed Ahmose's shoulder with his hand. "It's all right. Let him be, baby." Brim appeared on top of the table, shaking his finger and growling at Marcus, and then zipped back to the couch. "What was that about?"

"He said that he isn't a baby," Ahmose translated. She organized all the clothes that Brim had thrown. Folding the empty shopping bag, she set them on the counter behind her.

Slade grabbed them. "I am going to help you out here, Mom, and make you look like a hero." He called out, "Brim, it looks like my mother did get you something." Brim zipped to the top of the counter. "Here you go."

Brim did a little happy dance, grabbed the shopping bag, and zipped back to the couch, tearing off bite after bite while watching the game. When he was done with one bag, he zipped back to grab another. This went on until all the bags were gone.

Ahmose looked at Slade confused. Slade answered, "He will eat anything. That's what they do with the garbage in your quarters."

"And I thought he liked my sandwiches." Ahmose was a little hurt finding that out.

"Your sandwiches were the only thing I have heard him say 'yum, yum' about, and he liked them so much that he made it so you can talk to him," Slade said to console his mother.

It worked. She smiled again and went back to the clothes she had bought. "I didn't know your style, so I got a bunch of things. I didn't know your size, so I just guessed. I want you to go and try them on for me so I can see what they look like."

Slade took armfuls of clothing up to his room and looked through them. He didn't really have a style, but some of the clothes he would never wear. Some looked like they should be on skaters, while others looked like they should be on gangsters. He put them on anyway, and some of the pants were a little tight but not too bad. He smiled, thinking of a time not too long ago when everything he put on was too tight. He loved not having a big belly to work around any longer. He went downstairs to show his new mother one outfit at a time. To his relief she didn't like how they looked either.

"They looked different in the store," she would say.

Out of everything there were two pairs of jeans and a few shirts that were OK. He folded those and put them in the dresser in his room, grateful for having more clothes than what he was wearing. The rest he took downstairs to his mother.

"I'll take these back to the store, and then we can go shopping together when we leave," Ahmose said, folding and stacking the clothes on the table.

Slade wondered, "How can we afford clothes if we don't really have jobs?"

Marcus explained to him, "We own some of the biggest banks in the world. What we buy won't appear on the bank's computers as long we keep it within reason. We can hide most transactions. It's the only way we can buy what we need without drawing attention to ourselves. Any big charges take some finesse to hide. Usually a big charge needs a few months of tweaking the books before we can use the funds. Otherwise we draw attention to the banks, and then the vampire run institutions step in and take a look."

"So that's why you stole the car?"

Ahmose gave Marcus a look that said she was going to take his other hand. "You stole a car?"

"Didn't have much of a choice. It was either that or let Slade be on his own, and then you wouldn't have a son," Marcus spoke quickly, using Slade as his defense.

It worked. Ahmose calmed down and kissed Marcus on the cheek. "This time I'll forgive you, but I don't want to hear that you stole something again."

"I promise." Marcus said it in such a way that Slade wondered if he was crossing imaginary fingers with his missing hand.

Ahmose didn't believe him. She followed it up with, "Uh huh." Then she turned her attention to Slade. "Do you want to help me cook dinner? We can talk and get to know each other better."

"Is Dad going to help?" Slade said. He looked sideways at Marcus, knowing that he was uncomfortable with being called "Dad."

Marcus looked like he was going to say something but just breathed a heavy sigh of frustration and went to sit down next to Brim. Slade loved smelling the annoyance pouring off Marcus. Brim offered Marcus some shopping bags as if it were as simple as offering a piece of pizza. "No, thanks," Marcus said. "I'll wait for dinner." Brim shrugged his shoulders and went back to eating his bags.

"Marcus wasn't a good cook with two hands; I'd hate to see what he would do with one," Ahmose said, going into the kitchen and pulling out some pots. She filled them with water and put them on the stove.

"I can hear you," Marcus said, playfully offended.

"Samuel and your father tell me that you had a girlfriend before joining the order?" Ahmose didn't warm up first; she just jumped right into the fire with personal questions.

"Kind of," Slade said. "She was the only girl who was nice to me, and we hung out once."

"Is she pretty?"

"Oh, yeah," Slade said, suddenly realizing how he sounded and turning bright red.

Ahmose laughed. "Maybe you'll meet again and things will work out."

"I don't see how. By now she thinks I'm dead," Slade complained.

"Things have a way of working themselves out," Ahmose began, as she started cutting vegetables. "Take me and your father. I saw him when I was a serving girl. Right away I loved him. The way he walked and presented himself was so regal. There was no doubt when you saw him that he was emperor. He did his business in Egypt and moved on without even glancing my way. I thought for sure he didn't even know that I existed until after I had been a warrior for many years. I was assigned to come here, and I saw Marcus again. This time he came up to me and told me how he remembered me from Egypt. He wanted to talk to me then, but he would have ruined the negotiations if he was seen talking to a serving girl. He had to put aside his interests for his empire. But as warriors he was able to court me, and we were able to get married. So things have a way of working themselves out. If it's meant to be, then it's meant to be."

"What if it's not meant to be?"

"Then you'll have some heartache for a time. That will go away, and you will find the one you should be with. Your young and have plenty of time to worry about this kind of stuff later."

"Yeah, especially since I'm immortal."

As they cooked together, Ahmose asked all sorts of questions about Slade's former life. He told her of his childhood and his friends, then of Almira marking him and how all of that changed. When he spoke of his family basically disowning him and his friends betraying him, Ahmose was furious.

"If I was there, I would have torn those boys apart, and your family had no right to treat you like that," Ahmose said as her eyes briefly changed to golden, the scent of anger pouring off her.

"They weren't my family," Slade said. "They were just people I was staying with. You have been more of a family to me in these few short hours than they have ever been. Like you said, I wasn't meant to be with them; I was meant to be with you guys."

Ahmose's eyes changed back, and the scent of anger went away. Marcus gave Slade a quick thumbs-up before turning back to watch the game with Brim. "Thank you," she said, wiping a tear that was forming in the corner of her eye.

She went to the fridge and looked around for a moment. "Brim, dear." Brim appeared by her side immediately upon hearing his name. "Would you mind terribly running and getting me a few things for dinner?" She wrote some things down on a piece of paper and handed it to him. Brim grabbed the list and disappeared into the shadows.

"They can read?" Slade asked.

"I believe so. I usually left a list of what I wanted on the counter, and by the time I got home, everything from the list would be sitting on the counter."

Marcus saw a chance to make himself look better. "You know, the gremlins are more than likely stealing that stuff."

It did not help.

"I'm not married to any gremlins; I am married to you."

That second, Brim appeared, placing milk, butter, and ground beef on the counter and then disappearing again into the shadows. A second later he appeared with flour and some fresh herbs. He disappeared and reappeared again holding a box larger than himself. He set it on the counter and sat next to it.

"That is for you, Brim. It's a booster seat," Ahmose explained, hoping Brim would be pleased.

He smiled a large smile, showing all of his sharp teeth, and then he bit a huge portion out of the box.

Ahmose quickly grabbed the box away from him. "No, you can eat the box after I get the seat out."

Brim held his head low, and his ears drooped as he pouted. She took the cereal boxes off the chair Brim had used earlier and set up the booster seat. When she was finished, she handed the box back to Brim. He immediately began to eat it again. His ears perked back up, and he was happy that he got his food back.

As Ahmose cooked Brim squatted on the bar, eating his box and watching everything she was doing. It was like he had never seen anyone take separate ingredients and combine them before. With a full mouth, he pointed at what she was doing, grunting with his mouth full.

"I am making Marcus ravioli. It's his favorite." Ahmose hoped that was what Brim was asking.

It seemed to appease him. Brim went back to his box, keeping his eyes on Ahmose's hands. She cracked some eggs and went to throw them away, but Brim yelled at her to hand the shells over, which he quickly scarfed down. After the third time of trying to throw something away and getting yelled at, Ahmose just gave up and started handing the garbage to Brim. He kept one hand on his half-eaten box, guarding against anyone trying to take it away again while he grabbed the garbage from Ahmose. After he ate the empty can of spaghetti sauce, he realized that he wasn't going to be handed anything else and went back to eating the rest of his box.

When dinner was finished, Ahmose called, "Marcus, dinner is ready."

Brim zipped to Marcus's side and pulled on the fingers of his good hand to get him up and to the table. Brim then popped into his new booster seat. He shook the seat a bit and tapped it with his claws, deciding he liked it. He then turned his attention back to Ahmose putting the food in front of all of them. Ahmose had to tell Brim twice to wait for a blessing on the food first. After the prayer, when Brim saw everyone else begin to eat, he picked up his large bowl and poured the ravioli into his mouth. Within a few seconds, his bowl was licked clean.

"Yum, yum," he told Ahmose.

"I'm glad you liked it, Brim. I think the next thing we need to teach you is to eat slowly at the table. What are you going to do now that you are finished?"

Brim grumbled as he went back to the couch to watch more television while the rest of them sat and talked. Mostly they talked about what a transition it was for them to become warriors and how their life had changed. Ahmose voiced her concern for Slade and hoped that Samuel would be able to do something. Marcus reassured her, but even he didn't sound too sure himself.

After dinner was over, Marcus told Slade of his life when he was little and how much the world had changed since then. More than once he said, "Everyone became spoiled with the invention of indoor plumbing. Never having to go outside to get water or go to the bathroom makes men soft, and people don't appreciate what they don't have to work for."

Ahmose rebutted, "Well, I love indoor plumbing. It is the best invention."

Then Marcus and Ahmose would talk about their other favorite inventions and how easy humans' lives had gotten since their time. To Slade, they sounded like really old grandparents complaining to their grandchildren. Afterward, Marcus went to watch more football with Brim while Slade helped Ahmose with the dishes.

"I thought you didn't like football?" Ahmose asked.

Marcus answered, "I didn't realize that these men were like gladiators. This big one here just smashed this little one into the ground. I don't know why the big one helped the little one up afterward. He should have taken advantage and broke his neck or stabbed him. Then he would be finished with the fight."

"It's just a game," Slade said. "There is no killing, but there might be some broken bones."

"Well, at least there is that," Marcus said, keeping his eyes on the game.

After he was finished with the dishes, Slade tried the best he could to explain the game to both Marcus and Brim. Brim seemed to get the game faster. Marcus kept wondering when the person in charge would ask for the termination of the men on the field.

"*No* deaths," Slade had to keep telling him.

Marcus complained but continued to watch the game. When it was over, Marcus and Ahmose excused themselves to their own quarters and told Slade to get some sleep.

Finally with them gone, Slade was able to turn off all the lights and take off his glasses. "That's better," he said, looking down at Brim, who did the same. They went up to Slade's room where he got ready for bed and watched as Brim curled up at the foot of his bed. "Well, I guess that's where you're going to sleep. There are other rooms, if you want a bed of your own."

Brim shook his head. "Me protect." Then he fell asleep, purring a little as he slept. As he breathed, little puffs of smoke would rise in the air.

Slade was impressed at how fast Brim fell asleep and hoped he could do the same. He also hoped that he would see Chris again so he could figure out where the vampires were keeping him.

Chapter Twenty

Nothing eventful happened during the night, which worried Slade. He wanted to see and speak with Chris again, but instead he slept peacefully through the night. Now he worried that Chris had either died, which was why he hadn't dreamt of him again, or it was all a dream to begin with. From how Chris looked, he hoped it was a dream. It would have been better if Chris had died rather than go through anything like that.

Slade slipped out of bed, trying not to wake the sleeping Brim, who was still curled up and purring a creepy, growling sound. The room was starting to smell like burnt charcoal because of the puffs of smoke that came from Brim while he slept. Slade showered and dressed in a pair of his new clothes, knowing that his new mother would be happy to see him in his new clothes. Brim awoke as Slade sat on the edge of the bed to slip his shoes on. The groggy gremlin came and sat next to Slade on the edge of the bed. Brim's ears hung a little low as he rubbed the sleep from his eyes. He looked up at Slade with one eye partially closed.

"You can stay and sleep if you want. I have to go to class," Slade said.

Then he watched as the tired Brim laid his little head on Slade's pillow and pulled the covers over him. Half a second later, he was purring that creepy, growling sound again. Slade hoped that his pillow wouldn't smell like smoke when he came back to bed.

Downstairs, Slade went through his cupboards but didn't feel hungry. His mind was on Chris, and he was too worried to have an appetite. He stepped out of his quarters and found Samuel waiting for him.

"Do you ever sleep?" Slade joked.

"Not last night. I was reading my father's journal."

"Anything interesting?"

"Nothing I am willing to share at this moment, but it has been confirming some of my fears."

"Then what's with the visit? I know my way to class."

"We checked Chris's house, and it was vacant. All the furniture was there, dishes in the cabinets, and even dirty dishes in the sink. The back door looked to be forced open. Next we checked on that girl you told us about, um…"

"Amy Thompson."

"Right. We went to see if she was home, or at least the last time her family had seen her. Her house was also vacant, but with her house there were signs of a struggle. Lamps were broken, and furniture was either overturned or broken. It looks like they tried to fight back against whoever broke in. No signs of blood means the vampires abducted them."

"Why would they abduct Amy's family?"

"Often to show loyalty, a newly made vampire will consume the blood of their family."

"That's horrible!"

"Yes, it is horrible. These are the demons we must protect the world from. But it also confirms that you are not just dreaming. They are keeping Chris somewhere, and he is resisting. There is only so long he can resist. I will double my efforts to find him. You need to consider what must be done when we find him."

"What are you talking about? What is there to consider?"

"There is no out for Chris; nothing can save him now. Either he lives the rest of his life in misery craving blood every single minute, or he dies."

"You want to kill Chris, after all he's been through?"

"Especially after all he's been through. He needs mercy. Killing him will be the most merciful thing you can do for him. I did not mean to anger you. I'll leave and let you think on that as we search for your friend." Samuel started to walk away.

"May I ask, why search for him at all if you are just going to kill him?"

Samuel stopped to look at Slade and answered sincerely, "To save his soul. If you learn nothing else while you're here, I want you to leave with this knowledge: we fight every day to save the souls of every person on this earth, to save them from damnation and destruction." Samuel left Slade and went into the cafeteria.

The weight of the world seemed to press down against Slade's shoulders again. With Samuel's words came back Almira's. He was the only one that could save the warriors and the world from destruction. Slade had no clue how he was supposed to even start. He was going to take Samuel's advice and concentrate on what he currently needed to do and hope his next step would reveal itself.

He hurried to class, sitting away from everyone. Jack was now in the midst of the others. He gave Slade a wink when the others weren't looking. It was good to know that Jack was still on his side. Jack pointed at Slade and made a crack about his inability to transform. The rest of the small group broke out in laughter, thinking the joke was so funny. Slade flopped into his seat feeling more like Brian than Slade at the moment.

Madelyn walked in and began writing on the board. "We are going to be learning about witches today," she announced.

"Wait, there's witches?" Slade asked, astonished. The others seemed just as eager to find out as well.

"Oh yes," she answered. "Half of the things you learn in here will give you nightmares for some time. Not to worry though; I will also teach you their weaknesses and how to defeat them."

Just then the door opened to interrupt the class. Cyrus strode into the room like an emperor before his subjects.

"Cyrus, sir. To what do we owe the pleasure?" Madelyn said, obviously a little taken aback by his presence. Her face might not have shown her dislike for Cyrus, but her scent gave her away. The anger poured off her.

Cyrus walked across the room and stood before Slade. "One of these children doesn't belong here. Slade, if that is what you are choosing to call yourself now, remove yourself from this class immediately."

Madelyn tried to protest, "He needs this class if he is to survive."

"This class is for warriors. He cannot transform. He is not a warrior," Cyrus yelled.

Slade could smell the anger pouring off him now. As Cyrus turned to look at him, his eyes briefly changed golden. A new smell was added with the first. It smelled like something was burning. Cyrus didn't hide the hate he had for Slade from his face.

While looking down at Slade sitting in his desk, Cyrus added, "A warrior that cannot transform is a useless warrior."

"What is he to do if he is not in this class?" Madelyn asked, urgently trying to keep Slade where he was.

"That is not your concern."

Cyrus grabbed Slade by the arm and forcefully removed him from his desk and marched him out of the class. Dennis saw Slade being marched out of class from across the hall. He ran up to Cyrus.

"What is going on here?" Dennis raged. The smell of anger was strong with him. Cyrus was upsetting everyone, and the day hadn't even started yet.

Cyrus breathed a heavy sigh, like a response was beneath him. "If he cannot transform, then he does not go to class."

"Where is this rule? As far as I know, this is the first time this has ever happened."

"This is the first time this has ever happened, and as your leader it is my job to make the rules. My new rule says a warrior is not a warrior if he does not transform. I will be seeking death."

"Doesn't the rest of the council have to agree to that? What has Jaya said about it?"

"My wife is none of your concern, and the council will agree with me. Until that time Slade will not be allowed to attend any classes."

"Leave him with me then. I could use his help. Or should I find Samuel and ask him?"

Cyrus looked like he was about to strike out at Dennis just for hearing Samuel's name. "You take him, but I don't want him to participate at all."

"How can he if he can't transform?" Dennis said, mocking Cyrus.

Cyrus turned and stormed to the elevator, the smell of anger and hate leaving with him.

Dennis slapped Slade on the shoulder. "You all right?"

"I feel a bit like Rudolph," Slade joked. Dennis looked confused. "You know he wasn't able to play in any reindeer games?" That didn't help. "It's a classic kids Christmas movie. Never mind."

"You can help me set up for class," Dennis said, leading Slade to a small storage room inside his classroom.

"Do you think Cyrus will get the council to put me to death?"

"I wouldn't worry about it. The council doesn't like it when Cyrus comes up with new rules without consulting them."

In the storage room, Dennis showed Slade which containers he wanted for class. They were small, light containers. They moved one per warrior into Dennis's classroom.

"What are in these things?" asked Slade.

"The best teaching tool ever invented," Dennis answered.

"What is it?"

"You'll have to wait and see with the others."

While the two waited for the other class to get out, Dennis talked with Slade about his days as a Viking. He missed his days on the ocean discovering new places. He talked about his friends that had long since passed away. Slade, in turn, talked with Dennis about a certain red-nosed reindeer. Dennis looked more confused than ever.

"Just watch the movie," Slade finally said, giving up.

After some time sitting in silence, Dennis decided that he could not teach Slade how to fight like a warrior, but he could teach Slade how to fight like a Viking. He was teaching Slade as a man not as a warrior. He taught Slade the basics of how to throw a punch and then moved on to how to take a punch.

"It's just as important to know how to take a hit as well as give one," he said.

By the time the other class was finished, Slade was making progress. When the others went to the cafeteria to eat lunch, Slade didn't feel like eating and wanted to continue with his instructions. Dennis didn't want to continue while the others were done with their class. He didn't want any word of what they were doing to get back to Cyrus. The two of them sat on the floor instead and talked more of Dennis's Viking days. When the others got back, Slade was instructed to stand in the corner and watch as Dennis welcomed the class to their second day.

"In front of you is the greatest teaching tool I have ever come across. Once you have transformed, Slade will open the containers."

"What's he even doing here? I thought he wasn't allowed to be in classes," Brandon said smugly. Slade had flashbacks of when Chris started to think he was better than him too.

"You worry about what you need to do and not what others are doing," Dennis replied.

All the men transformed, and Slade began taking the tops off the containers one by one. Brandon breathed hot, wet air down on Slade to mess up his hair. A few drops of drool dropped on his head. It took all Slade's energy not to turn and punch Brandon as hard as he could, not that it would do any good while Brandon was in warrior form.

"What are we supposed to do with these?" Clive asked in his deep warrior voice.

Slade looked into the container for the first time to see. "Legos?" Slade looked to Dennis, who had a grin on his face. "This is the best teaching tool?"

"This is the greatest teaching tool. I used to make warriors work with small tools to build something, then some genius thought of these little things," Dennis said, as much to Slade as the rest of the class. "You are a giant, clumsy wolf. You have long, sharp claws and big hands. If you go into a fight, you will surely die. These plastic little beauties will help you to control your bodies. Now sit down and start building."

"Maybe after we could have nap time?" Jack joked, winking at both Dennis and Slade. Clive and Brandon laughed.

"That's a good one, Jack," Dennis said. "If you build something good, maybe I'll let you nap." He handed a container to Slade. "Run this next door to Rebecca."

As he left the room, he heard Brandon quip, "Yeah, go next door with the other girls."

Dennis yelled, "Enough!"

Next door, Rebecca was already in warrior form with Madelyn talking to her about controlling her breathing to help control her fear. "It works in any situation. If you find yourself completely terrified, just focus on your breathing, OK?"

Slade set down the container and took off the top, revealing the Legos. Rebecca looked from the container to Slade and then to Madelyn.

"You've got to be kidding," Rebecca exclaimed.

Madelyn answered, "It helps to build dexterity. Think of yourself as a new child needing to learn how to walk and move all over again. This will help. Just sit down and have fun with it. I'll be here to help you as you need it."

Rebecca sat on the floor, and Madelyn sat next to her, waving off Slade to go back to his class. Slade left and shut the door behind him. In the next room, he could hear the frustration as the warriors were having trouble building anything. They were finding that their claws were sharper than they realized. Their tails would gently sway back and forth until a Lego broke, and then it would become rigid. Pieces of broken Legos lay around each of them as they would break a piece, swear, and reach for another.

Slade thought if he had a camera, he would ruin the whole horror genre with one video. This scene was too comical to ever be looked at as scary. Huge, hulking, hairy beasts putting Legos together like six-year-olds on their parents' living room floor.

"Finesse, gentlemen. Finesse," Dennis announced. "You cannot kill your enemy with your awkward bodies. It takes finesse."

Jack was the first to realize to use his claws like tweezers and put the Legos in place with a gentle tap. He got three of them together when Dennis announced to the class that time was up. Hours were spent on the floor with Legos, and only one could put three of them together.

"Nice job, Jack. We'll pick up tomorrow doing this same thing until you all can build something in your warrior bodies like you can in your human form. Transform back and I'll see you tomorrow."

Dennis handed Slade a broom and dustpan to sweep up all the broken Legos. There were more than a few. As Slade did that, Dennis grabbed a large trashcan for him to dump them in. Slade swept and tossed the broken plastic pieces away as the class got dressed.

"I think this class has broken so many Legos that I might have to send out for some more; otherwise, there won't be enough for tomorrow," Dennis said as he watched the class leave. He looked at Jack and motioned for him to bump the trashcan, which he did, knocking the contents back onto the floor. "Jack!"

Brandon clapped Jack on the back. "That was so cool. That'll teach that loser that he's not one of us."

Dennis waited until they were out of earshot. "I think that helped Jack some more."

"What it did was make him look like a jerk and create more work for me," Slade yelled.

"Keep your voice down," Dennis warned. "What it did was make him look like he was one of them. If they think he is one of them, then maybe they will get word to Cyrus that he can be trusted. Hopefully then Cyrus will confide in him like he does the others." Dennis stopped for a second before saying, "Ahmose, what are you doing here?"

"I heard what Cyrus has done, and I came to check on my son." Her voice sounded very concerned. The scent of a freshly mowed lawn flowed from her.

"I'll be all right," he said, looking at his new mother. "I just feel a little like Rudolph."

She looked confused. "Rudolph?"

"Again," Slade was surprised, "do none of you keep up with children's classics? Do you just watch what the vampires put out?"

"I'm sorry, but we are usually too busy to worry about children's movies," Ahmose replied.

"When Christmas comes, I am making sure you see it," Slade said as he continued to sweep up the mess. "I can't have my own mother not know what I am talking about."

Ahmose came into the room and hugged Slade. "Whoever this Rudolph is, he probably just needed a hug from his mother."

Slade didn't know how to respond to that. He hugged his mother back and went back to cleaning the room. When he was finished, he went next door to clean. It looked like Rebecca had as much trouble as the guys did. After he was done, he walked with Ahmose down to his quarters, where Samuel and Marcus were waiting with Brim on the couch and watching more football.

"I think you created a monster," Samuel joked when he saw Slade, pointing at Brim. "He has been in front of that thing since I got here."

"He won't let any of us change the channel," Marcus complained. "I think he ate the controller."

Slade waved off their concerns. "That doesn't matter. Wait until you hear what Cyrus did to me today."

Samuel interjected, "We know already. I spoke with the council personally. They disagree with Cyrus, so you won't have to worry about him trying to put you to death. Unfortunately, as leader of all the warriors, he does have the power to keep you from being trained. The council will try to sway him, but I don't think he will budge on this. There is nothing they can do until they come back and speak with him personally, and that won't be until next year."

"I am not spending a whole year down here, am I?" Slade said, flopping down onto the couch across from Brim.

"No, you will leave next week with the others. I'll make sure of it," Samuel promised.

Slade believed Samuel wanted to help, but what could he do? Cyrus was the one in charge. If Cyrus wanted to, Slade believed he could keep him trapped down here forever.

Ahmose cooked dinner, and everyone ate together. It felt like a real family eating together. They talked over the table about each other's day. Ahmose made Slade describe who Rudolph was to everyone. No one had ever heard of the movie. They asked what Slade was doing now that he wasn't able to go to class. Samuel liked the idea of Dennis teaching him how to fight, even if it wasn't in his warrior form. After dinner everyone said their good-byes, and Slade went with Brim to bed. He had to grab a pillow from another room. His did smell like smoke when he tried to lie down.

Chapter Twenty-One

Cyrus met Slade at the entrance to Madelyn's class the next morning to make sure he didn't go inside. Dennis was there as well to make sure Cyrus didn't take Slade anywhere else. Dennis took Slade back into his classroom and taught him more about how to fight. It was beginning to be the only thing Slade looked forward to. He skipped lunch every day for an extra hour of instruction. Eventually Dennis thought Slade improved enough that he began to instruct him on how to fight with a sword.

"When I was made a warrior, I found that I had an easier time using my claws for fighting because I thought of them as a replacement for my sword. I think it could help you too if the time comes that you ever transform. If you never transform, at least you will know how to fight with a sword. I think everyone should know how to fight with a sword; it is a lost art."

The swords Dennis brought were his old Viking swords. They were huge and probably would make anyone pee themselves just by seeing them. Slade was thankful for his warrior strength; otherwise, he didn't know if he would have been able to lift it.

Learning to fight with Dennis kept Slade from going insane and kept him from hitting anyone when they made fun of him. Clyde and Jack were now doing it more with Brandon. Rebecca would say something in the hall when she saw him in passing. Whatever he heard didn't bother him. How many of them were learning to fight with a real Viking? It filled Slade with enough pride to make their insults run off him like water on a duck.

Every day Slade would hear some tidbits about the other class and what they were learning. Out of context he couldn't tell who or what they were talking about. They weren't allowed to tell him when he asked. When he did ask, they would always respond in the form of an insult.

While he was learning to fight, the others were getting skilled with more than just Legos. Every day, Dennis had them practice attacking dummies or learning how to run on all fours. The day always ended with everyone building with Legos. Rebecca learned faster than the others, and Dennis said that was because the women often had more finesse than the men. When training was getting close to being finished, each of them could build something out of the Legos—except for Clive, but he said he couldn't really build with them in the first place. Instead, he put together long, tall walls. He would call it the "Great Wall of Clive."

Every night Slade went to sleep hoping he would see Chris again, but no dream ever came. He was worried that Chris was killed or had fully turned into a vampire. He felt horrible hoping that Chris was dead rather than a vampire, but the latter would be far worse than death.

The closer the end of training came the more Slade worried about what Cyrus was going to do. This was offset by Ahmose and how much she made Slade feel like they were a real family. He felt more like he was born from Ahmose than adopted every day. Marcus, not so much. He was still resistant to the idea of being Slade's father, which of course egged Slade on to call him "father" whenever he got a chance. Slade enjoyed watching him squirm every time. Brim started getting in on it and calling Marcus "father," too. Marcus, of course, didn't know what Brim was saying, but Ahmose laughed every time she heard Brim.

Marcus would always ask, "What did he say?"

Ahmose would never tell him; she just said, "Don't worry about it." Every time Marcus would give off the cinnamon scent of irritation.

***

What seemed like an eternity had passed, and finally the two weeks were over. Samuel said there was a test the warriors would have to do, but since Slade couldn't transform, he would work something out with Cyrus.

They were all eating dinner for the last night in Slade's quarters when Jack burst into the room. He stopped when he saw Brim. "What is that?"

"My pet iguana," Slade answered. "Why are you here?"

Jack looked at Samuel, "I came to warn you. Cyrus talked to each of us. He wants us to kill Slade tomorrow. He said he will tell us tomorrow how he wants us to do it. I wanted to warn you now. I didn't know if I would be able to get a chance tomorrow."

"You did well, Jack," Samuel said. "I figured he might try something. Go to your quarters before he realizes you are here. I'll see you at the pit tomorrow."

Jack left just as quickly as he came. Slade waited a few minutes after Jack left before asking, "What are we going to do? And what is the pit?"

"The pit is the trial every warrior must face before going out into the world," Marcus answered.

"Should we escape with our son tonight?" Ahmose looked worried. The scent of concern was immediate and very strong.

Samuel shook his head. "If we run, we run forever and risk losing the chance to change things. Slade needs to be seen as strong by everyone if he is ever going to change the order. We need to stay close to Slade and keep him safe until we are allowed to leave tomorrow night."

"I guess we are staying here tonight, kid," Marcus said.

"Thanks, Dad," Slade said, causing Marcus to shift in his seat and let out a frustrated breath.

"Thanks, Dad," Brim echoed, followed by his gargled laugh, which made Ahmose giggle.

"What did he say?" Marcus asked. "Why do you always laugh when he says something after Slade does? Did he call me something?"

"Marcus, we have more important things to worry about at the moment," Samuel chided.

"Fine, after this is over, I want to know what he is saying," Marcus demanded.

Samuel stood from the table. "I am going to talk to Jaya and see if she can do something to help us."

Marcus got up from the table. "I'm going to grab some things for us in our quarters."

"Come back quickly," Ahmose said, standing to give her husband a quick kiss before he left. She looked at Slade. The smell of concern was very strong, but he didn't know what to say to make her feel better. What could he say?

Brim was the one to say something. "Me protect." He got down from his booster seat and disappeared into the shadows.

Ahmose squeezed her son's hand and put on the best smile she could. "You should shower and get ready for bed. I have a feeling you will have to be well rested for the morning."

Slade got up from the table and kissed Ahmose on the forehead. "Thanks for being the only person to want me. It felt good to have someone care about me, even if it was only for a couple of weeks. You are a great mother," Slade told her. He needed to say it in case he never got another chance. He made his way upstairs to his room and did what his mother told him: he showered and got ready for bed. When he was finished with his shower, Brim was sitting on the edge of the bed waiting for him. "Hey, buddy. Where did you run off to?"

"Me protect," was all Brim said.

Slade got into bed, while Brim curled into a ball like he had done every night. Almost immediately he was snoring with his creepy, growling snore. Slade had gotten used to it and found it starting to become a soothing sound to fall asleep to.

This night was not easy to find sleep. Slade would stare at the ceiling thinking about Cyrus and wondering what he was going to do. He tried thinking about Sarah and her beautiful smile, but that didn't help. He tried concentrating on Brim's rhythmic snoring. He even counted the puffs of smoke coming from Brim. Nothing. Slade got out of bed and paced the room. He felt exhausted. His body felt tired, and his eyes felt like they could snap shut and never open again. But when he laid down, sleep was gone. His mind went back to the warning about Cyrus.

When sleep finally did come, there were no dreams. It felt like he blinked and there was a knock at his bedroom door. "Yeah," he asked groggily.

"It's time to get up," the wonderful voice of his mother said from the other side.

"OK," he answered back. It was the first time since he was little that a mother woke him up. After he was bitten and his parents decided that he wasn't part of the family anymore, he was never woken up by his birth mother again. He was usually woken up by hearing his birth mother waking up his siblings.

Slade sat up in bed, feeling the exhaustion pulling down on his body. He went and splashed cold water on his face and got dressed. He expected to see Brim sleeping in his place just like every morning, but Brim was gone. Slade put on his sunglasses and left his room hoping last night wasn't the last time he had seen his little friend.

Something smelled really good. He went downstairs to see a huge breakfast made for him. The table was set with pancakes, eggs, sausage, and T-bone steaks. Marcus was already eating with Samuel. Ahmose waited for Slade to come down before she began to eat. Brim's seat was empty.

"Serve yourself. The blessing has already been said," Ahmose explained.

"Anyone see Brim this morning?" Slade asked. None of them had. "Samuel, any luck finding out what Cyrus has planned."

Samuel swallowed what he was chewing before answering. "I haven't. I have spoken with Jaya, and she has said that she has spoken to Cyrus. You will be free to leave after the ceremony today. They do expect you to attend and witness today at the pit."

Ahmose breathed a sigh of relief. "That is great news."

"It doesn't mean we can let our guard down. I still think Cyrus will try something." Samuel looked around the table at each of them. "From what I have read in my father's journal, Cyrus is more of a threat to us than the vampires, and I have been a fool far too long."

"What is that supposed to mean?" Slade said.

"Now is not the time. I will explain everything tonight when we leave. This place is no longer a sanctuary for us, especially not you."

"What is the plan? Where are we going?" Slade asked.

Marcus spoke up, filling Slade in on what they were going to do. "Ahmose," he began to say, but Ahmose was giving him the stink eye. "I mean your mother would like you to finish school. She would like to have the experience of having a child in school. You still look the same age as when you were bitten, so it shouldn't be a problem. We have made documents for you to transfer in. She wants you to have as normal a life as you can, for as long as you can."

"All right, I guess. What school will I be going to?"

"The same one you have already been attending," Marcus said. His smile said that he knew what reaction was coming from Slade.

"What! You're kidding, right? My brother and sister go to that school. All the kids there hate—"

Marcus cut him off. "Our covers are still intact. I'm a gym teacher, and Samuel is an English teacher. It would be easy to have you come in as my son transferring from another school. You could be an extra set of ears for us."

"Don't worry about the other children," Samuel said. "There is no way they will recognize you. We still haven't finished our work there. I need to stay there until I can figure out what the vampires are up to."

"Does Cyrus know what we are doing?"

"He knows where we will be working, but that is as much as he will know. I am done asking for permission from him. He is no longer my leader." The smell of anger started pouring off Samuel.

When they first got here, Samuel was a stickler for the rules. He bent the occasional rule, but for the most part, he was faithful. He didn't like Cyrus, but he stood up for him as the leader. Something in his father's journal had made him change his view on Cyrus, and Slade was dying to find out what it was.

After breakfast they all walked down the hall in the opposite direction of Slade's usual walk to class. They went past the cafeteria and continued down the hall. Slade was counting all the doors to the different quarters. He wanted to know how many could be housed down here. He counted thirty-two before Samuel informed him that they build quarters as needed for the warriors. They continued past the last door for some time before they reached a set of giant metal doors.

A crowd was gathered before them. There were so many faces that Slade had never seen before. Robin was with Madelyn at the front of the crowd with the new warriors, who were wearing bathrobes. Cyrus was standing off to the side with Jaya trying to look as important as he could. While everyone else was dressed casually, Cyrus was dressed in his suit and looking over the crowd. Being in charge wasn't enough; he wanted to look the part as well. The rest of the crowd was talking with each other about how exciting this was.

"This must be a big deal," Slade stated as he looked over the many faces in the crowd.

"It has been some time since new warriors faced the pit and joined our ranks. With the technology now, we can see what is actually going on in the pit," Dennis said, walking up behind them. He greeted Samuel, Marcus, and Ahmose. He whispered to Samuel so Cyrus couldn't hear over the crowd. "Careful, Cyrus is up to something," Dennis said before making his way through the crowd to stand next to Robin.

Cyrus began to speak, and the crowd went silent to listen. "Welcome, warriors. It has been some time since we have had this time-honored trial. These new warriors will be lowered into the pit to fight three half-breed vampires. They will prove they have learned the lessons they were taught and do what war requires of them to do. We will all witness as they come from the pit triumphant and welcome them into our fold."

The doors behind Cyrus opened, revealing the gigantic pit. A large screen was hung over the pit to show what was going on below with night-vision cameras. From what could be seen from the cameras, the pit below looked to have stone walls running all through it. They didn't want to make it too easy for the warriors going below. The vampires had places to hide and attack from. A vampire suddenly appeared and looked into the camera. It startled Slade, but the other warriors booed when they saw him. In the camera the vampire looked up to where the booing was coming from and ripped the camera out of the wall. The screen switched to the next camera available.

Behind the pit, carved into the rock, was a small room that reminded Slade of a VIP box at football games. Robin, Madelyn, and

Dennis said something to the new warriors and made their way along a small path around the pit to the small room. Inside, Dennis grabbed some controls, and a platform was lowered from the ceiling and swung over the side of the pit.

"Warriors, if you would please transform and step onto the platform," Cyrus announced.

This wasn't like the first day when they had so much trouble changing forms. It was almost instantaneous. The four of them dropped their robes and changed without any trouble. Their huge forms looked down onto the crowd with their golden-yellow eyes. The crowd cheered when they saw the newly transformed warriors. The four of them stepped onto the platform and were lowered into the pit with thunderous applause from the crowd. They could be seen on the screen getting off the platform before it was lifted back up into the ceiling.

Cyrus looked over the crowd until he saw Slade. "Oh, I'm sorry. I think we forgot one. Slade, will you please come forward." The throng of warriors turned to look at Slade.

"He can't do this," Ahmose said.

"Not here, Ahmose," Marcus replied, grabbing his wife's shoulder.

"I will go up with him," Samuel said, putting his hand on Slade's back and leading him through the crowd. Once to the front, Samuel looked from Jaya to Cyrus. "What are you up to, Cyrus?"

"You want to leave here with Slade, then he needs to join his class."

"You know he can't transform. Plus, you wouldn't let him go to any of his classes. He wouldn't know what to do. You can't expect him to face the pit."

"I am the leader, not you. My word is law." Cyrus stepped forward until he was almost touching noses with Samuel, separating him from Slade. "If you want to leave with him, he needs to face the trials."

That's when Slade found out, too late, that he was standing in the wrong place. Cyrus pushed Slade as hard as he could, sending Slade flying backward into the pit. Slade heard the screams of Ahmose over the gasps of the crowd as he fell.

Chapter Twenty-Two

The limousine pulled in front of the large blue house. It was the biggest house on the block, but it still looked like every other house to Amy. The lawn was well manicured, and flowers were planted next to the house, just like every house on the block. Despite being well lit by the street lamps, a few of the houses had their front porch lights on, including the house they were stopping in front of. As the limo came to a stop, Amy could see a few of the neighbors' curtains move. The neighborhood Gossip Watch was wanting to know everything going on so they could have something to talk about. Amy wondered if those neighbors were on the phone right now talking about the limo in their neighborhood.

"Why here?" Amy asked.

Jaden gave Amy a stern look. "I have business here. For now, that's all you need to know."

Donovan opened the door and stood beside it as Amy and Jaden got out of the vehicle. He closed the door behind them and followed them to the front door. The door flew open as they reached the top step. The man, a brunet with blue eyes, behind the door was around six feet tall. Obviously he was keeping an eye out for Jaden and knew better than to keep him waiting.

"C'mon in," the man said.

"Thank you, Charles," Jaden said as he walked through the door and turned left, entering the man's office.

It was a small office with an oak desk in the middle of the room. A large leather chair sat behind the desk with two small leather chairs in front for guests or clients. Jaden walked around the desk and sat in the large leather chair, giving no question as to who was in charge. Amy came around to stand at one side of Jaden with Donovan standing at the other. He motioned to one of the chairs in front of the desk.

"Please sit," he said as if it were his office. Charles didn't say anything; to the contrary, he closed the doors behind him and sat in one of the guest chairs. "Charles, now is the time to advance our plans."

"Now?" he questioned. "Are you sure the people will vote for me?"

"The people will do whatever I tell them to do. Who do you think owns the news companies, the TV networks, Hollywood? Anything I want the people to believe will be broadcast into their homes. Humans are nothing but cattle. You push them in a direction, and that's the direction they will go, even if it leads to their slaughter." Jaden snapped his fingers, and Donovan left the room, closing the doors behind him.

"Where's he going?" Charles asked.

"Here's my dilemma, Charles. I don't think you can be trusted. You have a lack of morals and the hunger for power, which I admire, but it seems that you can be swayed if given enough pressure. So I am going to do you a favor and remove that pressure."

Donovan opened the door and held a woman by her neck off the ground. She was a shorter woman, with long blond hair and blue eyes that made her beautiful face seem even more beautiful.

"What are you doing with my wife?" Charles was starting to panic.

"While you are…what is it they say these days…oh yes, a slime ball, your wife is a good soul. She was going down the right path with you, but something changed in her. I can't have that kind of negative influence on my future governor, now can I?"

"Please, let her go," Charles begged.

Jaden ignored him. "I have recording devices all over this office. I know all about the other son you had hidden away in this house. You didn't want anyone to see him. That I can respect. He was an embarrassment to you and your family, and most importantly, your business. You didn't let emotions get in the way of business. Even when one of my people killed your son, you didn't shed a tear. This woman, on the other hand, doesn't have the same point of view that we do. That I cannot stand."

"I'll do anything you want. I am begging you not to hurt my wife."

"You came to me! You knew who I was. You knew what I was, and yet you wanted to do business with me. What was the number one rule I gave you if you want to do business with me?"

"You are in charge."

"Exactly. I will not be questioned by an insignificant little ant like you. Your lack of morals, your willingness to do anything for power—I can work with that. I just need to get rid of your conscience."

"Charles," April squeaked out with as much air as she could. Her face was beginning to turn purple with the lack of oxygen. "What have you…"

Jaden laughed. "What has he done? Let me tell you, my dear. He has literally made a deal with the devil. He wanted money, fame, power, but couldn't he get them on his own, so he came to me. Most humans want one or two things, but not your husband. He wanted as much as we could give him. He didn't care what the cost."

"I can't get elected without my wife," Charles tried to bargain. April kicked her feet at her husband, knocking a chair over.

"Donovan, please sedate her," Jaden ordered.

When April saw Donovan's fangs extend, she tried to scream. Donovan's hand around her throat prevented her from that. Donovan used his finger to get some venom from his fang and put it into April's mouth. Within a few seconds, April's eyes glazed over and she stopped fighting. Donovan let go of her throat and let April stand on her own. She stood in place, staring at nothing.

"What did you do to my wife?" Charles asked.

"Drugged her," Jaden replied. "Set her down in the chair, Donovan, and then go police outside. I lost a good soldier a few weeks ago, and I want to make sure that warriors are not watching the house."

Donovan picked up the chair and sat April down before he left the room. Jaden got out of his chair and sat on the edge of the desk in front of Charles.

"You can get elected without your wife. Have you ever heard of a sympathy vote? You, a single father raising your children after a tragic accident takes the life of their mother. The humans will feel so sorry for you that they will be lining up to vote for you."

Charles looked from his wife to Jaden. His whole demeanor changed. "And this will work?"

"Of course it will work. We will paint you to be the reluctant hero just wanting to be governor because that's what your late wife wanted you to be. Every news station will run with the story because I own every news station. We will do programs and television specials about you. The humans will be eating out of your palm by election time."

Jaden stood up and looked down at Charles. "I can't trust you. You have lied to me about your son, and who knows what else you are trying to hide from me. You work for me, and I cannot stand my employees lying to me. Second, you are the type of guy who will turn on me if a better deal comes along. So, to fix that, I tell you what I am going to do. Your wife will get in a horrible car accident, but we are going to plant evidence that shows you murdered her. The police work for me. You step out of line at all, and you will be spending the rest of your life in prison. As a bonus, I brought Amy here. She will be going to school with your children. You step out of line, and I promise you she will not hesitate to eat them. I know that you don't care about your children; they are just there to make you look good. I agree with that thought, but if your children die and it looks like you are the one that killed them, you would be the most hated man in the world."

Charles hung his head in defeat. "What do you want me to do?"

"Everything I ask," Jaden said. "In return you will get everything you asked for." Donovan came back into the room and shook his head. "Great, you are not being watched. Good thing for you, otherwise I would have to terminate our contract right here. And by terminate your contract, I mean you and your whole family. Donovan, take Mrs. Porter here in her car and cause an accident. Make it look like she was trying to swerve away from a dog and hit a pole or something like that. I want the voters to love and miss her. Call Amy when you are done. Then your punishment begins."

Donovan grabbed April by the arm and led her out of the office. Charles didn't look at her as she was escorted away. Jaden smiled. "That's what I like to see. No emotions, only business. One of my people will be your campaign manager. Do whatever she tells you to. She should be by first thing in the morning."

Jaden walked out of the room, followed by Amy. Before she shut the door behind her, she said to Charles, "I look forward to eating— oops, I mean, meeting your children."

Chapter Twenty-Three

Slade slammed against the ground with such force that it cracked the rock floor. His sunglass shattered, spreading across the floor at the same time pain shot through his entire body. He would have cried out in pain upon impact, but the ground knocked all the air from him. A dead silence came from his open mouth as he tried to cry out in pain. For a moment he laid motionless, looking up at the bright light coming from above and waiting for the air to return to him. He couldn't believe that he had fallen so far and was still alive.

As Slade rolled over, he wished he had died. The pain was so intense that he felt every inch of his body scream at him. He got to his knees and looked at his surroundings. To anyone else it would have been too dark to see anything, but not to Slade. He could see everything perfectly. Every detail of the pit was revealed to him as he looked at the tall walls and the long pathways before and behind him. It felt like he had fallen into a maze.

The air was cold and damp, and there was a stench in the air that smelled like rotting meat. The smell was so unbearable that Slade covered his mouth with his hand. The smell was getting stronger. Slade gagged on the stench. His already-sore body hurt every time his muscles seized as he gagged. He leaned onto his hands and felt like he was going to vomit when he was suddenly knocked to the ground.

Instinctively, Slade rolled, keeping his elbow high and knocking whoever was on top of him off. He was very grateful for the time

Dennis took to train him. No sooner had he knocked off his attacker that the attacker jumped on him again, as fast as a cat on a mouse.

Now Slade could see his attacker clearly. It was a male vampire, very pale with long fangs. The vampire had short, messy hair and was wearing a business suit that was torn in places. The stench that Slade had smelled was coming from the vampire. Slade wanted to gag again, but for the moment, he had much bigger problems.

The vampire straddled Slade with his mouth open wide, pushing down with all his might. Slade was much stronger and tried to hold the man by the shoulders, but the vampire writhed and wiggled way too much to keep a hold on him. It was like trying to hold on to an attacking snake. He slipped through Slade's grasp and almost had a bite. Slade brought his knees up hard, hitting the vampire in the butt and sending him over Slade's head. Slade jumped to his feet quickly, ignoring the pain he was feeling. The vampire obviously couldn't see as well as Slade. It took him an extra second to find where Slade was standing. The vampire launched himself at Slade, but this time Slade was ready and too fast for him. Slade grabbed the vampire by the throat and swept the vampire's leg, slamming the vampire against the ground. The vampire bit the air and hissed. Slade was surprised to see his fingernails turn dark black and grow out to form long claws. The vampire was even more surprised as the claws grew into his throat. Slade pulled back, tearing the vampire's throat out. The vampire twitched on the ground as Slade stood and stomped his foot as hard as he could, crushing the vampire's skull. The vampire twitched for another second before becoming still.

Slade looked down at his very first kill and couldn't believe what he had done. He had acted on instinct and reacted faster with his body than his mind. He vomited, but it wasn't from the stench. It was from seeing the aftermath of what he had just done. This vampire was evil and had to be killed, but it didn't bring him any joy to do what was necessary. He looked at his hands covered in blood and his newly formed long, black claws. He wiped the blood from his hands onto his pants.

Cheers boomed in the air above him, and Slade looked around to find a camera hidden in the wall. They were cheering for him. He had killed the first vampire by himself instead of with a group. Slade felt like breaking the camera but instead smiled and waved like a kid on camera for the first time, hoping it would piss off Cyrus. He wasn't dead, and he had killed a vampire on his own while still in human form. Laughter echoed from above. He imagined Cyrus brooding while the rest of the crowd laughed.

It was time to focus on what he needed to do. The rest of the group was out there with two more vampires. If he could get to them, he could help. One problem was his claws, which had retracted, and the other was that he didn't know which way to go. Finally, he just picked a direction and began walking down the pathway. As he went he picked up a fist-size rock that had broken out the floor from his fall.

While he walked Slade tried to get his claws back. If it wasn't for his claws, he would more than likely be a vampire meal right now. He concentrated and did everything he remembered Dennis teaching the others to do. He pictured his claws growing, pictured his fingernails turning black and growing into claws. Still nothing. What had he done differently that made his claws grow in class this last time? Slade didn't know and wondered if he would ever find out. They seemed to come out on their own. There was time to worry about that later. Right now he needed to find the others and help, if he could.

The same stench he had smelled before came to him again. It was faint, but he recognized it immediately. *This must be how vampires smell,* Slade thought as he sniffed the air. He felt like a drug dog sniffing its way around as he followed the horrid stench of rotting flesh.

The smell would lead him down one path only to be a dead end. The only option was to follow the path back and hope it opened the way he needed to go. As soon as he came to a bend in the path, he followed his nose again. He would turn right, then left, come to a dead end and try to find another way. It was a dance that Slade did for almost an hour before the stench was really strong. The vampire had found him.

There it was, running toward him. The stench was so bad that he wanted to gag again. The vampire was a woman in a tight dress with her make up smeared. She had messy blond hair down to her shoulders. She ran barefoot directly at Slade, but her attention was behind her. She was being chased.

From around a corner popped out two warriors chasing after her. They were running on all fours and gaining on her. The vampire turned to see Slade and hissed with her mouth open to show her long fangs.

"I have a problem hitting a girl," Slade said. "I don't think I can hit a girl, let alone try and kill one."

The vampire jumped at Slade with her mouth opened wide and ready to bite. Without thinking Slade swung with the rock in his hand, striking the vampire against her head. He crushed the side of her head and sent her flying against the wall.

"Never mind. It looks like I'm over it." Slade dropped the bloodstained rock. He was proud of himself this time for not vomiting.

The vampire staggered to her feet. The side of her head caved in where she was hit with the rock. She collapsed back to the ground when the two warriors fell on her, clawing and biting. They shredded the woman until there was nothing recognizable left. Bone and flesh were scattered all around them. This time Slade did vomit. He wasn't proud that it was in front of the others.

"What are you doing here?" one of them asked. The deep, growling voice made it almost impossible to tell which warrior it was.

Slade looked at the one who asked the question. "Which one are you?"

"He's Brandon," the other said.

Slade could almost hear the difference in the voices. Brandon's voice still had his surfer way of talking, while this one sounded slightly more feminine. "Rebecca?" Slade took a guess.

"Yep, it's me," she affirmed.

"Where are the others?" Slade asked.

Rebecca was the one to answer. "They're around the corner. This one broke off from the other, and we chased after her. We still need to find one more."

"No you don't. I already killed him." Slade almost vomited again thinking about what he had done. He thought about something else quickly to keep his food down, if there was anything left. "Let's go back to the others and get out of here."

Brandon and Rebecca led Slade down the pathway to where the others were waiting with another shredded vampire at their feet. Slade couldn't tell if it was even a man or a woman.

Keep your eyes up, and keep the rest of your breakfast, Slade thought as he walked closer to the others.

"Runaway? What are you doing here?" It was obvious to Slade that the one on the left was Jack. That meant the other was Clive.

"Cyrus was very insistent that I be here," Slade answered.

"You shouldn't be here," Jack said. "You need to run."

It took a minute to register what Jack was saying. Falling into the pit and getting attacked by vampires wasn't how Cyrus planned to kill Slade. It was the warriors he had recruited. He didn't have time to run before he was backhanded by Brandon. He flew in the air, crashing against a wall. Brandon ran after him, swinging his claws down at Slade. Once again Dennis's training helped. Slade grabbed his furry arm, brought his feet up, and sent Brandon into the wall headfirst. The impact was so hard chunks of the wall broke off and hit Brandon on his back and head. He shook them off and turned again toward Slade.

Slade was already up on his feet and running away from Brandon. He couldn't take two steps before another warrior was in front of him. In their warrior forms, Slade couldn't tell if it was Clive or Rebecca. The warrior took a swing across Slade's midsection. Slade was able to jump back a step, narrowly missing the claws. He hit the warrior as hard as he could in the chest, knocking the warrior down and making it slide a couple of feet.

Slade looked at his fist. He couldn't believe how strong he was. "Did you guys see that?" This was not the time nor the crowd to brag to.

Another warrior raked Slade across his back, tearing his shirt away. Luckily they barely touched his skin. The one he had knocked down was back on its feet again. The others rushed around him to make sure he couldn't run anywhere. The warriors were down on all fours, growling as they surrounded him. Slade uppercut the warrior to his right, slamming his fist into the jaw of the warrior. The warrior fell backward onto the floor, not moving. Slade had just knocked out a warrior with his bare hands.

The celebration was brief as claws tore at his legs and arms. The pain was intense and immediate. Slade was able to catch or block every other hand that swung at him, but there were too many. He was knocked to the floor and closed his eyes, knowing that this was his last moment on earth. Then they all suddenly stopped. The warriors were yelling at each other to get something off them. Slade looked around to find hundreds of gremlins crawling over the warriors, biting and clawing at them.

Brim was at Slade's side. "Me protect." He ran and joined the others, biting one of the warriors in the ankle. The warriors yelled out in pain and tried to swat and claw back at the gremlins, but they proved too fast for any of them. They would move before the warriors even got close to touching them.

From above Cyrus could be heard yelling, "Get the flood lights on."

Giant lights in the ceiling above turned on, burning Slade's eyes. The gremlins ran toward the shadows away from the light. Brim didn't want to go, but Slade, through watery eyes, told him to run. Without the gremlins to keep them away, the warriors turned their attention back to Slade.

"We will not let your evil into the world," one of them said. Slade thought it was Clive.

"Who are you calling evil? You attacked me!" Slade yelled back.

They started clawing at him again. Slade was losing consciousness with the loss of blood. He could feel himself slipping away. A voice came into his mind, saying, "The world needs you. Live!" It was the voice of Almira. "This is not your natural form, little one. You are a warrior. Your human form is where you hide. Let go of your human form and show them who you truly are. Show them!"

As the light was getting dimmer in Slade's eyes, he did what Almira told him to. He didn't think of this human form as anything but camouflage to walk in. He didn't imagine transforming into a warrior like Dennis instructed. He imagined shedding his human form and stepping out of his skin. His skin was hiding his true self.

The light was coming back to him. He felt his body changing, and he welcomed it. His body popped and grew. Not one part of it was painful. It was the opposite. It felt like a surge of power rushing through him. Slade opened his eyes to see fur growing out of every pore. It wasn't gray like all the other warriors. It was dark black fur.

The other warriors stopped attacking to watch what was happening. Slade got to his feet, as they grew and ripped through the shoes he was wearing. What was left of his pants ripped off and fell to the floor. He stood a foot taller than the other warriors. He looked down on them while his giant snout and ears finished forming. If he thought he had great vision before, now it was a hundred times better.

He could see so much better and found that the light didn't bother him as much as before.

Over their shock the warriors began their attack again. Slade felt through his tail as one of them moved behind him. What would it take to make them stop attacking? He didn't want to hurt any of them. The warrior behind Slade took a swing, but Slade was much faster now. He grabbed the warrior by the wrist and threw it into the other two, knocking them down. They got back to their feet and all charged Slade at the same time.

Anger rushed through Slade, and he instinctively let out a mighty roar. The earth shook and the lights above shattered, casting darkness upon everything. The warriors fell, the earth unable to control their forms any longer. The roar Slade let out forced them back into their human forms. Even the one lying unconscious, which happened to be Jack, changed back into his human form.

Cyrus yelled from above, "Get some warriors down there and help our new recruits."

Slade needed to hurry before Cyrus sent more warriors to kill him. He jumped on top of the large wall. It was nothing for him to jump so high now. He proceeded to run across the tops of the walls until he came to the edge of the pit. Using his sharp claws on his hands and feet, he climbed the edge of the pit. His claws had no trouble slicing into the rock. Hand over hand and foot over foot he clawed up the edge until he reached the top. He pulled himself up and over the edge as the crowd gasped. There stood Slade, the only warrior covered in black fur, looking down on them.

Cyrus didn't look shocked; he looked terrified. The sweet smell of fear poured off him. "Take this beast into custody," he yelled. "I want him executed."

"No, you don't." Samuel came to his defense. "We all saw Slade get attacked by your warriors. He fought back in self-defense. He did your challenge and won. Now he is coming with us."

Slade felt angry, and the feeling grew as he looked at all the faces staring at him as if he were a freak. It was the same look he had gotten his whole life, and he hated it. Cyrus made him angrier by stopping him from training, not to mention trying to have him killed. The voice of Almira came to his mind. "It's time to announce yourself to the order. Show them who you really are and that you are here to change this order. No one can stop you from doing what you were created to do. The days of following Cyrus are over. Announce loudly so there will be no question left in anyone's mind."

Full of rage Slade let the wolf instincts guide him. He stomped, shaking the ground near him, and let out a mighty roar. This was not the same roar he had used in the pit; this was much stronger. Everyone that stood before him fell to the ground as his roar shook them to their very frames. Lights shattered one by one as his voice carried down the hallway. Darkness fell upon them all as the lights went out.

Chapter Twenty-Four

The crowd couldn't see Slade in the dark, but he could see each of their frightened expressions perfectly. Their emotions flooded the room. One was different from the rest, the smell of fresh cut lumber. Slade looked to the back of the room to see Ahmose still on her feet looking in Slade's direction. She had a smile on her face, and she clasped her hand below her chin. She was filled with pride for her son.

"Emergency light!" Cyrus screamed, pushing himself off the ground.

Running lights along the edges of the hallway illuminated to give off a dim light. It wasn't much, but it was enough for everyone to see. The group got off the ground and stared at Slade. They were still frightened of him, but not one could take their eyes off him. He hoped that they all realized that change had finally come to the warriors, a good change.

The smell of hate came to Slade's nostrils. He turned, too late, to see Cyrus throw his suit coat open and pull out a silver dagger. It was a long dagger with an intricate design of a warrior on either side. The hilt was wrapped in leather so the user would not touch the silver directly.

"Die, abomination!" Cyrus yelled out as he plunged the dagger into Slade's heart.

Burning pain shot through Slade. He roared with pain as the fur around the dagger singed and burned. Cyrus let go of the dagger and grinned, obviously pleased with himself until Slade grabbed the dagger with his giant clawed hand. With effort he was able to pull the dagger out and drop it at his feet. The burning went away as soon as the dagger was out. The wound sealed back up with fur once again growing back in place. Before a second had passed Slade looked as if nothing had happened.

Samuel, seeing the shock on Cyrus's face, used this moment to pick up the dagger. "Why did you bring this? You had this planned all along."

Cyrus buttoned his coat, acting as if he had done nothing wrong. "That is the dagger of leadership your father gave to me. Why should I not have it?"

"This dagger is only used for executions of warriors. There would be no reason to bring it to an initiation…unless you planned from the beginning to use it. It was your back-up plan in case your recruits couldn't kill him, wasn't it?"

"I had a feeling that I would need it," Cyrus stuck his nose in the air as if he was beyond being questioned. "This abomination must be destroyed."

Samuel looked past Samuel to Jaya. "Surely you can see reason, Jaya."

Jaya came forward by her husband's side. "From what I have just seen, my husband was acting in self-defense. His actions were justified. He is also right that this boy is an abomination. If silver doesn't hurt him, then he is not of the holy warriors. He will be treated like the feral warriors of old and be put to death."

Slade began to growl looking down at Cyrus and Jaya. He stopped when Samuel put a hand on his shoulder. Ahmose and Marcus had made their way through the crowd to stand next to Slade. Samuel motioned for them to stay silent.

"Feral warriors were found guilty by the council before being executed. The only thing Slade is guilty of is self-defense and," Samuel looked directly at Cyrus to see if he would get a reaction from what he said next, "coming out of darkness."

It worked. Cyrus's eyes showed the shock on his face; it was easy for anyone to read. What Samuel didn't expect was the shock that was also on Jaya's face. Both of them were at a loss for words. They looked at each other as if saying, "How could he possibly..."

Samuel continued before they could speak. "Slade has done everything you have asked of him." He was speaking loud enough for the whole crowd to hear. "Your recruits attacked him in the pit after you had given your word that Slade did not have to go down until he learned to transform. Lucky for us he learned before he was killed. We will be leaving today with Slade as you promised, or are you no longer a man of your word?"

Cyrus looked to the crowd, then to his wife. He spoke so the crowd could hear. "Of course you may leave with him. That is what I have promised, and I am a man of my word." He lowered his tone so the crowd couldn't hear what he said next. "He will be put down like a rabid dog. The council will agree with me. Until then Slade will not leave my sight. I will see him executed."

Slade growled again getting Cyrus's attention. Cyrus looked up at Slade defiantly, as if he had won a great battle. "You try, and I'll remove your head," Slade said. His voice was much deeper than any other warrior before him. The others around were startled by how different Slade's voice was. The defiant look on Cyrus's face was gone, and the smell of fear once again came from him. Slade thought of it as a small victory.

Marcus grabbed a robe left on the ground by one of the other warriors. He held it up as best he could with one hand. "Come on, Son. We best be going."

It was the first time Marcus had called him son. By the look he gave Cyrus while he said it, it seemed like a challenge had just been issued. It was his way of telling Cyrus that he would protect Slade, even if that meant going against him.

Slade closed his eyes and pictured himself putting on human skin as if it were an outfit. He put human legs on like pants and pulled a shirt of human skin over his head. Human form was his disguise from the world, and if picturing shedding his skin helped him transform into a warrior, then picturing putting it back on should help him turn back. He opened his eyes to find himself shrinking. His fur was receding back into his skin, and his body popped as it shifted into his human form. His claws were the last to change, and of course, his eyes would never change. He found, once again, that the light bothered him, even the little light that there was. He wasn't covered in sweat like the other new warriors. That was his true from, not this.

His mother saw his discomfort. "We'll get you a new pair of sunglasses as soon as we can."

Slade smiled in gratitude as Marcus put the robe around Slade's naked frame. As Samuel, Marcus, Ahmose, and Slade made their motion to leave, Cyrus stopped them.

"Not so fast," he said. "Samuel, I will need that dagger back."

Samuel looked at the dagger that his father had made. He remembered his father collecting the material for it and melting it down. Many days and nights his father spent making the right mold to poor the melted silver into. On one side was Samuel before he could take human form, and on the other side was his sister, Almira. His father had taken so much care to craft such a beautiful dagger. Back then it was only for show. Something for the leader to have and pass down. It wasn't meant for executions until after silver became deadly for the warriors. Samuel wondered if his father knew how deadly silver would become for them when he started to make it. His father never lived to see the day when silver would become the warriors' greatest threat.

Samuel turned to Cyrus, "You forget that I was there when my father made the rules that went along with this dagger. It is no longer yours." Samuel motioned his head toward Slade. "It is now his." Samuel walked off with the others, ending the conversation and leaving Cyrus stewing in his anger.

Cyrus looked over the crowd and saw their faces look to Slade and then back to him. They parted to let Slade through. Cyrus needed to do something to show the warriors that he was still in charge. He couldn't have any warriors question his authority. His word was law, and he needed to say something now before this group of warriors began to doubt that.

"That was our newest warrior," Cyrus announced over the crowd. He took satisfaction in all the faces turning to look at him, their leader. "He is different than any other warrior that we have had. We don't know why. Just finishing the trials of this pit does not make him one of us, does it? We fight with a righteous cause. I promise all of you that I will be watching this new warrior to make sure he fights with the same cause as the rest of you. After all, shouldn't we be able to come to our sanctuary to get away from the evils of the world? We should not have them follow us down here. If this new warrior proves not to be one of us, I will personally take care of him. I promise you will not have to fight an enemy from within our own ranks. I will keep you safe."

The crowd clapped after Cyrus's remarks. Marcus looked to Samuel. "What does this mean?"

"This means we need to hurry and get out of here. I need to get something from my quarters. Get Slade to his quarters so he can get dressed. I'll meet you there." Slade's stomach made a loud grumbling. Slade grabbed his stomach with hunger pains. Samuel added, "Marcus, go tell Mick to bring Slade's last order to his quarters. You might need to tell him that Slade is Brian first."

They separated, and Samuel went to his quarters while Marcus went to the cafeteria and Ahmose took Slade to his quarters. Brim was waiting inside Slade's quarters with his ears drooping and his head hanging low. As soon as he saw Slade, his ears perked up and then drooped back down again.

"Me no protect," Brim said.

Slade got down on his knees and scratched behind Brim's ear like he would a dog. It was the first time he tried it, and it seemed that Brim liked it. "You did protect me, buddy. If it wasn't for you, I would have died," Slade said, hoping that would comfort his little friend.

Ahmose kneeled beside Slade and rubbed Brim's back. "We all saw what you did on the monitor. It was very brave. Slade would not be alive if it wasn't for you."

Brim's ears perked right up, and he looked from Ahmose to Slade. "Me protect?"

"You sure did, buddy," Slade responded. "And I think you're going to have to come with us to make sure I stay safe. Right, Mom?" Slade stressed the word "mom," hoping that Ahmose would get that he was trying to make his friend feel needed.

She understood. "That's right, Brim. We are leaving right now, and we need you to come with us. We need your help to protect Slade."

Brim jumped in the air. "Me come. Me protect."

Marcus came through the door, hearing the last part of the conversation. "He is not coming with us, is he?"

Ahmose got up and kissed Marcus on the cheek and walked into the kitchen. She turned the light on low until they could replace Slade's sunglasses.

"That's not an answer," Marcus complained.

Slade quickly ran upstairs to get dressed with Brim. By the time he was done and ran back down to the kitchen, Mick had already dropped off an elk carcass. Slade's stomach grumbled and made him grab his sides from the pain. He had never had hunger pains before. Ahmose saw Slade grab his sides.

"That transformation really took a lot out of you. You need to eat," she said, pulling out a chair for Slade to sit.

He didn't need to be asked twice. His teeth grew into sharp canine teeth, and once again it didn't seem like he noticed the transformation. He tore into the carcass with the black claws that grew from his fingers. Chunk after chunk of meat Slade tore away. All the while Brim danced around his chair like a dog waiting for scraps. When Slade cleaned a bone of all its meat, he would drop it down to Brim, who eagerly accepted and ate the bone like it was a potato chip. Brim's teeth went through the bone with no effort, making small crunching noises as he chewed. Between the two of them, the eight hundred-pound carcass went quickly away, leaving only a puddle of blood on the table where the carcass had been. Ahmose wiped up the blood with a paper towel, which Brim also ate.

When Samuel got there, he asked, "Is Mick going to bring Slade his elk?"

"He already came and left," Marcus answered, shaking his head. "If I didn't see it, I wouldn't believe it. Where in the world do these two put that much food?"

"Two?" Samuel asked.

"Yeah, two. Slade ate the meat, and Brim ate the bones," Ahmose replied.

"Makes sense," Samuel said. "Gremlins at one time would devour entire livestock to anger ranchers. All that was found was the hides of the livestock. That was so long ago I almost forgot about it."

Brim sat on the floor and let out a loud belch before rubbing his stomach with both hands. "Nice," Marcus remarked. Brim grumbled something that Marcus couldn't understand, which made Slade and Ahmose both laugh. "What did he say?" Marcus asked, looking back and forth between his wife and Slade. "I know it was about me."

Before anyone could answer, Dennis came through the door. "I have a blue SUV waiting for you in front of the building. Here are the keys to that." Dennis handed Samuel car keys before continuing. "The key to your house is under the potted plant by the front door. Cyrus knows nothing about where you are staying. Slade's documents have all been sent to the school, and he is ready to start. I made sure to make him a solid C student. I didn't want to make him stand out."

"Smart," Samuel said. "Thanks for your help."

"How are the others?" Slade asked.

Dennis was a shocked that Slade would worry about the others after what they had done. "You're a great kid, Slade. Don't let anyone make you feel otherwise. I have never seen anyone care about others as much as you. To answer your question, they are fine. You knocked out Jack pretty good, so he missed your whole transformation, which is good because Cyrus still thinks Jack is on his side. He wanted to keep them all close. I convinced him to keep Jack close, but the others he allowed me to send far away. Rebecca is being sent to Paris, Clive is being sent to London, and Brandon is being sent to Tokyo. He wanted to be a ninja so bad that I am sending him to work under the original. If it makes you feel any better, they all regret their actions. Cyrus had told them that the vampires put you here and that's why you couldn't transform. He said you were some kind of unholy abomination. They really thought they were doing what was right. That's partly why I want to send them far away, so Cyrus won't be able to influence them anymore. Oh, and before I forget…"

Dennis pulled out of his pocket a pair of sunglasses for Slade. Slade quickly put them on. Even with the light low, his eyes were still hurting. "What are you going to do now that you have no more warriors to train?"

"You have changed things. Cyrus is freaking out so much that he is sending out warriors to recruit as many people as possible. He doesn't care about the rules he put in place. Age no longer matters."

"He can't do that," Marcus complained.

"I told him that," Dennis responded. "He then told me that I would no longer be training. Madelyn and Robin have been removed as well."

"He needs the council's approval to do that," Ahmose stated.

"After what Slade has done, he no longer cares about the council. Slade has really put fear into him."

"Then I have a job for the three of you," Samuel said. "I need you to find a new sanctuary, one that Cyrus will have no knowledge of—one that he will never be able to find. I have a feeling that we will be needing it soon."

"I will leave right after you are on your way."

"Once it is up and running, bring only those you can trust into the new sanctuary. Even if it only be a handful of warriors, I want only those that we can trust without question."

Brim grumbled something that Slade translated for Dennis. "He said that the gremlins will go to the new sanctuary. They will no longer help the warriors here."

"Perfect." Dennis clapped his hands with excitement. "Having the gremlins will make short work of creating a new sanctuary."

"We need to leave before Cyrus comes looking for us." Marcus looked at his watch and then at the door.

"Brim, meet us at the blue SUV in front of the building," Slade said.

Brim ran quickly into the shadows. The rest of them made their way out the door and quickly to the elevator. They were in the lobby of the bank before one of the security guards stopped them.

He was a short, stocky man. He had a very serious look, as if smiling would literally crack his face. "Samuel," he said. "Cyrus told me to stop you from leaving. I already told him that you had left, so you better hurry and get out of here."

"Thanks, Scott," Samuel said as he ushered everyone out the door. He threw the keys to Marcus. "Marcus, you drive. I need to talk to Slade."

Marcus got behind the wheel with Ahmose sitting in the passenger seat and Slade in back with Samuel. Brim was already inside, sitting between the front and back seats. He was wearing Ahmose's sunglasses again. He grumbled a few words that Ahmose and Slade understood.

"Great job, Brim," Ahmose said. She looked at Marcus. "He said that Cyrus was coming up in the elevator until Brim and some other gremlins severed the elevator cable."

Marcus smiled and actually gave Brim a compliment, "That is great work, Brim."

They drove away from the building and made a few turns down different streets before driving in the direction that they wanted to go. Once they were well on their way, Samuel opened his father's journal and showed it to Slade.

Slade looked at the writing on the pages. "It looks like letters and hieroglyphics and a bunch of others stuff I've seen."

"It is the original language. All other languages come from this even writing. Let me read to you what my father had written before he died."

Samuel cleared his throat before starting to read. "Cyrus is not the man he pretends to be. He has falsely led me to believe that a few feral warriors dwell here in the depths of hell. He has betrayed me; he has betrayed all of us. Once we were down deep enough, I found that he had stolen the dagger from me and had pierced my heart. It took me off guard, and I transformed back to my human form. He took the dagger with him and left me here to die. The environment here is hostile to humans, as you know. My wound is keeping me from transforming back into my warrior form, and the environment is stopping my wound from healing. I am afraid I will suffer a long, painful death. If it was not for the kindness of the gremlins that I freed so long ago, I would not be able to write my last words.

"Cyrus desires the mantle of leadership. My son, you were meant to be the next in line, the rightful leader of the warriors. I am afraid that you will also fall to the lies of this man and not take your rightful place as my heir. I am also afraid of what Cyrus has planned for my beloved order, and I am afraid he is not alone in his deceitful workings. As Cyrus stood over me celebrating what he had done, my mind was opened, and I could see clearly what was to come.

"I spoke aloud to Cyrus. 'What you have done here will reverberate through the years, nearly killing off our order. Your selfish greed for power and your bigotry will make our enemy stronger. But one shall come to remove this mantle you have taken for yourself. He will be a warrior unlike any other before him. Out of darkness he shall climb to stand before the warriors with fur black as night. With a mighty roar, he shall announce himself. He will be the most powerful warrior ever. He is the rightful leader and shall save the world from all the evil you shall bring upon it. You shall fight against him, but he will destroy you and all that follow you. This is your warning, and if you do not repent for what you have done, it shall be your future. You shall know him by his golden eyes that will never change, not even in human form, for he will never truly be human, but a chosen warrior. The dagger belongs to him, and in your anger, you shall give it to him.'

"Cyrus did not listen and mocked me before leaving with the dagger to take the leadership he had not earned. I entrust these words to my little friends and have instructed that they give them to you, my son, when it is safe to do so. I go now to see my beloved wife and stand before my maker."

Samuel shut the journal. "He writes some more, but those words are just for myself. When you came out of the pit, Slade, you fulfilled the prophecy my father spoke of. That's why I said you were only guilty of coming out of darkness. I wanted to see Cyrus's reaction.

I wanted him to know that I knew what my father had said. I didn't expect to see Jaya react to the same words. I knew that she was not a good woman. That's why I told you the women of our order can be beautiful on the outside, but I did not expect her to be a part of this." Samuel pulled the dagger from under his pant leg. It was wrapped up so the silver would not touch his skin. He unwrapped it and showed it to Slade. "When Cyrus stabbed you and let go of the dagger, it became yours once you took ahold of it. He fulfilled the prophecy of my father. He gave you the dagger."

Ahmose looked from Samuel to her son. "So you're saying—"

"That Slade is now the leader of the Holy Warriors."

www.ingramcontent.com/pod-product-compliance
Lightning Source LLC
Chambersburg PA
CBHW071518110726
47908CB00003B/878